The Street Singer

Singer

Kathleen Neely

The Street Singer
COPYRIGHT 2018 by Kathleen Neely

Contact Information: titleadmin@pelicanbookgroup.com

All scripture quotations, unless otherwise indicated, are taken from the Holy Bible, New International Version(R), NIV(R), Copyright 1973, 1978, 1984, 2011 by Biblica, Inc.™ Used by permission of Zondervan. All rights reserved worldwide. www.zondervan.com

Cover Art by *Nicola Martinez*

Harbourlight Books, a division of Pelican Ventures, LLC
www.pelicanbookgroup.com PO Box 1738 *Aztec, NM * 87410

Harbourlight Books sail and mast logo is a trademark of Pelican Ventures, LLC

Publishing History
First Harbourlight Edition, 2019
Paperback Edition ISBN 978-1-5223-0131-8
Electronic Edition ISBN 978-1-5223-0129-5
Published in the United States of America

Dedication

To Brian, Stephen, and Darren
I loved having three sons, and I'm so proud of the men
you have become.

Prologue

There was magic in the grooves. Every disk looked the same, but the grooves made all the difference. Each fashioned for distinctiveness of sound. Trisha held two black vinyl disks to the light, trying to see the variance. Pap's eyes flickered with amusement as she puzzled over the grooves. His raspy voice called to her. "Little girls need to learn how to dance." With that, Pap chose the album, pulled the disk from the cardboard cover, removed the paper sleeve, and placed it on the phonograph with the care of fragile glass. "Adaline. Now there's a lady that can sing."

The soft tinkling sounds of a piano, high on the keyboard, entered first. The soft hum of the brass joined them next, followed by the thump of percussion commanding a steady beat. Then Adaline's gentle tones tiptoed into the living room, as if testing their welcome.

Pap stretched his hand toward her. "May I have this dance?" He angled into a slight bow. Trisha stepped into the circle of his arm and rested her right hand in his work-worn left, her left hand touching the shoulder of a flannel shirt, leaving space between them for propriety.

"You know, I taught your mama to dance in this very room. She was about your age. Your Grandma watched us, calling out directions." He exhaled a deep, sad sigh. Grandma wasn't watching today. Trisha hungered for memories of her mom, but they always made Grandma cry.

"Shoulders straight. Don't watch your feet." Pap danced with smooth and practiced fluidity. As they danced, he murmured cues to Trisha. "Right foot, left foot, side step, back." Soon she no longer needed the cues. Miss Adaline's voice grew in crescendo, its richness filling the room with sound until it penetrated deep inside her.

When the end of the song came, Pap dipped her while she laughed, keeping hold throughout the eternity of the last note. *Just call me Baby. Baby.* How could anyone hold their breath that long and then close it with perfect pitch? Only Miss Adaline.

1

Trisha had way too much to do, but Julie practically dragged her to the ice cream parlor anyway.

"You need to take a break. Everything goes better with a cool, creamy gelato."

Trisha shook her head. "How do you stay so skinny?"

"I burn it off at the gym." Julie did a couple high-step jogs to demonstrate.

They ordered and sat across from each other at a round table as bright sunlight spilled through the glass windows.

Trisha rubbed her neck to ease the tension, twisting it from side to side to get a good stretch. "I'm so overwhelmed right now. This final semester has been intense, and the bar exam is looming closer all the time. But all I can think about is the mess at Pap's house. There's so much to clean out."

Julie's eyes softened. "It's only been a week since his funeral. Give yourself a little time."

Trisha tasted the cool lemon flavor of her sorbet. "I really want to have it done before the wedding."

"You couldn't have anticipated this. Your Grandpa wasn't in bad health."

"No, but he just shut down after Grandma died. I think he couldn't take one more loss."

"How about your uncle? Will he help with the

house?"

"Uncle Brendan?" Trisha shook her head. "I doubt it. I think he's still upset that they left me the house."

"But you said they evened things out with other assets. He probably got the better end of the deal. You get an old house in ill repair and the task of disposing of it."

Trisha gave a mock smile. "Well, thanks for cheering me up."

"You have Grant to help you. Four months 'til the wedding. That's plenty of time to take care of your grandpa's place."

Trisha tilted her head up. "Grant? He's not exactly the roll-up-your-sleeves kind of guy. He's more inclined toward 'call a disaster relief service, and I'll write the check.' Maybe it'll come to that." She crumpled her napkin and put it in her empty bowl. "For some stupid reason, I thought one month after graduation would be a great time to get married."

"Honey, you're marrying Grant Ramsey. Anytime would be a good time to marry that man."

The tension eased and the corners of her lips lifted into the slightest grin. "You're right, Jules. I need to relax and enjoy the anticipation."

"Let's attack that house this weekend. I can gather about a half-dozen friends, and we'll tear through it in no time." She snapped her fingers rapid fire.

Trisha shook her head. "I'm not ready for other people to tear through there. I need to see what I'm dealing with first. But I'll take you up on your offer. And this weekend works. But Jules, I have to warn you, it's not pretty. My grandparents were pack rats. They could've been featured on one of those hoarding shows."

"That bad, huh?
"You have no idea."

~*~

Trisha turned left toward her grandparents' home—or what had been their home before it became hers two weeks ago. The sparse gravel and lack of rain brought a billow of dust when the tires hit the driveway. Now she'd have to add "carwash" to her to-do list.

"It's a mess, Julie. I'm almost ashamed to take anyone in there, but I do need your help." She shrugged her shoulders but kept her eyes on the winding drive.

"I'm no stranger to work. We'll roll up our sleeves and have it done by the end of the week." She rubbed her palms together like this would be an adventure. When Trisha picked her up this morning, she came out wearing patched jeans, a flannel shirt with a variety of paint colors, and a bandana on her head. She grasped the handle of a bin with paper towels, rags, disinfectant, and window cleaner. A grocery store tote bag filled with snacks swung from her arm.

Trisha gaped at the load. "I told you I'd order lunch and have it delivered."

"Humph. You think I can make it 'til lunch without eating? Just a healthy little bag of chips, cookies, and doughnut holes. Oh, and a little, bitty one-pound package of to-die-for peppermint bark."

Trisha gasped in disbelief. "I don't know how you can eat like that."

"Well, you'll know as soon as we get working and

break into the stash. It's actually pretty easy." To prove her point, she pulled out a doughnut hole and popped it into her mouth.

The two-story house came into view. Why hadn't they downsized? Trish had only suggested it hundreds of times. A cynical answer sprang to her mind—*because then they would have had this chore instead of me.*

The house sat on three acres of overgrown grass, untrimmed shrubbery, and about forty large oak trees. Trisha glanced up at the new leaves welcoming spring. She thought about fall when the assault would come, filling this yard with dead leaves and acorns. Her eighty-seven-year-old grandpa had still planned to rake them. Every fall for two months, he used a wooden-handled rake, picked a small section of yard, pulled them into a pile at the far end of the property, and set them on fire. Then he repeated the process day after day until green peeked through the single layer of dead brown leaves remaining. At that point, he abandoned the task and allowed them to rot on the ground. Would the house be sold by then, or would that job be hers?

He mowed the lawn in much the same way. Three acres and no riding mower. He walked his push mower over a section at a time, starting with a rectangular square to mark the invisible boundaries he had chosen that day. Then he mowed from the outer boundary to the center, each day choosing a different spot until all three acres had been mown. By then, the original place towered so high it was time to start over.

"Wow. Big house." Julie stared before retrieving her supplies.

Trisha reached over and relieved Julie of the bag. "You know, it only looks that way. It's tall because some of the basement is out of the ground, ceilings are high, and there's an attic where we can stand upright—which is a good thing because it's full."

Trisha started toward the side door that entered the summer room off of the kitchen. Julie scanned all of the supplies they had to carry and pointed toward the front door, raising her eyes in question. "That door's closer."

Trisha shook her head. "Porch boards are rotten. It's not safe. Pap didn't worry about it since he always used the back."

Julie's mouth gaped open. "Shouldn't it be cordoned off? What if someone comes to the door and gets hurt?"

Trisha gave her a sad smile. "That's what I asked Pap."

They walked into the kitchen and set all the supplies on the table.

Julie looked around at the dated appliances, the rounded white surface of a refrigerator door with the tiny freezer tucked on the inside, the six-burner gas range laden heavy with grease. The linoleum flooring squares didn't always line up, and the chrome table legs had pitted over the years.

"This isn't so bad. Old but quaint. Feels kind of homey."

Trisha took a deep breath. "That's because I already did the kitchen. I couldn't leave food and dirty dishes. Believe me. It was nasty."

Julie ran her fingers over an antiquated, embroidered dishtowel. "Give him a little slack, Trishie. He must have missed your grandma so much."

"I know, but I also know it wasn't much different when she lived. Now, if you're ready, brace yourself and take a walk into the living room."

Julie went first and, before Trisha reached the doorway, she heard laughter.

"Are you kidding me? He must have just done this. Maybe he started packing to downsize and didn't tell you."

They stood and perused boxes on top of boxes. Lamps and knickknacks cluttered the tables until there was barely any wood visible.

"Five years ago? That's a slow-mo downsize."

Julie shook her head in disbelief. "Tell me where to start and what to do with the stuff?"

"Most of it will be discarded, but I can't dump a box and assume there's nothing of importance. I'll take the ones beside the desk. They're most likely to be important papers. Just pick a spot. Or, better yet, clear all of the knickknacks. Anything you like, take it. Everything else on the tables and shelves can be tossed away." She glanced around the room as she spoke. "Except this." Trisha picked up an antique bud vase with tiny pink flowers. "I always did like this piece."

"What about your uncle? Will he want anything?"

Trisha narrowed her eyes. "Do you see him here helping? Toss them."

An hour into cleaning, the stash of snacks had been opened and consumed. Trisha and Julie sorted through boxes and loaded them into the car to take to the shredding facility. They could see tabletops again, the surfaces cleared of all clutter.

Julie had a little packrat in her, too. She kept a few items and boxed the rest for donation to a resale store.

Trisha uncovered a deep box filled with old vinyl records. "I remember these. Pap loved his music. He used to play them when I was a little girl. Technology's come a long way. I remember the skipping and scratching. Oh, and sometimes it would get stuck and play the same line over and over. Pap's trick was to put a penny on the arm of the needle and weigh it down."

Julie came over and knelt beside the box as they leafed through the stack. "Does he have an old phonograph? These albums might be valuable."

"Somewhere. You don't think he would have thrown it out, do you?"

"It'll surface. If we try them, we can see which ones still play well and sort them to sell."

Trisha crossed her arms. "Are you crazy? There's got to be over a hundred of these. Do you know how long it would take to test each one?"

Julie held both arms out, palms up. "Just trying to be helpful."

She went back to sorting table drawers and boxes for donating. Trisha sat cross-legged on the floor, pulling records out as memories sparked to life. A smile crossed her face as her vision shifted from the stubborn old man that died to the grandfather who raised her.

"We danced the Polka to this one. He said every girl needed to learn to dance. Oh, and this one he used before my first high school dance. He said I'd waltz like Ginger Rogers by the night of the dance."

She fingered the album covers, lost in memories of her grandfather swinging her around the small space and counting out loud to help her remember where to place her feet. Flipping through the vinyls, she pulled one out and stared.

"This was my favorite." The lady on the cover had always mesmerized Trisha. Her singing held mourning, deep and sorrowful, a longing in each note as though she sang directly to Trisha's heart.

"A lot of black singers performed jazz or gospel, but Adaline sang ballads. She could capture an emotion like no one I ever heard."

Trisha dug through the box, certain there were others by Adaline. She pulled out two more records. Scanning the songs, she closed her eyes and remembered…so many feelings, so many years ago.

"I wonder what Adaline is doing now."

Julie called over her shoulder. "If she's alive."

"I guess it's possible she's not, but she's pretty young here. I can't find a date."

Julie rolled her eyes. "It's a vinyl record. That ought'a tell you something." She carried a box to the car. When she walked back into the living room, she clutched a large carton in both arms, a conspiratorial smile on her face. "Wanna guess what I found?"

"Montgomery Ward catalogs? Newspapers from 1945? Last month's dirty dishes?"

"No, but those first two would be pretty cool to find. Close your eyes."

Trisha shot her an impatient look. "Just show me!"

"Close them or no more peppermint bark."

She obeyed and heard the rustling sound as Julie emptied the box.

"OK. Open."

With the pride of a fisherman showing his catch, Julie held the old phonograph in her extended arms.

It took only a few minutes to clear the dust and discover it still worked. Soon they sat listening to Adaline crooning about a love lost. Had the tones always been this scratchy? How would Adaline sound on today's advanced technology? Yet even through the grainy sound, deep emotion drifted into the room.

Trisha closed her eyes and listened in hushed stillness. She was a teenager again, singing into a makeshift microphone that doubled as a hairbrush, doing her best to mimic Adaline's pensive tones.

The mood in the room became subdued. Trisha was contented to rest in the quiet for a few more moments, but Julie's abrupt movement broke the hypnotic spell. "Time to order lunch." She reached over and lifted the needle from the phonograph as if she couldn't bear the sadness.

Four hours later, they called it a day. They would deliver some boxes to the resale store and some to the dump. Trisha set her last two boxes on the step and dug in her handbag for the correct key to lock up. She would take the vinyl records home with her, not certain why. She wouldn't keep them long term, but so much of Pap lived in the music he loved.

Julie took a box to the car and then returned to help. Trisha heard a gasp and turned. Julie held the top album and stared at Adaline's picture. Adaline posed, slender in a royal-blue, close-fitting gown covered with sequins, bronze skin glowing beneath the close-shorn hair. Her face tilted sideways, gazing at something outside of the album's perimeter.

"Trisha, I know her!"

"Adaline? She was famous in her day, but you're a little young for that. I only know her because of Pap."

Julie shook her head. "No. I mean, I know her! She's the street singer over on the east side. Crawford Street area. She sings for the crowds and has a box to collect donations."

Trisha shook her head. "No, Jules. Can't be. First of all, I doubt she was from around here. Second, she'd be pretty old by now." She reached for the album cover. "I'm sure she doesn't look like this anymore."

Julie's crooked finger tapped the picture, unwavering. "She doesn't look like that anymore, but it's her. She's not as thin and her hair is longer and graying, but it's her." Her hands went to her hips. "Trust me. You don't forget those eyes."

Trisha tilted the album and searched the eyes, as if they'd tell her the truth. "No, I don't imagine those eyes would be easy to forget. But what in the world are you doing over in that area?"

"Walking through that area when I'm going from work to my sister's cuts off a few blocks. I never do it at night. You know, she can still gather a crowd. Sometimes I'll see six or more people just standing, listening."

Trisha stared, contemplating the possibility. Then, with great care, she placed the album back in the box. She turned her key to lock the door, hoisted the box to her hip, and walked to the car. She would have to make a trip to Crawford Street.

2

On her last birthday, Grant told Trisha dressy attire was in order and left the rest a surprise. He arrived in a chauffeured limousine that took them to an airstrip, and then a chartered plane whisked them off to New York City for dinner and a Broadway show.

That evening in New York, Grant proposed, and she accepted. A fairy-tale evening, perfect in every detail, until the show ended.

As the crowds began to disperse, Grant suggested they relax and wait until the people thinned out. In their seats, he leaned in and pulled her close. He stroked her cheek, his face close to hers.

Trisha brushed his lips with hers. "Thank you for such a nice surprise. It's been a perfect evening."

"You're welcome, but it's not over. I took the liberty of reserving us a room. I know you didn't pack, but we don't need much. The Piper Cub will be ready in the morning."

Trisha pulled back. "Grant, we've had this conversation. You know what I want."

With gentleness, he pulled her back, lifted her left hand, and tapped her ring finger where the 1.5 carat diamond rested. "Doesn't this make a difference? You know I love you."

She placed a soft kiss on his lips. "Then be patient. Please."

He lifted one eyebrow and spoke with a steady tone. "Trish, I've been patient. It's time."

"Grant, I want our—"

"It's time," he repeated it with authority.

Trisha stiffened. "It's not time until the time is right for both of us. Do I need to return this?" She began to remove the glimmering jewel.

"Stop it." He raised his voice and enclosed his hand over hers. Then he softened his tone. "Honey, that's not what I meant."

Trisha stopped removing the ring but looked him square in the eye. "I don't think I've misunderstood any of this conversation. We've talked about this."

Grant ran his hands through his hair, the cut so precise each hair retreated back into place. He pulled his cell phone from a pocket and hit a few keys.

"Can you have the aircraft ready tonight? We're heading back home."

After a few aloof days and some conversation, Grant came to terms with Trisha's desire to wait until the wedding night. She compromised by agreeing to schedule the wedding for an earlier date.

~*~

Trisha and Grant reserved Saturdays as their date night. He always found someplace special for dinner. It provided an evening of respite from classes, studying, and errands. They ate dinner, lingering and catching up on the week past. With their schedules so full, sometimes that was all the time they had.

The glass pillar in the center of the table held a single candle with rivulets of wax melting down the side. Trisha loved dripping candles. They held a story, lit and burning for so many different reasons. Whether happy or sad, a sweet aroma drifted into each story.

Grant took her hand, running his finger over the diamond she wore. He did that often. He had been raised with affluence, but she had never owned anything this valuable.

The candle flickered as the waiter cleared the table and refilled their wine glasses. Grant ordered crème brûlèe without asking. He knew how Trisha loved it. The subtle lighting and soft music provided a perfect backdrop for romance. But their busy schedules left them little time together, and there were things they needed to talk about. He leaned back and crossed his legs at the ankle.

"So what's the status of the house? I have a realtor friend who will come to list it. The sooner we get it on the market, the sooner you can focus on what's important."

Trisha rolled her eyes. "You wouldn't believe it. I've only touched the surface. You know how much clutter they had."

"Honey, this is way too much distraction. Why don't you let me take care of it? I can have it emptied in a day."

"No. I know how you'd empty it. You'd order a dumpster and a crew of workers, list it 'as is,' and be done with it."

"You have to admit, that's not a bad plan. Tax liability should be better if it's sold before the wedding."

The waiter arrived with their crème brûlée. He placed ramekins filled with the creamy custard on the table before them. Trisha's spoon pierced the crusted, brown topping to reach the cool crème beneath.

"No, I have to do it myself. Once I find what's important, it will go faster."

Grant twirled his wine, sniffed, and took a sip. "Your grandfather had all his important papers in the safe deposit box along with the will. That should be all you need."

She placed her elbows on the table, entwined her fingers, and rested her chin on them. Leaning forward, she locked her gaze with his. "If this were your parents' home, would you hire someone to discard everything and arrange a quick sale?"

Grant shifted, crossing his leg over his knee. "That's different."

"Why?"

"Come on, Trish. You know there's nothing of value there. My parents have an art collection, valuable antiques, things you don't toss out."

She shook her head. "Take off your financial hat for a change. My life is in that house. They have things my mother made and pictures of her and my dad. That's all I have left of them. Things I can't reduce to a dollar value."

He took her hand in his. "You're right, honey. I don't mean to dismiss that. I'm worried about you. You can only stretch yourself so far." He lifted her hand to his lips. "I love you, Trish. You know that, don't you?"

She stroked his face with the hand he had lifted. "I know. I love you, too. This is a season in life I have to walk through. It will be over soon." Her eyes misted. "You know, I miss him so much. He called me his princess."

Grant leaned in close. "You're my princess now."

~*~

Trisha stood, stretched, and looked at Chester, his tiger stripes designed with precision. Curled across the back of the sofa, his whiskers twitched as she rubbed the top of his sleeping head. "Chester, maybe you can sleep, but I have to get out of this apartment for a while."

Sliding her feet into her shoes, Trisha reached for her keys and phone. As she headed to the door for a brief walk, she saw the box of albums that she had pushed into a corner. Stepping past them every day kept Adaline fresh in her mind. Could she be the street singer Julie saw? It didn't seem possible, but this just became the perfect time to find out.

Heading into the city, she set her GPS to Crawford Street. She could probably find it herself, but she'd better not take the chance of getting lost. Turning a bend, the Asheville skyline materialized before her, always a pleasant sight. While much smaller than big cities, it boasted a double skyline—cities in the forefront, mountains as a backdrop.

She approached Crawford Street, an older ethnic neighborhood. Some attempts had been made at revitalization, but it still fell short of attracting new residents.

Trisha turned left onto Crawford Street. Julie hadn't told her what intersection, but it had to be this one—Julie probably traveled this way from her workplace to her sister's home. She slowed the car as she scanned the sidewalk.

The Mendino apartment building sat back from

the road, providing more depth for the sidewalk—a wide triangular walkway fronting the corner entrance. There was a street singer, but not necessarily Adaline. Trisha wasn't yet convinced it was her.

The singer sat on a folding chair, a microphone lowered to her seated level, and a speaker providing instrumental music. Two pedestrians had stopped to listen, perched on a bench built around a tree trunk. Others walked by, slowing to catch a few moments of song.

The parking garage was up ahead and Trisha merged into traffic to switch lanes. She parked and waited for the light to change so she could cross the four lanes, her ear strained to hear the faint sound of music. As she crossed and walked closer, the sound grew louder. She gauged the familiarity of the vocals before she reached a position where she could see.

She approached The Mendino and found an empty bench. The voice was older, the aging evident, but as Julie said, it was the eyes that convinced her. Trisha made eye contact…and there was the younger woman who graced the cover of the album she loved.

Heavy traffic whizzed by, cars and buses sounding their horns and the repetitive beep of a siren. Trisha, lost in the music, tuned everything else out. Ten minutes passed, then twenty.

Adaline reached over and pushed a few buttons between songs, took a sip from her container, and began again. Each song mirrored the pattern Trisha remembered—starting softly, growing to crescendo, and ending on a note not quite as long or clear as in her youth.

Some people dropped cash in a box placed in front of her chair. After almost thirty minutes, she thanked those listening and said there would be a short break. She would be back in one hour.

The singer stood, eased herself out of the chair, and found her balance. Then she began breaking down the microphone and wrapping the cord from the speaker that sat on a little wheeled cart. Trisha dug in her handbag for a few dollar bills. As she approached the box, she made eye contact.

"That was beautiful. Do you need some help?" It seemed like a laborious task to break down and set up again in an hour.

The singer shook her head. "No but thank you." She turned her back and began to roll the speaker toward the side of the apartments, each step slow and careful. Adaline disappeared in the side alley.

I can't believe it. Pap and I danced to your music.

~*~

Trisha left the east side and took the rural road that led to Pap's house. Her house. She needed to begin thinking of it as hers. She would get the old phonograph and take it to her apartment.

The gravel driveway provided the reverse of the city she had visited. Clean air and natural beauty swallowed up the tension. Even knowing what she faced inside, there was still a sense of coming home.

Trisha entered the quiet of the farmhouse. "Maybe I should study here." She spoke aloud. "Turn my phone off. No distractions." She could bring Chester along in his cat carrier. He'd have new territory to explore. Pap never allowed an inside cat, but the house belonged to her now. She began to feel a new sense of ownership.

She went through the pantry and retrieved a tea bag. The jar of honey looked antiquated, but didn't they say honey never went bad? She looked for an expiration date. Finding none, she set it beside her mug. Trisha lifted the tea kettle from the stove and peered inside. Rust. She tossed it in the trash and set a pan on the stove to boil water.

While she waited for it to boil, she pulled back the curtains and opened the window blinds. If this was hers, she would take all of this down and let that beautiful sunshine flow in. It allowed a panoramic view of the neighboring fields with some mountains in the backdrop.

But it is mine. Trisha reached up and dislodged the curtain rod, taking the curtains, rod and all, to the summer room. The room flooded with light.

What would it take to renovate this old home? Would it qualify to be labeled historic? Trisha reached down and peeled a corner of the uneven linoleum squares to discover hardwood beneath. The same thing was true with the carpet in the living and dining room. Why would anyone cover that?

Her water started to boil so she poured it over her tea bag and turned the gas stove off. While it steeped, Trisha walked from room to room with growing excitement. The house was run down, no question about that. But it had so many quaint features—an original carved mantel over the brick fireplace with weeping mortar joints, stain glass panels topping the dining room windows, crystal knobs on each door.

The huge wood beams on the living room ceiling always struck her as dark and ominous. But today, she threw open the curtains and sunshine poured in. The windows were old and drafty, but they were abundant. With all of the clutter, she had never seen the potential before.

Trisha retrieved her tea and brought it to Pap's old recliner. Sitting back, she breathed in the spicy ginger aroma before taking a tentative sip to test the temperature. "Grant would never agree to live here like this." Again she spoke aloud, filling the silence surrounding her. "But if I can convince him to see what I see—maybe. Or perhaps I should begin renovations and bring that up when it's restored."

Pap had left some money. It wouldn't be enough to finish, but it would get her started.

One thing was certain. She wouldn't sell this house as is and get next to nothing for it. It had too much potential. Tomorrow she would call Jimmy Wallace from church. He'd worked as a builder all his life before retiring two years ago. He'd give her some good advice.

Trisha finished her tea and washed her cup. She gathered the old phonograph in her arms and locked the door of her house.

3

The morning sunshine woke Trisha. She stretched her sluggish limbs and lingered in the bed. Thoughts of Adaline entered her mind. What could have plunged a recording star from fame to poverty? She hadn't been a household name like Ella Fitzgerald or Patti Paige, but she'd had some fame in her day. Trisha had an early class but then would head back over to The Mendino.

After class, Trisha drove east, crossing through the city to Crawford Street. She once again used the parking garage and walked back toward The Mendino apartments.

The sound of the city faded to the background as the music took over. Trisha heard nothing but the song. The familiar sound of Adaline's voice whisked her back in time. Sitting on a bench with people passing back and forth between them, Trisha glimpsed some of the features of the younger woman on the album cover. Adaline kept her hair brushed smooth, cut to just below her ears, the top swept back off her face making the graying age spots of her skin prominent. No longer the slender beauty posing on the album cover, she looked like an ordinary lady with an extraordinary voice.

Trisha looked around for anything indicating her name. No display identified her but written in marker on the side of the speaker was the name *Adda Marsh*.

The block lettering claimed ownership, not notoriety. When she announced a short break, Trisha pulled ten dollars from her wallet and walked over to the box.

As Trisha dropped the money in, the singer looked up at her and smiled. "Thank you, ma'am."

"No—thank you! That was beautiful. You're very gifted."

The woman acknowledged with a slight bob of her head and continued to pack, winding up the cords.

"Adda Marsh?" Trisha pointed toward the words written on the speaker. "Is that your name?"

The singer answered, but continued packing. "Yes, ma'am. That's me."

Trisha rambled, trying to keep her for just a few moments of conversation.

"Charming name. Is it short for something?"

Adda picked up the chair with her free hand and turned Trisha's way. Her jaw tightened, and she stared for a moment. "No ma'am. Just Adda. That's my given name."

"That's quite a load to carry in and out each time you break. Do you have to take it far?"

"Just right to that doorway. I rent some space for it."

Trisha took the chair and microphone stand from her. "Please, let me help."

Adda hesitated then nodded. "Thank you. I seen you here yesterday?"

"Yes, I came yesterday."

Adda stepped toward the door.

Trisha followed. "Your music, it's…it's special. It touched me."

Adda stopped walking. "That so? Well, guess the old girl still got something left." She muttered and continued her steps.

They reached the doorway of what looked like a storage room. The side door was tucked off of a walkway away from pedestrian traffic. "How nice that they let you use this space."

"Let's me use it for fifty dollars every month. You just leave it right there. I'll get it from here." Adda retrieved a key from her pocket.

"So, are you done for the day?"

"No ma'am. I'll be back on out there in about an hour. My throat needs a rest every now and then."

Trish set the chair and microphone down but lingered, not wanting to leave Adda's presence.

Adda didn't unlock the door. She stood there, hands on hips looking Trisha in the eye. She gave a determined nod. "I've got this now. I hope you'll come back again." She made no attempt to open the door with Trisha standing there.

"Well, thank you again. I'll be back sometime." She turned to walk back to the corner. When she stole a glance backward, Adda opened the door and began pulling the chair and microphone inside.

~*~

Julie sat at the high-top table across from Trisha. She leaned forward over her plate to take a bite from the two-fisted burger. Trisha pushed a fork through her salad, spearing a tomato.

"So where did you say that man of yours is off to?" Julie dabbed the juices from her chin.

"Grant? He's at a conference in Dallas. He'll be back Friday. But Jules, I have lots to tell you."

She took a sip of her ice water and opened her handbag.

"First, drumroll please...here's the final decision." She pulled out a swatch of sage green fabric and a sketch of the bridesmaid dress.

"Nice! That's the pattern I liked. The swatch? Eh?" She moved her hands up and down. "It'll do."

"Yes, it will do because the decision is final. Schedule your fitting ASAP."

"What else? You said you have lots to tell." Julie dipped her fry in ketchup and plopped it in her mouth.

"I went down to the east side. You're right. It is Adaline."

Julie furrowed her eyebrows. "That's not news. I already told you."

"I know, Jules, but I just had to see it for myself. I talked with her. Her name is Adda Marsh. She didn't say anything about Adaline. I got the distinct impression that topic was off limits. She said Adda isn't short for anything. It's her given name."

"Well, now you know. But you could'a known before, if you believed a friend."

Trisha laughed. "A little sensitive, are we?"

"Is that the end of your news?"

"No. Here's what's really on my mind. I'm thinking of renovating Pap's house." Trisha let that sink in, scanning Julie's face for any reaction.

Julie leaned forward. "Well that's the best thing you've said this morning. That could be an awesome old house."

"I called Jimmy Wallace, a retired builder from Pap's church. He's going to meet me over there this Thursday."

"And I'll be there with you. What time?"

Trisha laughed. "You don't have to come, Jules. We won't be doing any work."

"Hey, I'm all into that stuff—fixing old and making it shine. I want to hear what he says. I bet we can do some of the work ourselves."

Trisha tipped her chin. "You mean in all of my spare time?"

"Just saying," she spoke before plopping the final bite of burger in her mouth.

"Ten o'clock Thursday morning."

Julie crossed her arms and put on a pout. "You know I'm working."

"Sorry, my friend. That's when he's free."

They both paused while the waitress came and filled their drinks.

When she finished, Trisha resumed, "Speaking of 'just saying,' we're not saying anything to Grant about this. Not yet."

Julie's eyebrows shot up. "Uh-oh. Trouble in River City?"

"No. Nothing like that. I'm just not sure he'll be able to envision it until I have something concrete to talk about."

"You think you two will live there?"

"I don't know, Jules. Just don't know." She pushed her remaining salad aside.

~*~

Trisha's phone rang, showing Grant's name on the caller ID. She'd been listening to music and hesitated before picking up the phone.

"Hello?" she answered on the fourth ring.

"Took you long enough to answer the call. I hope the delay is because you're deep into studying...or pining over my absence."

Trisha laughed. "Right and right. I'm pining while I'm studying."

"With music on?"

"Just some of Pap's old music."

"And that doesn't break your concentration?"

"Let me worry about law school. I've done OK so far."

"Miss me?"

She closed her laptop and reached for the phonograph to reduce the volume. "Of course. I'm just too busy to notice I'm missing you."

"I'm not quite sure how to take that."

"Just take it as honest truth. I made some wedding decisions. I selected fabric and patterns for the dresses and chose the flowers."

"Progress! That means you're one step closer to becoming Mrs. Ramsey."

Trisha moved to the sofa, curling her legs under her. "How's your conference going?"

"Typical. Just keeping up with changes in annuities, money market, IRAs. Speaking of which, if you aren't still set on family law, there's a huge market for attorneys in the finance world."

A sigh escaped her. "Are you serious? Me? I'm much more suited to watch over the needs of children. Divorce can be pretty ugly, and kids tend to be used as pawns."

"Yeah, poor parents scraping to meet child support payments. You could end up a starving lawyer. There's a lot of money in finance, or even corporate law."

"I'll let you do the money making. It'll stoke your ego."

"My ego's just fine, thank you."

"The corporate world's too demanding. I need something that will give me flexibility when we have a family."

"Way down the road, my dear."

"Not too far down. Are you forgetting we talked about this? I told you I won't stop with one child. I'd give my eyeteeth for a sister. I won't do that to our babies. Three minimum. I want a full house."

"You'll change your mind after the first one."

~*~

Jimmy Wallace walked through the house with a clipboard in hand and a leather tool belt strapped to his waist. Trisha followed him around while he pushed, probed, and peeled. Sometimes he would stand scratching his chin, thinking, then write on his clipboard. He stood in the living room running his hands over the intricacies of the mantel, then staring up at the massive wood beams.

"Trish, you got yourself a diamond in the rough. I was never inside when your Pap lived, just pulled into the driveway once or twice to pick him up. This house has good bones. If it were mine, I'd hold on to the parts that give it character while adding updates to make it more livable."

"That's what I'm thinking, but I don't know where to start. Should I get a contractor or an architect? Should I do it in baby steps or dive right in and have it all done? And what in the world am I looking at in cost?"

Again, Jimmy scratched his chin and swept a wide gaze around.

"Well, Trishie, if you want a contractor, I can give you a few names. Most of what a contractor is going to do is to outsource the work. He coordinates and pulls it all together. Gets the workers, checks the quality, keeps them on schedule."

He absently pulled open a hidden pocket door between the living room and the dining room. "Slides pretty smooth." Pushing it shut, he continued, "I keep looking for a project since I retired two years ago. I still know lots of tradesmen. I'd be right happy to help you out on this. It would save you a bundle. A regular contractor will take off the top of every tradesmen that works here, and then some."

"You?" Trisha asked.

Jimmy retreated. "Sorry. Didn't mean to be presumptuous. I'll get you some names."

"No, Mr. Wallace, that's not what I meant. I was just surprised you'd take on such a big project. I'd love to hire you as contractor."

"Oh, it won't be hiring. You're church family, and I got nothing but time." He craned his neck to view the beams again. "I'm getting kind of excited thinking about how this all might look."

Trisha shook her head. "I couldn't let you do this without being compensated. That wouldn't be right." She followed his eyes toward the beams. "And I know what you mean. When I started thinking about it, I kept imagining the potential. As a teenager, I just saw an old house. Now I see what it could be."

"Then it's a deal. We'll talk about compensation when the house is done. If you have your grandma's recipes, I wouldn't be opposed to some of that graham cracker pie she always made."

Trisha reached up for a quick hug. "Thank you, Mr. Wallace. When do we start? How do we start?"

"We can get started right quick. Let me do some pondering this week and I'll come up with a plan."

Trisha dug out an extra key and gave it to Jimmy Wallace. As she locked the door, she thought of Grant. This would take some explaining. *How long can I dodge this conversation?*

4

Trisha had no time or reason to visit Adda Marsh on Crawford Street, yet a magnet force pulled her. Adaline to Adda, top ten hit to street singer—the mystery intrigued her as much as the lady's music.

Trisha packed two lunches. Turkey and Swiss on whole wheat with lettuce, tomato, and pickle on the side. Two honey crisp apples, two bags of baked chips, and two bottles of water. She managed to squeeze it all into her canvas lunch sack and placed it in a tote bag.

A rare parking space opened on a side street, allowing her to avoid the garage two blocks away. Trisha heard the music before she saw Adda. She perched on the edge of a bench surrounding a massive planter. Adda glanced in her direction and gave an appreciative nod without missing a beat. Music filled the square, overshadowing traffic and pedestrians. She brought a sweet flavor to this corner of town. Adda sang some of the familiar tunes from Adaline's album, but Trisha waited and waited to hear her favorite. It never came. The song that had been her biggest hit, "Just Call Me Baby," didn't make her repertoire.

After fifteen minutes, when Adda announced she would be taking a break, Trisha grabbed her tote bag and hurried over "Can I help you, Adda?"

She eased out of the chair, holding on to the arm until she was balanced. "I'd be right grateful."

Trisha knew the routine and began wrapping up the microphone and folding the chair.

"Let me drop these at the door, and I'll be back for the speaker."

Adda shook her head. "No need. All this moving keeps this old lady going. Just drop them at the door, and I'll be taking my time getting this over."

Trisha hurried to the storage closet but came back to Adda who inched her way forward, pulling the cart with the speaker.

"Adda, I brought two lunches. It's a beautiful day. Would you join me? There are some café tables on the sidewalk right over there." She pointed to an ice cream shop two doors down.

Adda stopped walking and turned narrowed eyes toward Trisha. "I can't recall you saying your name."

"Trisha. Trisha Mills."

"And Miss Trisha Mills, what kinda work you do?" She stood in place, eyeing her.

"I'm a student. I go to Garlington Law School just north of here."

"You ain't a reporter?"

Trisha's mouth opened with understanding. "No ma'am. I'm just someone who loves your music. It helps me to remember my Pap."

Adda stroked her chin with her hand. "That so? All right. Then I'd be happy to share a meal with you."

When they reached the storage room, Adda turned to Trisha without unlocking her door. "I'll just be sliding these in here. You go on and get us one of them tables."

Trisha glanced at the empty tables. She started to speak, to offer help putting the equipment away, but Adda's feet stayed planted, her stance adamant.

"Sure. I'll get us a table and meet you over there."

At a table farthest from the street, Trisha pulled out her packed lunches. She placed them on the napkins she'd tossed in her tote bag.

"This is a real fine treat. Thank you." Adda bowed her head in silent prayer.

Trisha followed her example.

"So Adda, do you live close by? You seem to be here every day."

"Oh, I'm here every day for sure. Even Saturdays. Don't sing on Sundays. Leastways not for money."

Trisha repeated the first part of the question. "So do you live close by?"

"Can't get much closer. I live right there in the Mendino."

"How nice." She braved the subject she wanted to talk about. "You know, I lived with my Grandma and Pap, quite a bit older than me. Pap loved music and gave me an appreciation for it. We danced to music on his old phonograph."

"That so?" Adda continued eating.

"Pap had lots of music, but our favorite songs were from Adaline."

Trisha studied Adda's eyes for some reaction. They gave nothing up. Adda looked down and opened the bag of chips. With great deliberateness, she smoothed her napkin and poured half of the individual-sized bag onto it. Just when Trisha started to give up hope that she would respond, Adda lifted her eyes to Trisha's.

"I done figured you knew. You wore them questions all over your face." She opened her water bottle and took a long, slow drink. "Here's what you gotta know. There ain't no more Adaline. I'm Adda, my given name. That's all I am."

Trisha nodded but remained unsatisfied. "Can I ask what happened?"

Adda laughed. "Honey, age happened. You too young to understand. The body goes. The voice goes. The energy goes."

"I know, but your records, they sold...maybe millions."

Adda chuckled at that. "Well, you be givin' me too much credit, but yeah, they did sell back in the day." Adda looked at her watch and took a bite of her sandwich.

"So, I guess you're wondering where all my money went?"

Trisha backpedaled. The bluntness made it sound so callous. "That's none of my business, but..."

"You right there. It ain't none of your business. But I'll tell you anyways. My daddy, he was a sharecropper in Mississippi. We young'uns had to help when we got big enough to hold a shovel. I never got me past primary schooling. Them record people knowed it and all them fancy papers I signed didn't give me much left over."

Trisha gasped. "That's terrible."

Adda looked up from her lunch. "Oh, they treated me good. Real good. Set me up in a fancy place to live, bought me clothes and food. Dressed me for pictures and took me to the studio. But they never let me go places where I'd get to talk and never let me talk in microphones where I went to sing. Didn't want me having no friends. I knew they feared my poor schooling would show.

"Them fancy papers I signed said I worked for the record company and only got my paycheck. After time, my voice weren't as sweet, and I weren't doing new records. I had no paycheck at all."

Trisha stared at her, dumbfounded. How could they do that? This lady had an unparalleled voice. They were nothing without her. She deserved more than this. "Adda, I'm so sorry. That just doesn't seem right."

"Ain't right. But it's so. The good Lord watchin' over me anyways." She smiled. "I'm still using my singing to make me some living money. And you," she spread her hands over the table where they had just finished eating, "you blessed me with this feast. Now I gotta be getting back to my spot."

Trisha stood. "I'll help you."

Adda held her hand out, palm forward. "No ma'am. You done enough for one day. Thank you for your kindness."

With that, Adda disappeared into the crowd. Trisha swept her remaining chips into the bag of trash, still in disbelief.

~*~

That evening, Grant knocked on the door to her little apartment near campus.

"Well, welcome back, stranger." She held the door wide for him to enter.

"I hope you looked through the peep hole before opening?" He phrased it as a question.

"Always."

Grant scooped her into his arms, his lips meeting hers. "Missed you."

"I missed you, too."

She motioned to the cup of tea she had just prepared. "Coffee? Tea?"

"Isn't that supposed to be 'coffee, tea, or me'?" He reached for her playfully.

Trisha stepped out of his embrace. "I'll take that as a no. Sit down. I've got to tell you something."

Grant pulled his jacket off and tossed it over the back of a chair. "I hope you're going to tell me the house is ready to list."

Trisha had no desire to talk about selling Pap's house. "Do you remember me telling you how Pap used to teach me to dance? We'd spin around right there in the living room."

Grant gave her a lopsided grin. "I don't know how you managed without tripping over clutter."

Trisha scrunched her face and shot him a look, otherwise ignoring the remark. "Well, our favorite—both of us—our favorite was Adaline."

"I think I've heard of her."

"She was more famous in my Pap's generation. When I went through the albums, Julie recognized her. She's now a street singer over on the east side. I had to know if that was true, so I went there and met her."

He furrowed his brows. "By yourself? There're some rough neighborhoods over there."

"Not where she is. And yes, by myself. I'm a big girl, you know. Anyway, I've gotten to know her. We had lunch together today. Do you know why she's singing on the street?"

Grant crossed his leg over his knee. "No idea."

"The record company duped her. She didn't say it like that, but that's what it amounts to. They gave her a paycheck. A paycheck, for goodness' sakes, one of the biggest stars of her day. She got nothing for record sales, radio time, or appearances. Nothing! Just a paycheck like a grocery store clerk."

Grant shook his head. "Well, that's unfortunate. But Trish, I hope you satisfied your curiosity. I don't like you going over there alone, and you can't afford the time. Have you gotten enough sorted that we can list the house? Have you finalized the plans for the caterer and musicians at the wedding?"

Trisha sat back on the sofa and crossed one arm over the other. "Let me worry about my time management. Shouldn't there be two people planning this wedding? What have you done to get a caterer or musicians?"

Grant ran his hand through his hair. "Honey, don't make this ugly. I'm just telling you that I worry."

"I don't need your worry. But I do need your help planning a wedding."

"I've been in Dallas all week with a full itinerary and my boss at my side. What did you think I could do from there? You might have accomplished more if you weren't having lunch with street people."

Trisha jumped up from the sofa and faced him. "Street people?" The volume of her voice rose. "Adda's not homeless. She has an apartment. And what if she were homeless? Would that make her less important?"

"Not less important. Just not our kind of people."

She stood before him, chin lifted and hands palms up in front of her. "Really? I didn't know we had a kind of people. What kind would that be?"

Grant exhaled a huge sigh. He stood and reached for her hands. Trisha pulled back, crossing her arms over her chest.

"My father's a state senator. Ramsey's a household name in this state. Everything we do reflects back on him."

"So wouldn't it be a good thing to reach out to someone in need?"

"No, it wouldn't. They come with baggage. A quick check into their background and the media will splash it all over the news side-by-side with our picture."

Grant sat down and patted the space beside him. Trisha sat, but her back remained ramrod straight, her arms still crossed.

"Trisha." He put on his patronizing tone. "I was raised with the understanding that any flaw in me reflected directly back to Dad. You know he had a failed attempt at the governor's mansion. Eventually, he'll give it another shot. I have to live carefully."

Trisha hadn't given thought to his dad's career and how it might affect her future. "I'm not accustomed to measuring every word."

"That's why you have to stay out of situations you know nothing about. My dad dropped some gold nuggets about you to the media. When our wedding comes, they'll capitalize on the background of your grandparents' owning the mom and pop hardware store. People will love to hear the story of your humble beginnings and how you rose above that blue-collar mentality."

Trisha lurched to her feet. "Rose above it? That makes it sound like…" Anger surged, and she couldn't find a word to complete her thought.

"Unambitious?"

"That hardware store served this community. My grandparents worked hard. I'm proud of that background."

"And you should be. But you're not part of it

anymore." Grant stood again, his tone escalating. "You'll soon be a Ramsey. You need to start thinking about that."

Trisha walked toward the door. "What I need to start thinking about is studying." She held the door open for him. "We can talk at dinner tomorrow."

Grant walked to the door. He leaned in to kiss her but only caught her cheek.

When Grant left, Trisha went to the box of vinyl records. The cardboard carried a musty smell from whatever closet the box had been buried in. She leafed through the covers and retrieved the three albums by Adaline. The same record label recorded all three—Haven Records, founder and CEO Ernie Gillen. Pulling out her laptop, she typed in *Haven Records*. Their website appeared. A brief perusal indicated they were still in business, but they listed the CEO as Frank Gillen. Perhaps a son.

Trisha logged onto a site with archived legal cases. She entered a search for recording artist contracts. It listed dozens of cases where artists had sued record companies and record companies had sued artists.

After reading a few cases, she closed her laptop, opened the same site on her tablet, and slipped into her pajamas. She fell asleep reading archived legal cases involving record companies, hoping somehow this would double as studying for the bar.

5

Seated in the high-backed booth, Trisha sipped her vanilla cappuccino. She would have opted to head straight to Pap's house, but Julie insisted that coffee and a bagel would come first. The time spent sitting here was worth Julie's help.

Julie swallowed the bite of bagel and washed it down with coffee. "So, where's the Saturday dinner this week?"

Trisha smiled. "Blowing Rock. I love that little town."

"Wow, that's about two hours away. Long drive for dinner."

Trisha nodded. "Not quite two hours. We're leaving around four. We'll have dinner then mosey around some of the shops. It's a drive, but it's worth it. There's something relaxing about Blowing Rock, like stepping into the past."

Spreading cream cheese on her last half of a bagel, Julie raised her brows. "So, are you telling him about renovating the house tonight?"

Trisha rested her chin on her hand. "I hope to. I think I need to test the waters—see what the mood is. He got upset with me last night for visiting Adda." She drummed the table as she frowned. "Then I got annoyed at him for telling me what to do."

"Uh-oh." Julie leaned forward. "Did you smooth

things out?"

Trisha grimaced. "No. I asked him to leave."

Julie widened her eyes. "You didn't!"

"Did."

"Girl, what are you thinking? You gotta work through those things. And, did you ever think he might have a valid point? You've got a full plate."

Trisha set her mug down. "I can't explain it, Jules. I keep thinking of Adda, of her beautiful voice, how Pap and I both loved it. It makes me so mad that they didn't treat her right. Just because she was uneducated. Or maybe it's because she's a person of color."

"I hear you, but you've gotta take care of yourself right now."

Trisha glanced at her phone to check the time. "Ready when you are."

Julie took a final sip of her coffee. "Ready. Let's get some work done at the house before Romeo whisks you away."

~*~

Adda rested on her mattress, too fatigued to get up. Chills had started during the night, and her joints ached. Her throat felt like it was on fire and everything sounded hollow. There would be no singing today with a fever burning in her head. No singing meant no money.

Her mind went to the girl—Trisha Mills. Sure had been nice to sit across from somebody while eating a meal. Adda couldn't remember the last time she sat at a table with another person. Didn't appear to be a soul in this whole world that cared much about old Adda

Marsh. Maybe Trisha Mills did. Maybe the music did connect them.

The girl had some kinda spunk, getting all that schooling to be a lawyer, learning how to take care of herself so no scheming man would fool her. She must be one smart lady. At her age, Adda had been spineless. Spineless and foolish. Good looking white man, swept on in and sweet talked her, and she melted like last winter's snowman. Ernie, he was no fool. He played her well.

Adda managed to swing her feet to the floor and sat there until the dizziness passed. She tested her footing before trying to step. When she felt secure, she walked over to her tape player and put in the song she never sang anymore, the one she wrote for him. It didn't win him over, but no doubt made him rich. She almost won a Grammy for it.

Sitting on the side of her bed, Adda closed her eyes and went back in time where she had refused to go. That was before Trisha. The girl brought it all back, fresh and new. And painful.

I just want to walk hand in hand
Let everybody see that you're my man
And everyone will know that I'm your lady.
You say that we're just friends, that's how it has to end.
But I just want to hear you call me Baby.

It was the second year the awards were given. He'd brought a satin gown for her to wear, alabaster white. The fit showed every curve of her hips, her buttocks, her breasts. Ernie said it made her honey-brown skin shine like gold. She sat beside him, a vulnerable eighteen-year-old caught up in a world she didn't know, smitten by a white man twice her age.

When they called the names of those nominated

for female vocalist, they said Adaline right there along with the others.

Ernie squeezed her hand, and she sat there clinging to it, scared of not winning and disappointing him, and half scared of winning and walking up to that stage. Everybody else who went up did some talking. Ernie said if they called her name, she was only to say 'thank you' and sit down. When they announced the winner—Ella Fitzgerald—Ernie dropped her hand. He shifted away from her touch with a weak clap of his hands. She'd agonized, not because she hadn't won, but because he'd pulled away. Later the press criticized her for refusing to applaud.

Adda turned the tape off and pulled on the wrinkled clothes from the floor where she'd discarded them. Sick or not, she needed to get up, use the bathroom, and get something hot to drink.

She hoped she would see Trisha Mills again.

~*~

Daffodils, hyacinths, tulips, and crocuses peppered the landscape on the road leading to Blowing Rock. Yellow forsythia bloomed along the sides. Spring had burst through this mountain town.

Stealing a sideways glance while Grant drove, Trisha smiled in appreciation. He wore khaki's and a black polo shirt, his RayBan's shielding the sunlight. So urbane, he could model for a magazine ad.

She stroked his right shoulder. "I'm sorry I was snippy last night."

Grant reached up and took her hand, lacing his fingers through hers. "No worries. Let's just have a nice evening. What did you do today?"

She separated their fingers and placed his hand on the steering wheel. The mountain road curved while it inclined. "Julie and I worked at Pap's." She wanted to hold this conversation for over dinner.

"How's that coming?"

"OK. Sorted through a lot. Are those mountain laurels? Look—there's the statue with the flower pots." Nice topic shift. If he noticed, he gave no indication. "Did you manage to get those three accounts you tried to secure?"

"Two of the three. I think I've lost the third. They're going with another financial planner. At least, I signed the two larger ones."

The intersection came into view and conversation shifted to which road to take.

~*~

Grant held the door for Trisha as they entered the restaurant. They slid into a booth across from a counter with every imaginable beer on tap. British flags hung limp without the wind to lift them.

The English Pub drew a crowd. The locals recommended it for having the best fish and chips this side of the Atlantic.

It was an indulgence, but both Grant and Trisha ordered the fish and chips. Served steaming hot in baskets with tartar sauce and malt vinegar, the meal justified every fried calorie.

Adda Marsh and renovating Pap's house occupied Trisha's mind, but she hoped to avoid both topics for now. It wouldn't be good to start dinner with tension.

Law school should be a safe subject.

"My classes seem to have eased up some. I worked ahead on my project and have a little breathing room."

Grant sipped his water. "Are you feeling prepared for the bar?"

Trisha hesitated. She never knew what would set Grant off these days. "The bar? Well, I'm just not sure. I may have to do the next sitting. That seems to make sense. I could concentrate on classes and the wedding. Then this summer, after the wedding, do a bar exam prep workshop and take the test in the fall."

Grant's lips pressed together. Trisha could see the tightness fill his jaw before a staged smile replaced it. "Honey, that's fine with me, but I've heard the sooner you take it, the fresher the content will be. There are better success rates during the final semester or soon after it."

Trisha fingered the lantern throwing a dim light on their table. The iron base and white dome were replicated throughout the pub. "I know, but factor in Pap's death, the wedding, the house. I think I'll have a better chance of success if I do it this way."

Grant picked at some invisible spot on his sleeve. "If that's what you decide, it's fine with me. Maybe the house will be a non-issue. It should be taken care of before all that occurs."

For some reason, Grant obsessed about selling this house. Trisha's chest tightened, and she looked him square in the eye. "I'm not planning to sell the house right away."

She waited, trying to gauge his response. He picked up his glass and gave her nothing beyond neutral. He sipped his water then dabbed his napkin on the condensation that settled on the wooden table.

"What will you do with it?"

Was he really OK with that? Trisha's excitement mounted. "I've been looking around, and I think that old house has potential to be restored."

"Restored? Are you kidding me?"

Trisha leaned back and crossed her arms. "Yes, restored." Her eyes bore into his, her tone resolute. "I've talked with a contractor, and he agrees."

Grant rubbed his temples. "Trish, of course he agrees. Did you expect anything different? Someone comes to me and asks if I think he needs a financial planner, what do you think I'm going to say?"

Arms still crossed, she focused her gaze on his. "I hope you'll give an honest answer, just like Mr. Wallace gave me. And, you can put your cynicism away, he isn't charging me anything."

Grant moved forward, closing some of the space she had created. "Well, my cynicism is common sense. He's getting something out of it. You just need to dissect the contract and find out where."

Trisha unstiffened, placing her hand on his. "Let me start over. I didn't phrase that well. I called Jimmy Wallace from church. He's a friend of Pap's and a retired contractor. He's willing to coordinate the subcontractors and oversee the work, just because he needs a project. Well, that and because everyone there loves me." She ended with a tilted head and slight grin.

Grant sat looking at her, not responding. He shook his head as if clearing cobwebs. "Whatever."

She leaned forward. "No, not whatever!" She raised her voice. "What in the world do you mean by that? This is my house, Grant. Mine. You can't rush me into selling it."

"Your house? Well, silly me. I thought as man and

wife, what was mine would be yours and yours would be mine."

"And it will be. When we're man and wife. In the meantime, I want to see what that old place can become."

"And then we'll sell it?"

"And then, we'll see."

After dinner, they visited a few shops, avoiding conversation. The ride home was silent as Trisha nursed resentment.

6

It was designated project week, and Trisha had no classes. She did have an appointment with her professor to discuss her project and goals. When they finished, Trisha took time to ask a few questions.

"Where would someone go to get free legal help? I see ads all the time, but I'm not sure what would be the best route to take."

He sat across from her at his office desk. "Is this for you?"

"No. Someone I met. She can't afford to pay."

"As you well know, some attorneys won't charge up front, only a percentage of what they secure for you. That's the most conventional route. But if you want *pro bono*, I'll give you a name. He was a former student, sharp as a whip, and required to do some *pro bono* work at his firm." He opened his desk drawer and searched until he came up with what he sought.

He handed Trisha a business card. Russell Bergstrom, Attorney at Law, Brackston Law Firm. "Call Rusty and tell him I sent you. He'll do what he can."

Trisha left his office knowing that she couldn't call Rusty or anyone else without talking this over with Adda Marsh. She picked up two lunches and turned her car toward Crawford Street. Parking, she walked toward the apartment complex but heard no music.

Adda must be on her break.

Trisha took a seat on a vacant bench and waited. After an hour passed, she began to worry. She stood with her tote bag of lunches and watched the revolving door. The doorman came out occasionally to hail a cab or help someone from their car. When she saw him, she quickly flagged him down before he disappeared again.

"Do you know where Adda Marsh is today?"

"Is that the lady that sings?"

Trisha nodded.

"Haven't seen her today. That's strange. She's always here."

"I know this is asking a lot, but could you tell me her apartment number. I'm worried about her."

He looked perplexed. "She doesn't live here. Just rents a storage closest for her equipment."

"I think you're wrong. She told me she lived at the Mendino. This is the only one, isn't it?"

"Only one I ever heard of. But I know all the residents, and she's not one of them."

That was puzzling. Trisha sat again on the bench where she had waited, trying to decide what to do next. She looked toward the storage closet that Adda rented. The door opened from the inside, and Adda came out. She walked slowly, almost painfully, crossed the street, and entered the fast food restaurant. Trisha had not seen her stop to lock the storage closet.

When Adda disappeared inside the restaurant, Trisha walked toward the door and opened it just a crack. She was intruding, even trespassing, but she had to know if her suspicions were founded.

Inside there was a closet with Adda's equipment, her chair, a utility sink, and cardboard boxes. A twin-sized air mattress rested on top of the boxes. Three more boxes served as a table/nightstand combination.

"There a reason you nebbing into my space?"

Trisha jumped at the voice behind her. Adda stood there with her one hand on her hip, the other holding a steaming Styrofoam cup.

"Adda, I, um, I …" she stuttered.

"You, um, what?" Adda mimicked her stutter.

Trisha composed herself. "You live here?"

"Yeah, I live here, and if you don't mind, I'd like to get back on in there."

Trisha stepped aside. Adda passed and walked into the small space.

"I brought lunch. May I come in?"

"You can come on in if you want, but you better be knowing that I'm sick. Not much place in here for these old germs to go."

Trisha scanned quickly. Adda was right. No windows and little air flow. She couldn't afford to be sick right now, yet she entered anyway. "You OK, Adda? You don't look good."

Adda tipped one side of her mouth into a half smile.

"I didn't mean it like that. I meant you don't look like you feel well."

Adda sat on the side of her bed. "If I felt well, I'd be out there singing." Her voice was raspy and an occasional cough escaped. "Now where's that lunch you talked about?"

Trisha opened her tote bag and pulled out two chicken-salad sandwiches, two side salads, and two bottles of water.

She began to set them upon the boxes serving as a makeshift table. Glancing down, each box had a label:

things to wear, things to eat, things to remember. Before Trisha could fill up the space, Adda lifted the lid on the top box labeled 'things to eat' and dropped the bottle of water into it. Inside were pretzels, a can of soup, and a box of crackers.

"Well, long as you're here, might as well have a seat." Adda motioned to the canvas folding chair beside the bed, the same one she used for singing.

"I thought you had an apartment in this building. Why didn't you tell me you lived in here?"

"Ain't none of your business. Don't need nobody fretting. I got everything I need right here." She lifted her sandwich for a bite.

They ate in silence. Adda just picked at her food. When Trisha finished, she stretched her head, craning to look around the closet apartment again. "You don't have a bathroom in here."

"I got me a sink with running water to wash up, and I got me a bathroom right across the street. They's open twenty-four hours. And sometimes they give me stuff that's gonna get throwed out. And I got me one electric plug right over there." She pointed to the one plug along the wall.

Adda cleared off the box top and put the trash in a plastic garbage bag. "I take my trash back on over when I use the bathroom. Now if you're finished eating, I need to get me some sleep."

Trisha stood to leave, but then pointed down to the bottom box. "What's in there? Things to remember?"

Adda looked down, a shadow crossing her face. Trisha was almost sorry she asked.

After a long silence, she answered. "That's my remembering stuff."

Only a moment ago she was sorry she had asked, but the box held the mystery. Trisha was certain of that. "What kind of remembering stuff? Is it about your music?"

"It's stuff that helps me remember all the parts I don't wanna be forgetting."

"Would you show me?"

Adda looked at her for a long minute. "Guess there ain't no secrets since you know I was Adaline. Yes, Miss Trisha Mills. I show you. I show you another day. You come back sometime after singing's done and see."

Trisha resisted the urge to hug her. She left behind her own unopened bottle of water and closed the door. When she reached her car, she locked the door, pulled out her wallet and retrieved the business card for Mr. Russell Bergstrom. She changed her mind. She would call him before talking with Adda. No sense getting her hopes up if he wasn't optimistic. She set the card on her console and drove home.

Trisha's phone started ringing as she unlocked her apartment door. She reached into her handbag to catch it before the caller hung up.

"Trish, it's Jimmy Wallace here. Is this a good time to talk?"

"Yes, Mr. Wallace. Just give me one moment to get in the door. I'm just getting home." She unlocked the door, dropped her bag, and reached to flip the deadbolt, a long-time habit since living alone.

Plopping onto the sofa, she returned to the call. "OK, now this is a good time."

"Well, one thing we need to be getting straight. You gotta start calling me Jimmy. Mr. Wallace makes me sound old. Never mind that I am. No reason I have to be reminded."

Trisha laughed. "It's a deal, Jimmy. So, what have you been thinking?" She used her toe to drop first one shoe, then the other before stretching her legs out and resting them on the coffee table.

"If you're ready to start, I see no cause to wait. The first thing is to have someone check for termites. That front porch concerns me. If that comes back clear, I would strip the carpet and all the flooring and see the condition of the hardwoods. Best case scenario is they'll need to be stripped and refinished. Worst case is some might need to be replaced, but we'll need to match the old original flooring with some reclaimed wood to keep the authentic look. You have some heavy-duty balusters on that stairway. We'll clean those up along with the rail and newel posts before we do the treads."

Trisha was nodding, but he couldn't see that. "Yes, yes, that sounds good. One question—not knowing how far my funds will go, can we start with things that can be finished and make a difference, possibly leaving other things for later?"

Jimmy responded. "Sure can, but not that front porch. That's got to be gutted and rebuilt. We can't save those floor boards or the rail. Fortunately, it's sturdy where it ties into the foundation. And you still have old fuses inside. We'll need to bring that up to code with breakers. I'll get you a price for those things—rebuilding the porch, upgrading the electric, and refinishing the floors."

"Great. I'm excited to get started."

"Oh, and Trish, even though the original porch didn't wrap around, that house is perfect for one. We could build a wrap-around porch on the front and the east side of the house. If you like, we could even open that dining room window into French doors to access that side of the porch."

Trisha hadn't thought about that possibility. The dining room window had the beautiful mountain view. Could she actually sit out there in the open air and gaze at their beauty? "Oh, that sounds interesting. Can you price it both ways?"

"Will do. Hope we can get workers in there next week."

"Jimmy, how can I thank you enough?"

"Already told you—graham cracker cream pie."

Trisha looked over at the stack of folders on her table. She needed to get working, but her mind was filled with Miss Adda Marsh and Pap's house. She picked up the card beside her purse and dialed.

A female answered. "Brackston Law Firm."

"May I speak with Russell Bergstrom, please?"

"May I tell him who's calling?"

"Trisha Mills. He doesn't know me, but please tell him that Professor Samuels suggested I contact him."

"One moment, please."

Trisha was connected with classical music while she waited. Every few moments, the music was interrupted to tell her how much Brackston Law Firm appreciated her, thanked her for holding, and rewarded her with more music. She was just about ready to give up when a male voice answered.

"Hello, this is Rusty Bergstrom."

"Mr. Bergstrom, thank you for taking my call."

He gave a short snicker. "How could I not? Brooke said Professor Samuels sent you. I graduated two years ago, and I'm still afraid of that man."

Now Trisha laughed. "Yes, he is quite an imposing

figure. I wouldn't want to go against him in court."

"My worst nightmare. How can I help you?"

Trisha's eyes traveled to the boxes of vinyl records. "It's complicated. I'd like to stop in to see you if I may. But I wanted you to know that I'm looking first for advice, and then for some pro bono help."

"Well, I couldn't turn away a friend of Professor Samuels. I have a certain amount of pro bono hours I'm required to fill. I'll be glad to talk with you, but keep in mind, there are always more requests than I can fit in. Let's schedule something for…" He hesitated, probably checking his calendar. "Actually, I have some time tomorrow morning. Is nine o'clock good?"

"I'll be there. Thank you." Trisha's hopes plummeted. Her request could be placed in a stack of hundreds waiting for some future decision. If she couldn't find someone to work pro bono, she wouldn't be able to help Adda. She'd be stuck in that unheated storage closet.

7

Adda drifted in and out of sleep. Well, now Trisha knew the truth about this closet apartment. There had been no lie. Adda had said she lived at the Mendino. But the box—why did the girl have to ask about that? Adda glanced down at that box like she could see right through it, see her seventy-five years of living all flash before her like a bad movie. She could have said no, but maybe it was time to watch that old movie again.

With no kin that cared or even knew the whereabouts of Adda Marsh, it was a good feeling to know that today, someone had been looking for her. She'd show Trisha Mills her "things to remember." But first, she had to look at them herself, pick the right order.

Adda slept, but at the first morning light creeping through the bottom threshold of that metal door, she swung her aching legs over the side of the mattress, pushed her feet into the slip-on shoes, and stood to walk across the street to her bathroom.

Carrying a cup of coffee and a biscuit that the manager slipped her way, she carefully set them on the concrete floor. That allowed her to move her food box from the top of the three. It had little openings on the side that made it nice for lifting. Next was her clothes box. That was a little heavier because she had herself an extra pair of shoes. She was able to slide that one right on over to rest on the food box.

Adda sat on the mattress to catch her breath before lifting the lid off of the remembering box. It was the fullest. There was a lot more to remember than there was to eat. Some of the remembering was good. But mostly it was hard.

Adda picked up a photograph of her family. She never questioned where they got it or how they had afforded such a fine picture. It was black and white with a white border around the whole thing. Little curvy cuts made up the white paper frame. There were her mama and daddy, standing straight in the middle, all nine of their children surrounding them, everyone smiling for the picture.

She started with the one on her left because that was the way she was told to read—left to right. Leila, Jamal, and Rosa were first, next to Mama. Then Daddy was standing with Berta, Kande, Kioni, and Luther, beside him. She and Minny were in front of Mama and Daddy. They were the littlest. Adda figured she must have been around four years old, and Minny just a tad younger.

Adda looked beyond the people and saw her growing-up home. There was that old house with the two windows that always stayed open, trying to get some air inside those three rooms. The front porch had big rocks pushed under the corner poles to keep it level. Adda remembered the time Luther slithered under that porch, hiding when he was a'feared that Daddy was gonna whoop him. Didn't take Daddy no time to find him cause that dry old dust started Luther coughing. Daddy whooped him, once for disobeying and twice for hiding.

The big pole furthest from the door had the

clothesline attached. Then it stretched out to a big old Elm tree. There were no clothes hanging on it, which was a strange sight. Adda never remembered the clothesline being empty.

She placed the picture face down and pulled out a frayed piece of fabric, no bigger than a hand towel. The floral pattern was faded beyond recognition, but Adda saw it clearly. She had those tiny pink roses burned in her mind, their green swirly stems all sewed with hand stitches. Mama had sewn the blanket when Berta was a little child, but when she tried to hand it on down, Berta threw a fit. Adda kept sneaking to use it, and Berta would snatch it back. That was about the finest thing inside that little old rough wood building. Adda held the scrap to her face and brushed its softness against her cheek. *Mama. Why didn't you help me?*

~*~

Brackston Law Firm was located in downtown Asheville. Trisha found the building and took the elevator to the third floor. The name of the firm was on a placard directly above the room number.

Trisha entered and checked in with the receptionist. After making a quick phone call, the young lady stood. "I'll show you to Mr. Bergstrom's office."

The doorway from the third-floor hall had been deceiving. It looked like a small firm with one entrance. However, as they walked back from the reception area, Trisha discovered a massive complex. They passed a number of closed doors and two open spaces that were clearly for conferences. Turning toward the left, she found herself in another hallway with more offices. One of those was labeled *Russell Bergstrom, Attorney at Law.*

The receptionist rapped lightly and opened the door. The man inside stood from his chair and walked from behind the desk. He extended his hand before he reached her.

"Trisha? I'm Rusty Bergstrom."

Rusty was not the stereotype she imagined attorneys to be—suit and tie, dressed to the nines, all business. Grant would fit that exemplar. But Rusty was dressed casually, his sandy-brown hair longer and curling at the nape of his neck. But it was his eyes that she noticed first. They had to be the bluest eyes she had ever seen—not gray-blue, or slate-blue—but bright sky blue. She could picture him working in a ski shop or a tennis club.

"Hello." Her voice sounded small as she spoke and accepted his hand shake.

Rusty motioned for her to have a seat, and he took the chair across from her, a small table between them. "Brooke, will you bring us..." he turned back toward Trisha. "Coffee, tea, soda?"

"Just some water, please."

Rusty looked back toward the receptionist. "Water and I'll have coffee. Thanks."

When the door closed, he sat back and smiled. "So, how's Professor Samuels doing, the old prosecutor of law students?"

His casual style put Trisha at ease. "Still demanding, but fair. He expects a lot, but he's there to help us through it."

"Oh, you're way too kind. But enough about that. How do you like law school?"

He was making small talk. Trisha had expected someone stuffy who would hurry her, counting the minutes he could have been billing someone else.

"It's a challenge, but I do love it. I enjoy looking at old cases and watching clips of real trials. They're not quite like TV court dramas."

Trisha had to look away to keep from staring at his radiant eyes. She glanced around the office and saw his law degree framed and hanging. A photograph of two children rested on his desk. They would have been born before he graduated law school if he was only out two years. She was going to ask about the children, but Brooke returned with their beverages, setting a tray on the table with coffee, sparkling water, and a dish with individually wrapped tea biscuits.

When the door closed again, Rusty looked at her with those penetrating eyes. "So where do you see yourself headed?"

"I'm inclined toward family law. It feels like a better fit for me than corporate."

He shook his head. "Unfortunately, it's a growing need. Too many families falling apart. Too many kids caught in the middle."

"I agree. It's heartbreaking."

He sipped his coffee pensively, then turned the smiling eyes back toward Trisha. "So, what's the complicated situation you wanted to discuss?"

Trisha wasn't sure how to begin. She grinned sheepishly. "I guess I'm sticking my nose where it doesn't belong, but I see an injustice that's eating at me. I met a lady...no, let me start way before then."

She recounted the story of dancing to Adaline's music so he'd realize why this was important to her. After telling how she met Adda and learning of the way Haven Records cheated her, Trisha brought up the question of a lawsuit.

"I haven't spoken to Adda about the possibility of taking legal action. I don't want to do that if there are no grounds."

Rusty was contemplative, jotted a few notes on a tablet. "Can you get your hands on a copy of her contract?"

"I can try. I suspect they crossed their t's and dotted their i's. It probably lays it out just as she told me. But that doesn't make it right."

"No, but it does make it legal."

"So, you don't think there's any use pursuing?"

He looked up with a twinkle in those blue eyes. "I didn't say that." He jotted a few more notes. "Let's start with the contract. If it's not rock solid, we can work there. If it is, we'll have to decide what argument is best. We'll need to know if that was a typical business contract for Haven. They don't have to offer royalties if they wish to structure their business in an atypical manner. But if they use a traditional pattern of royalties for all except Adda, then we may have an argument."

The more he spoke, the more those eyes became animated.

"So you'll take this on?"

"I'd love the challenge, Trish. But Adda would be the plaintiff. If she's not up to the fight, there can't be one."

It was a small and inconsequential manner of speech, but "Trish" instead of "Trisha" brought a flush to her face. Many people called her Trish. Why did it suddenly sound so personal?

"I know. And you'd do this pro bono? You said

there are more requests than you can fill."

"Yes, I would. It sounds like a worthy cause."

They sat in silence for a moment. She sipped her sparkling water, and he finished the last drop of his coffee.

"I better go." She stood, and Rusty joined her. "Thank you."

"Don't thank me yet. Talk with Adda. See if she's ready for a mêlée." But there was a sparkle in his eyes. "I'll wait to hear back from you."

Trisha left the building and walked to her car, amazed that he had agreed to take the case. That was one successful hurdle. But would she be able to convince Adda to go through with it?

8

Trisha pulled up the gravel driveway to the farmhouse to find Jimmy's pick-up truck parked there. She went in the kitchen door and called out his name.

"In here." He turned as she walked into the living room. He held sandpaper in his hand; a toolbox sat on the hearth beside him, and a tool belt was strapped around his waist.

"Jimmy, I thought you were getting subcontractors for the actual work." She peered over his shoulder. They hadn't talked about the mantel.

"Not for this. This mantel is a work of art. Tiger-eye wood. Don't see that too often. I'm just easing out some fine scratches and a few nicks. Then I'll rub in the bee's oil and bring back the original shine. Oh, and my nephew does chimney sweeping. I had him over here yesterday, and he cleaned it out. Didn't want to pretty this up 'til that job was done."

Tiger eye? Trisha looked closely at the mottled-brown background, the fine black lines striped throughout, curving into the optical of a cat's eye. "Is that what it's called? I can see why."

"It'll stand out even more after we bring the shine back. Look at the detail this has." He traced the curved supports that tied it into the brick firewall. Floral foliage was etched into the scalloped front, draping over the brick.

Grandma had always complained that it was a dust collector. Trisha remembered her using a feather duster to reach into all of the floral crevices.

"You got my message that the termite inspection was good?"

"Yes, that was a relief. I saw the prices, and we're fine to start with the floors and rebuilding the porch. And I've decided to do the wrap-around. The beautiful view of the mountains from that side will make it worth the extra money."

He motioned toward the end table with his free hand. "There's a brochure with railings. I circled a few I thought would match the architecture here. They're all in the price range that I sent. If you want the bigger ones, they're a little more money. But I don't think they would fit as well with the character of this house. Don't forget to pick out a post cap too. We'll only need them on the stair posts. All the others will tie into the ceiling."

Trisha picked up the brochure and flipped to the pages where Jimmy had placed little post-it notes.

"I kind of like the colonial spindles and the New England post cap. White spindles and posts. Woodgrain rail?"

Jimmy smiled over his shoulder. "Good choice. That'd be my pick, too. They'll be here to demo that porch on Thursday. I told them not to touch the box gutters. You don't see those anymore. We need to protect them."

He took a moment to dust the mantel. Then he rubbed his hand over the surface, walked the length of it, and eyed it closely. Finding some imperfection, he switched to a different grade of sandpaper and smoothed it out.

"I can't wait to see how it all comes together. Are you sure Mrs. Wallace doesn't mind you spending so much time here?"

"Kim? She's happy to have me out from under foot. Today I'm hiding out to get away from her book club. Ten ladies meeting at our house." He gave a mock shudder. "I hope to have another crew start uncovering the hardwood floors this week. When we see how your funds are holding out, you might want to look at the windows and siding next."

Trisha cringed. "Sounds expensive."

"Yep, both of those things can be expensive. May not need to replace the siding if we can power wash it. Depends on how well the wood handles it."

"Do you think all of the windows will need to be replaced?"

"Eventually, yes, but we can start with one room at a time. I'll save you some labor cost. When we buy the windows, my boy will help me slide the first-floor ones in place. Nothing to it. I can't handle doing the second floor. Not quite steady enough on a ladder."

Trisha shook her head. "I don't want you doing that. Just hire it out."

He put the sandpaper back in his tool belt and ran a dust cloth over the smooth top surface. Then he turned toward her with a little grin. "We'll see."

~*~

Trisha pushed the shopping cart down the aisle with canned goods. She could pick up some things for Adda's box, but how would she prepare them? Cold soup had little appeal. *A slow cooker. That's what she'd do.* She had a small, one-quart slow-cooker at home that she seldom used. That opened up many possibilities.

Trisha maneuvered around two shoppers who obviously hadn't seen each other in a while. She reached for canned soups, vegetables, and fruits, all with easy snap-off lids. Moving around the bend toward the next aisle, she threw two bags of dried fruit and a can of mixed nuts in her cart. She added a box of crackers and a package of rice cakes. An end-aisle displayed a sale on tissues. As Trisha wheeled past, she tossed a box into the cart.

Adda might take offense to the charitable gifts, but she hadn't objected to the lunches. And she did live off of donations.

Rain was falling when Trisha reached Crawford Street. She drove slowly past the Mendino. Adda was not in her typical spot outside of the building. She may still be sick, or she may not sing in the rain. There was an overhang where she sat, but no one would be likely to linger. Trisha parked and walked toward the storage closet, balancing her umbrella and groceries. She lightly rapped on the door.

"Adda, it's Trisha." She was beginning to wonder if Adda might be across the street when the door crept open.

Adda looked terrible. Her hair was flattened against her head, and skin sagged beneath her eyes. "I ain't accustomed to no one knocking on this door. Don't get many folks come a'calling."

Adda held the door open for Trisha to enter. Then she walked slowly back and sat on her air mattress. She motioned to the tote bag. "You bring lunch?"

Trisha set the tote bag down. "Yes, I did. And a

few items for your 'things to eat' box."

If Adda was offended, she showed no sign. She opened the top lid and said, "Just put 'em on in here."

Trisha placed each item in the box under Adda's careful gaze. When she reached the bottom of the tote, she pulled out her slow cooker. Adda's eyebrows arched in question.

"I never use this. No sense it sitting in my apartment if you can make some use of it. You can heat soup and vegetables with it."

Adda eyed it suspiciously and nodded. "Just sit it on over yonder." She tilted her head toward the plug.

"Adda, how are you feeling? Are you still sick?"

She flipped her hand forward. "I'm old. That don't get better."

Trisha smiled. "But is the flu gone? Are you gaining strength?"

"Healing comes slow. Now where's that lunch?"

Trisha opened two bowls of hot vegetable soup from the corner deli. She pulled out crackers, applesauce, two giant chocolate chip cookies, and two half pints of milk. Adda bowed her head before picking up the plastic spoon and pulling the lid off of the bowl of soup.

When they finished eating, Trisha pointed to the bottom box. "You said you would show me your 'things to remember.'"

Adda nodded. "There's too much remembering for one day. We can start today, but ain't nothing in that box that means anything without the remembering. That takes some time."

Trisha nodded. "I have the time."

"Then move them first two boxes off."

~*~

Adda watched the girl lift the boxes as though they didn't weigh a thing. She remembered that feeling, when everything wasn't a task that wore a body out. Why did Trisha Mills keep coming? Adda had been foolish trusting folks before. She hoped she wasn't being foolish again. But then she found herself thinking of the girl, hoping she would come around. Sure enough, every couple days, there she was. Miss Trisha. She brought a spark to living that Adda hadn't experienced for a while.

Adda saw the food. It was more than her eating box ever held at one time. She probably should feel bad about taking charity, but she hadn't got any singing money for most of the week. The apartment manager would still be looking for his fifty dollars.

Trisha started to lift the lid off of the remembering box, but Adda stopped her. No sense her looking in when this would only be starting. Adda took the lid, tilted it, reached inside, and pulled out four items. She could see Trisha's eyes glancing down to take a peek, but this was her telling time. They would do it her way.

She turned the photograph up for Trisha to see. After naming all of her brothers and sisters, she pointed. "This is me in the front, right close to my mama, and Minny right close to my daddy. We was the youngest."

Trisha ran her hand over the old photo.

Adda pulled it back. "Didn't no one tell you, you ain't supposed to touch the picture part?" Today's pictures are different, but these old ones weren't meant to be touched.

Trisha flinched, putting her hands in her lap. "Sorry." She craned her neck forward to see the picture. "You all lived in that house?"

"Yes, ma'am. All eleven of us in three rooms. Most of the sharecroppers' families were the same. Some of them had more kids, a few had only a couple. But all the houses was the same."

When they finished with the picture, Adda lovingly stroked the swatch of fabric that had once been a blanket. She described her mama's fine stitching and how Berta never let her use it.

"When I left home with that record man, I sneaked in and took the blanket. I knew it was stealing, but I couldn't stand not having something that made me think of Mama. I'm sure Berta was boiling mad when she found it missing."

Trisha shook her head. "My mom died when I was twelve years old. I clung to things that reminded me of her. I still use the quilt that she kept on her bed. She didn't make it, but she loved it. Some days I rub my hands over the pattern, and I still cry."

Adda stared at her and nodded slowly. "Ain't nobody like our mamas."

"What else do you have, Adda?"

Adda carefully set the fabric on top of the picture and then turned her next item. It was a child's storybook, a little golden reader. *Guess we ain't getting past our mamas yet.*

"We never had much reading stuff in our house. No money for it and no space to keep things like that. But Mama kept this book for all of us young'uns. She read it to the older ones, then to Minny and me, telling us about the good Lord, Jesus. Then she'd pray out loud that He be watching over her babies, even when they weren't all babies no more."

Trisha scanned the book and took it from Adda's hands. She turned the pages—pictures of Jesus with children surrounding him, Jesus in a boat, and Jesus talking to a crowd of people. The pages were old and one was torn, held together with yellowing tape.

"Other people come and go. They ain't always there when you're needing them. But this book's reminding me that Jesus was everywhere I was, even when I wasn't thinking of Him."

Trisha handed the book back to her. "That's so true. I should keep something handy to help me remember that. It's easy to get so busy that we forget."

Adda placed the book gently on top of the fabric. She held up a crumbling piece of white plaster, stared at it, and placed it on top of the book.

Trisha reached for it. "Adda, you didn't tell me why you keep this. Is there a story here?"

She turned the plaster in her hand, looking for some meaning, but she wouldn't find it. It was just an old piece of plaster about four inches long, the story only in Adda's head. But she had promised she'd tell the remembering part.

"That was from a plaster cast when I got my arm broke. I was thirteen years old." Trisha turned it over and examined the fragments of fabric still clinging to it. That old piece of cast seemed to fascinate her.

"They don't use plaster ones like this anymore. I've never had a cast. How did you break your arm?"

Adda was silent, staring at something beyond the walls of this room. She spoke without looking at Trisha. "Like I said, my daddy was a sharecropper. The landowner let us stay there and make a living. It weren't much different from the time when there was slaves, 'cepting slaves weren't allowed no more. Still, if he didn't let Daddy stay, we wouldn't have no home. So that landowner done whatever he liked."

Adda reached for the piece of plaster and took it from Trisha's hand. She set it back on the stack of rememberings as if it burned her fingers. "That landowner started liking me when I was thirteen. After the first couple times he used me, I said no more. Then he done twisted my arm 'til I heard the break."

Trisha gasped. "Adda!"

"That's just the way it was. That's what my mama told me when we come back from the clinic. I lay crying on my cot, my big, old cast heavy as a workhorse laying on my arm. She said, 'Adda, we just gotta keep them white folks happy. That's just the way it is.' So, I kept him happy. 'Til he took a fancy to Minny a few years later."

Trisha covered her mouth and tears gathered in her eyes. Was she more upset about the landowner or about Adda's mama turning her head? They were worlds apart. Trisha's mama may have died early, but she probably never turned her back when the girl needed her. She sure had a soft heart, crying about an old lady's trouble from more than fifty years ago.

Adda reached over and touched her arm. "Don't be fretting for what's done, girl. The good Lord will have His say." Then she lifted the corner of the box and slid the four items back in.

That was enough remembering for this day.

9

Driving home, Trisha couldn't stop the tears. They blurred her eyes, but she kept going. An old urge to run gripped her. She had joined the track team in high school but stopped running when law school became all-consuming. But today, she needed to loosen the tight muscles and outrun the anguish.

She had her own grief at thirteen years old. Some days she harbored irrational anger at her parents for dying, for leaving her, uprooting her, making her change schools. But her logical mind knew it wasn't their fault. They loved her beyond measure. She grew up with that assurance. How could a mother turn her head away from a daughter enduring abuse and simply say, "That's just the way it is"? It made Trisha so angry she wanted to throw something, to lash out. But there wasn't anyone to throw anything at. Even the injustice of Haven Records didn't match this.

That reminded her...she hadn't broached the subject of the contract or seeking retribution. It would have been the wrong time. Too much pain.

Trisha turned into her apartment complex. She had been so consumed with Adda Marsh that she barely remembered the ride home. Grant's car sat right next to an empty space in front of her apartment. What was he doing here? Trisha pulled her car beside his.

For a moment, Trisha wished she hadn't given Grant a key. She turned the knob and walked inside. Grant stood in front of her sofa.

"Trish, I thought I would find you here studying." But one close look and he rushed to her side. "Honey, what's wrong? You've been crying." He pulled her into his arms and stroked her head.

Trisha melted into his embrace.

"Oh Grant, it's just been a hard morning." The tears threatened to return, but she refused them.

Grant led her to the sofa and sat with his arm around her.

"Tell me what's wrong. It can't be that bad." He held her hand with his free one, his thumb caressing her wrist.

"It's Adda. She just shared some awful things about her past." Trisha looked up at him, ready to share her sadness. Until she felt him stiffen.

"Trish, did you go back over there? I asked you not to. Now look at you. Why don't you ever listen to me?"

She pulled away and stood. "You asked, but I never agreed." Trisha paced, looking out the front window before turning back to Grant. She sat on the table in front of him and took his hands in hers. "Grant, when I walked in that door, I needed more from you. I didn't need your condemnation."

He exhaled a loud sigh. "Honey, I'm sorry, but you should've listened to me. I'm concerned about you."

"You know what? 'I'm sorry' shouldn't have a 'but' after it. That's designed to support your position instead of supporting me."

He scratched his ear, rested his head on his hand.

"I am supporting you. Someone has to be logical here."

"Can you stop being logical for one minute and show some compassion? You didn't even ask me about her, about what kind of trauma would make me so upset. Are you that callous?"

Grant stood.

"Callous?" He raised his voice. "If I were callous would I be so concerned? Maybe you're the one who's callous, ignoring my worries."

Trisha took a hard look at him and walked into the kitchen. She stood at the sliding door to her patio and tried to cool down.

After a few minutes, Grant's hand closed on her shoulder, his breath close to her neck. "I'm sorry." He kissed her neck. "I shouldn't have said that." His lips traced her neck to the side, and he whispered in her ear. "Forgive me?"

Trisha turned into his arms.

He kissed her.

When they pulled apart, she leaned against the door. "Why are we always sparring?"

He gathered her hand in his. "Because we're two strong people. I think we both need to learn how to give a little. Did you wonder why I'm here?"

She hadn't asked what would bring him here in the middle of a work day. She smiled up at him. "So why are you here?"

"I took today off work to help with wedding plans. Come here." He led her back into the living room and opened a folder. "Here's our band." He held up an advertisement for one of the three they had considered. "Signed, sealed, and paid for."

"Wonderful. One thing to check off the list."

"And Saturday night dinner is here." He handed

her a business card from the folder. It had the name of one of the caterers they had discussed.

"Where?" The card identified their place of business, not a restaurant.

"In their headquarters. They have a tasting room to sample menu choices. They assured me we would go home satiated."

Trisha beamed. "You took off work to do that?"

Grant tilted his head and the corners of his lips rose. "There's an awful lot I'd do for you, Trisha. I can't wait until you're Trisha Ramsey."

~*~

Trisha sat in her morning class. The phone in her pocket vibrated. She sneaked it out and glimpsed at a text from her uncle. *In Asheville on business. I'm at my parents' house. Thought I should let you know. You sure emptied it out in a hurry.*

He didn't say *hope to see you* or *nice job cleaning it up.* Trisha wished she could read his tone through the cryptic text. She noticed he called it "my parents' house," not her house, the farm house, or the old house. And he didn't say *home.* A house is just a building, but a home's where memories live.

She would take a drive out there to see him after class. He might be quirky, but he was the closest she had to family.

Class ended and students closed their laptops and fed them back into their cases. Trisha wove her way around loitering talkers and went outside. She dialed her uncle's number, but it went to voicemail. The text had come in twenty minutes ago. He must still be there, but she didn't want to ride thirty minutes to the farmhouse without checking first.

"Uncle Brendan, I'd love to ride out there and see you. Class just ended. Phone or text me a time that's good."

~*~

Since she didn't hear back from her uncle, Trisha left class and headed to Crawford Street for the second day in a row. She heard the music before she reached the apartment entrance. Adda must be feeling better, but that meant they wouldn't have time for "remembering," as she called it.

Rusty Bergstrom came to her mind. Today, over lunch, she must talk about the possibilities. Rusty's reaction to Adda's situation had been so different from Grant's. No, that wasn't fair. Rusty would have a vested interest. Even if he didn't make anything from the case, it would bring him some professional acclaim. Yet, his concern for the unfairness seemed genuine. Grant focused completely on Trisha right now. That should make her happy.

As she walked toward the entrance, she glimpsed a man dropping cash into the box and then turning to walk away. Her heart caught. Was that Rusty? But that would be too coincidental. It's just because he had been on her mind. She watched the back of the man as he walked away. His hair curled at his neck, a relaxed swing of his arms with each step. It could have been anyone.

When Adda took her break for lunch, they carried her equipment to the side of the building and Adda unlocked the door.

"Might as well help me get it all inside since you know what you're gonna see."

Trisha grinned at Adda's straightforward, almost cantankerous temperament, but a bond was forming. This season of life must be so lonesome for Adda. Where were all those faces she had seen in the photograph? With that many siblings, there must be a large extended family. Unlike Trisha who had no one. She longed for a big family, filled with voices and laughter at holiday gatherings.

With mild temperatures and the sun shining, they went to the outdoor café tables. Trisha opened the lunch pack and pulled out two fried chicken lunches she had picked up along the way. Adda's eyes lit up at the sight.

"Ain't had me no fried chicken in longer than I can recall."

"I try to avoid fried, but every now and then, I cave."

Adda nodded. "Back in Nashville, I weren't allowed to eat nothing fried. They kept me eating things that would show off the fancy dresses. Nothing fried, no desserts, no potatoes or pasta."

Trisha found the opening she needed.

"You know, Adda, they needed you more than you needed them. You could have stood up for your rights. In fact, you still can." Trisha paused, but Adda turned her chicken and bit into it, her eyes on her food.

"Haven Records cheated you. You could go after them and legally get what should have been yours. Even after all these years."

Again, Trisha waited for some reaction. Adda set the chicken bone down and picked up her napkin. She wiped her face, lifted her biscuit, and dipped it into the mashed potatoes and gravy.

Trisha watched and waited.

After taking a bite of the biscuit, Adda looked up. "Ernie's dead. Can't get nothing outta a dead man."

"The owner isn't the one who owes you, it's the record company. They're alive and well, maybe still making money off of Adaline."

Adda jerked her head up. "You saying people still buying my stuff?"

"Maybe. It's information that should be available to you as a recording artist. You should be able to track your record sales."

Adda finished the little cup of mashed potatoes.

"'Course they never told me nothing about no tracking stuff."

Trisha's eyebrows arched. "Adda, let's go after what's yours. You should be able to get yourself set up in a nice little home. You can't spend a winter in that closet."

Adda eyed her with suspicion. "And what you be getting for helping me?"

"Absolutely nothing. I wouldn't be the one to represent you since I don't have my license. And the attorney wouldn't get anything. Lawyers sometimes do something called pro bono work. That means helping people without taking anything for themselves. I know a man who would do that."

Adda picked up her cookie and took a bite. "I already spent a winter in my room. I got through it."

Trisha moved her empty lunch container out of the way and leaned forward. "But you don't have to. And Adda, if you fight Haven Records for what's yours, you might be helping some other young person. If they cheated you, no reason why they wouldn't cheat someone else." Trisha went on, "And I'll be with you every step of the way. You won't have to do anything. It's doubtful it would ever go to trial."

"I heard Ernie's son got the company. Frank." She looked at her wristwatch before continuing. "He was about ten when I knew Ernie. Foulmouthed kid. My daddy would'a whooped me for talking like he did, but Ernie acted like his kid set the moon. Frank looked at me like I was scum. Guess to him, a poor little black kid from Mississippi was scum."

"Do you have a copy of your contract with them?"

She glanced at her watch again. "I gotta get me back to my singing spot." Adda rose and gathered her trash.

"Adda, do you have that contract?"

Adda raised one brow. "It's in the remembering box. You come on by tonight, and we'll do some remembering."

"And we'll plan to go after Haven Records?"

"I said we'll do some remembering."

Trisha was walking to her car when the text came in. *Sorry. I'm tied up for the rest of today and leaving in the morning. Maybe next time I'm in town.*

She sighed. "So much for my only living relative."

10

Trisha answered her phone on the third ring.

"Hello, Trisha? It's Rusty Bergstrom here."

"Rusty. Hello."

She had nothing to tell him since Adda hadn't given her an answer. She hoped he wasn't backing out of his offer.

"I've been thinking of you a good deal since we met. I mean...thinking about this case. Have you had a chance to talk with Adaline?"

"I made the suggestion. Be careful not to call her that. She goes by Adda. She seems to want to distance herself from the other persona."

"Is she on board?"

Trisha covered her opposite ear to block out the noise from the coffee shop. "I'm not sure. I'm headed back to see her tonight. I asked if she had the contract, and she said to come back. I'm hoping to get a look at it."

"I've started digging into Haven Records. Much of the info I needed was either public record or easy to find. Seems their traditional contract is a royalty-based agreement. That makes it easy to present a case that they singled Adda out."

Trisha hoped Adda said yes, because Rusty had put in time for a case he didn't have.

"I haven't been able to get my hands on her record sales or live appearances, but if we file, it will all be part of discovery."

Trisha managed a quick sip of her cappuccino. "Record sales and airtime. Don't they track that info as well?"

"Recording artists don't get airtime royalties. That goes to the songwriters. But airtime increases sales. That's how it benefits the artist."

"Interesting. I didn't know that. So for Adda, we're just looking at sales?"

"Yes, unless she wrote any of the songs."

"I doubt that. She never mentioned writing. And she isn't very literate."

"Even for songwriters, music companies often include a controlled composition clause limiting their returns. But that won't have any impact here. Do you think she'll agree?"

"I hope so. I don't think she'll survive an Asheville winter in that unheated space. I planted the suggestion. I'll send you an e-mail tonight after I see what she's thinking. Oh, and Rusty, she's been taken advantage of and manipulated by people she trusted. I think it's left her skittish. She asked me what I would be getting out of it. I assured her I wouldn't get anything."

"I'll make it clear in the paperwork that there's no compensation for services."

"Thank you. And thanks for looking into this already."

Trisha imagined those sapphire eyes smiling. She disconnected the call and slid her cell phone back into her purse. Julie sat across the table from her in Brewsters Coffee Shop listening to her side of the conversation with her mouth gaping open.

"She's suing?" she asked with astonishment.

"I don't know, Jules. I've opened the door of possibility. It infuriates me that they treated her so badly."

"So who's Rusty?"

"A former student of one of my profs. He passed the name along to me." Trisha returned to her cappuccino.

Julie tapped a rhythm on the table between them. "Details. Details. You can't leave me hanging like that."

Trisha had no intention of sharing Adda's rememberings. She would stick to the record company's misdeeds. "I don't have any details. I went to see this attorney, and we talked about contract legalities. He thinks she may have a case. Much of it depends on Haven's traditional contract structure, which appears to be different from what they offered Adda. I dropped the suggestion, and she's thinking about it. I'll be seeing her tonight."

Excitement lit Julie's eyes. "I want to come with you."

Trisha shook her head. "No, Jules. She's still wary of people. I'm building a relationship based on trust and another person would set it back. Someday down the road, maybe. But not now."

Julie pouted and crossed her arms. "I'm the one who told you about her."

Trisha laughed. "Don't be a crybaby."

~*~

Trisha sat in the canvas folding chair across from Adda's bed, the remembering box waiting on the floor between them.

"Adda, you grew up in Mississippi then went to Nashville. How did you end up here in Asheville?"

Adda glanced down at the box. "We'll be getting to that. It's all part of the story. Now, here's the next things for us to have us a look at." She leaned over, one hand lifting the lid, the other pulling a few more items from the box. She sat up and rubbed the small of her back.

As Adda set them down and checked their order, Trisha tried to see if the contract was among them. Adda kept them well concealed. The timing would be hers. First, she turned over a paper menu. "This here's from the Cozy Café. I was fourteen when Rosa started waiting tables there. They had a lady who'd sing when the customers ate. Rosa kept telling me I sang as good, wanting me to talk to Miz Tizzie who runned it. Rosa heard me singing when I worked in the fields. I said it ain't the same as singing for people. But when Miz Tizzie heard me, she brought me in some days to sing for her customers." Adda grinned. "This is a good remembering. That was the first time singing got me any money."

I smiled with her. "So, singing came naturally, no voice lessons or teacher?"

She shook her head as she laid down the menu and reached for the next item.

"No lessons. I just sang to chase away all the sadness. Some days it worked. Some days the sadness was bigger than my voice could sing away."

She held an envelope in her hand. Trisha couldn't see in it but knew from the pained expression it would not be a happy memory. Trisha waited through the quiet moment and then asked. "Is this something that makes you sad?"

Adda gave Trisha a lopsided grin. "Oh, it has happy and sad all wrapped up together." She sighed and held the envelope for Trisha to peek inside. Trisha couldn't identify the black fuzzy material and reached to feel it. Adda pulled it out of Trisha's reach.

"You can't be touching that."

"What is it?"

She folded the envelope closed and placed it out of reach.

"Like I said, Mr. Gordon, the landowner, he been using me for two years. I started getting sick every day and Mama asked me if my bleeding stopped. That's when I first I realized I hadn't had bleeding for a while. Mama made me pull my dress up so she could be looking at my belly. She said I'd be birthing a baby for sure. Said she suspect I was about half ways ready."

Trisha felt the color draining from her face, nausea gripping her. Of course that would happen. No one would have been taking any preventative measures.

"Well, Miz Tizzie sent me away, said she couldn't have no sprite of a girl singing with a big old baby showing ready to come," Adda continued. "That ended my singing for money. When my birthing time started, Mama and another sharecropper's wife who done some midwifing were there. She sent everyone else away, which weren't too many, 'cause by now, just me, Minny, and Rosa lived at home.

"The midwife lady told Mama I'd be having trouble cause of being so little. We didn't have no doctoring money, so they done the best they could. My little one took a long time coming. It took two days, and I know Mama thought I was gonna see my reward in heaven, but then he came. He was so tiny and curled his little fists up tight. They took care of all the birthing stuff and laid him in my arms. He cradled against me just purring like a barn kitten. I ain't never loved like that a'fore." A sad expression crossed her face. "Or since."

She shook off the sad look and glanced at the envelope. "He was so perfect, tiny little toes and skin so soft. He'd take his little baby finger and wrap it around mine and squeeze. It felt real strong. But he weren't strong enough to live. In three days, we dug his resting place. Enam. I named him Enam 'cause it means gift from God. When I buried him, I added Job. Enam Job Marsh, cause the Lord giveth and the Lord taketh away."

Trisha pressed her palms to her eyes to stop the tears, but Adda's face was a shadow, hiding all emotion.

"Adda, what was in the envelope?"

She glanced at it again. "Didn't have no baby picture or nothing to remember my Enam. He had a full head of hair. I snipped me a piece before they wrapped him up."

Trisha wasn't sure she could handle any more memories tonight. But Adda held one other thing in her hand. When Trisha glanced at it, Adda shook her head as if that could remove the last memory.

"When I had me a baby coming, that's when Mr. Gordon started liking Minny. I didn't want Minny to have to go through all that, so I went to see him. Said to leave her be, and I'd be there iff'n he was needing. He just looked me up and down, up and down. He laughed and told me to get on home. After Enam died, I told Minny I'd be getting her outta there. I'd get me some singing money to take care of us.

"I wanted to get out of there right then, but I didn't have no means, so I planned to save up some to take me and Minny somewhere else, maybe to Jackson. I found some singing in a nightclub and told Minny it would be a couple weeks 'til I had enough for bus tickets."

Adda held out a cork coaster for Trisha to see. "One night after I finished singing, a waitress brought me this." She turned it over to show the note written in pen on the coaster. It said, "Stop by table seven. I can make you a star."

"Well, I stopped by table seven and met the record people. Oh, it weren't Ernie yet. But they sweet talked me about how famous I would be. I said I'd go but had to take Minny with me. I figured the good Lord sent me my answer. Turns out, it came too late. Minny's belly was swelling with child. I told her to come, and we'd get her a real doctor. But she wouldn't leave Mama. At least Mr. Gordon would be leaving her be."

Adda lifted the lid and placed the items inside.

Trisha wondered if Adda had forgotten their conversation from lunch. "The contract? Do you have it?"

"I'm reaching for it, girl." She pulled out a larger envelope with an old logo from Haven Records across the top. "I guess with you almost being a lawyer, you know what all this mumbo jumbo means?"

"Well, what I don't know, I can find out. May I see it?"

Adda handed the envelope over to her. Trisha slid the papers out and began to read. The contract dripped with intentional legalese, designed to be difficult for laymen. From her initial perusal, it looked like the record company had covered themselves by calling her an "employee" and repeating the term *work-for-hire* throughout the lengthy contract.

"Adda, may I take this to make a copy?"

"No ma'am. It ain't leaving my remembering box."

Trisha considered taking a picture with her phone, but the contract wasn't what she needed right now. She needed Adda's agreement to move forward. "Are you ready to let an attorney fight to get you what you deserve?"

"I've been a thinking on that since lunch. You said he don't get nothing?"

"That's right. And he'll put that in writing for you. I'll make sure it's clear and written to understand."

"And you said it wouldn't need to go to court?"

"Probably not. Record companies don't like the bad publicity. They prefer to settle these things out of court."

"I ain't wanting no trial. All I want is enough to get me a little room and some doctoring money when I'm ailing."

Trisha shook her head. "So you'll see him?"

Adda nodded. "I'll see him."

~*~

Even with the imperfections of the old phonography, Adaline's whisper-soft voice had a sweetness to it. Trisha closed her eyes and rested her head on the back of her sofa. She recalled hearing the woeful tones as a child. Maybe that's why she related so much to Adaline. Heaviness had blanketed her after her parents died, robbing her of the remaining years of childhood. She'd listened to the cooing of the mourning doves at Pap's as though they mourned for her.

When she'd first heard Adaline, it was like the mourning dove—someone who understood a broken heart.

Now she knew why. Adaline knew loss. She grieved for her lost baby and her lost childhood. They both craved the protective arms of a mother who should be there, shielding them from the hard side of life. Adaline's voice on the phonograph swelled, filling the room and the emptiness in Trisha's chest like the tunes of the mourning dove crying his sad notes.

Trisha wanted her mom to plan her wedding, to be there to help her dress and find something old, new, borrowed, and blue. She wanted her mom to pray with her as the music began. How she wanted to cling to her father's arm as he handed her over to Grant before kissing her forehead. She imagined looking up into his misty eyes and whispering, "I love you, Daddy."

Adaline's voice reached its crescendo, opening wide as all emotion broke through. Tears gathered and throbbed behind Trisha's closed eyes until she had no choice but to open them. Adda's heartache and her own converged, and Trisha shed enough tears for both.

When the song ended, Trisha opened her laptop, went to her e-mail and hit *compose*. She typed in Rusty's address and wrote, "She said yes."

11

With the first ray of sunshine, Trisha hopped in her car and headed to the farmhouse. Thursday had come and gone and she hadn't checked in to see what the workers had done. She pulled to the drive-thru window at the coffee shop and ordered a vanilla latte. As she turned into the driveway and her tires hit the gravel, she made a mental note to ask Jimmy how much it would cost to pave. Last winter's freeze and thaw filled the driveway with ruts.

Two vehicles had parked beside the house, a white work van and a pick-up truck. Men stood outside where the porch used to be. The rotted lumber had been discarded into a dumpster. Trisha parked and walked toward the elevated front door with nothing in front of it.

"Hi, I'm Trisha." She shook hands with both men. "You sure got that down fast."

The older of the two men chuckled. "It comes off faster than it goes up. We're waiting for the load of lumber to arrive within the hour."

"Anything done inside? I didn't get over here yesterday."

He nodded. "There were workers in there, but that's not us. We're just doing the porch."

"I'm headed in to take a look." Trisha walked inside. All the hardwood floors were now visible. They were rough, in need of work, but she began to envision what it would look like. "Wow." As she walked around, she couldn't keep the smile from her face. *Wait until Grant see's this. He'll know I was right.*

She turned and began to climb the stairs to the second floor. They had always squeaked, but now her footsteps echoed. With the carpet gone, only a few soft surfaces remained to absorb sound. The excess furniture had been taken to Goodwill, leaving minimal pieces.

"We'll take care of those squeaks," said a voice from behind her.

Trisha jumped. "Jimmy, you startled me. I didn't think anyone was here."

"Sorry, Trish. So, what do you think?"

"It's incredible. I can't believe how different it looks."

He wore a large grin. "I'm here to check out the hardwood. Carpenters told me they looked pretty good. Kitchen is the one spot where they'll need to replace some boards. Looks like some water damage got covered over. I'm checking it out, and then I'll start looking to see how I can match these boards. They were pretty high quality in their day."

Trisha decided she'd better look for Grandma's recipe, although it wouldn't be near enough reward for all Jimmy was doing.

"Oh, and watch the newel post at the landing. It's loose. I'd say it's a keeper, so I'll sand it up a little and tighten it."

Trisha looked over the rail at Jimmy. "I lived with that loose post for years. I always remember when I get to the top."

Trisha's cell phone rang as she talked with Jimmy.

She pulled it from the pocket of her jeans and answered.

Rusty Bergstrom's voice answered hers. He didn't identify himself, but she heard his enthusiasm. "I got your e-mail. Great news. When can we get together?"

Who in the world enjoyed doing free work? "I have classes in a few hours, and then it's the weekend. I guess the earliest we could meet is Monday."

"How about tomorrow morning. We can meet for breakfast."

Trisha sat on the step, her mind running through the weekend plans. Jimmy discreetly walked away from her conversation.

"Yes, I can do that. But Adda sings on Saturdays. I don't know if she'll give up singing to meet."

"We'll start with a meeting between you and me, and then we'll plan a time to meet with Adda."

"OK. Rusty, I've learned so much about her. I really want to see this work out."

"Were you able to get the contract?"

"I saw it, but she wouldn't let me take it. I considered taking a picture with my phone but didn't think it would be clear enough."

"No problem. We'll get it in due time."

Trisha went back to her initial thought. "Rusty, I know Adda, so that explains my involvement. But you sound like you're pretty motivated to take this on. Can I ask why?"

"Same reason I went into law. It's just wrong. If we can make it right, it'll be worth it."

Trisha smiled. "Thank you. It's the answer I had hoped for."

~*~

Adda woke. She tried to remember the day of the week. Sometimes they just seemed to run one right into the other. She went to the box by the sink where she kept her markings. Yesterday she wrote *Th* for Thursday. She learned that trick a long time ago so she wouldn't mix it up with Tuesday. Tuesday was just a plain old *T*. That made today Friday. She marked *F* next to it. Two more days before she had a break from singing.

Oh, she liked singing well enough, but a body got tired lugging all the stuff back and forth. What would it be like if Miss Trisha Mills was right and that spoiled little Frank had to give her enough to live on? She'd like to see his face when he had to hand some money over. Would it be enough to pay for a little place without getting singing money, or maybe she'd only have to do singing a few days each week. Right now, it would be good to just take a day off every now and then.

She hoped Trisha would come today. She didn't make it every day. Adda knew she couldn't always come, but it brought a real nice feeling to look up and see her sitting there. She never would'a thought about such a thing like getting her money from Haven Records without the girl. Maybe she was an angel God sent to help her through these years of being old. By her way of thinking, God owed her a little bit. She had expected she wouldn't be getting nothing from Him until the here and after.

Adda turned her eyes toward heaven. "Oh, I'm thankful for that, God. I don't mean no disrespect. But it would be real nice to get some of that reward on this side while things is hard."

She'd liked to have splashed some water on her face and freshened up a bit, and decided she'd better pull on some shoes and head across the street to her bathroom.

~*~

Trisha arrived to find Rusty waiting at the café. As Trisha walked through the door, he smiled as though they shared a secret and extended his arm with a closed hand. It took Trisha a moment before she caught on. She raised her hand to his for the "fist bump."

"Good work getting her onboard. I have a table in the back where we can work." Trisha stole a nonchalant look at him as he motioned her to the counter. Jeans, a Duke T-shirt, boat shoes, no socks. And eyes as blue as ever.

"Let's order. What can I get for you?"

"A vanilla latte sounds good."

"And?" His hand swept toward the menu items. "Don't make me eat alone."

She looked at the choices in the glass case. "Maybe an orange scone."

They waited for Rusty's breakfast sandwich then took the tray to the table in the back. Trisha's eyebrows raised when she saw stacks of pages waiting.

She turned toward Rusty and smirked. "I guess you really are an attorney."

"Oh, so the lady does have a sense of humor." His face lit with amusement.

"What does that mean?"

Rusty pulled her chair out for her. "You're quite serious. Humor's good."

Trisha wanted to be insulted, but he looked so relaxed that she sensed no offense had been intended.

"I grew up fast."

He sat across from her, pushing the papers to the side. "And why is that, Trish?"

There it was again. The familiarity, the intimacy of a close friend. "I thought you wanted Adda's story, not mine."

He touched her hand. "Sorry. Didn't mean to pry. We'll be working closely together, and I just want you to feel comfortable."

Her mind focused on one word. *Closely.* "What will you want from me?" When it left her lips, she realized how awkward the question sounded.

"Oh, sorry again. I may have jumped to conclusions. I thought you wanted to assist on this case. I know it's tugged at your heart. I also thought Adda might be looking for you to be involved."

"You're right, Rusty. I didn't mean it like that. In fact, I promised Adda I would be beside her all the way. And you're not prying. My parents died in an auto accident when I was twelve. My grandparents raised me, and they both died within the last year. Just six weeks ago for my Pap."

His face turned serious. "I'm sorry."

She put her elbows on the table and rested her chin in her hands. "That's three times."

He looked puzzled. "Three times what?"

Trisha leaned forward, a slight grin, forming. "We sat down approximately two minutes ago, and you've apologized three times."

Rusty tipped his head up and down, chuckling. "I learned early on that's a safe response. I'll be happy to have you work alongside me on this case in whatever capacity you have time for. I know you're finishing your final semester, but this would be great experience."

"You know, the semester started out pretty intense, but I feel like it's coasting now. I see the end in sight and think most of the load is behind me."

"I remember the same feeling. I suspect it's deliberate since they know you're prepping for the bar."

"Maybe."

His eyebrows rose. "Maybe? You're considering not taking it?"

"Just postponing. I'm not sure I'll be ready."

Rusty flicked his hand dismissing her concern. "Take it. If you don't pass, you just take it again."

Trisha's mouth gaped open. "I'd be devastated if I took it and failed."

He took a drink of his coffee and set the mug down. "Do you play video games?"

Where had that question come from? She laughed. "You mean in all my spare time?"

"No, I mean ever. Have you ever played one? One with different levels?"

"Well, sure."

"Did you ever get past the first level?"

Trisha crossed her arms, a playful smirk lighting her face. "Of course. Your point is?"

"Didn't you have to fail before you could succeed?"

"Ah, but that's not the same."

"Sure it is. No better prep for taking the bar than taking the bar. Many people don't pass the first time. You're looking at one."

Trisha pondered that. "I'll think about it. Now you

know a little about me. Tell me about Rusty Bergstrom."

His blue eyes twinkled with amusement. "My favorite subject. However, not much to tell. Grew up in Charlotte, business undergrad at Duke, law school here in Asheville, job with Brackston."

Trisha attempted an indiscreet glance at his left hand, but she couldn't see his ring finger. "Do you do anything for fun? Married? Kids? I saw pictures on your desk."

"You saw my niece and nephew. No wife. No kids. Love sports. Big football and hockey fan. You don't want to be anywhere near my brothers and me when the Panthers are losing. I still try to play a little deck hockey, but I'm getting older than everyone there. It's hard to match speed with twenty-year-olds. Hiking. I love these mountains. And I'll tell you a secret if you promise never to tell my brothers."

Trisha hesitated. "OK, I think."

He leaned in close and spoke conspiratorially. "I love going to musicals."

"And why is that a secret?"

"We're a football family. They moan and groan and carry on when their wives make them go to anything cultural."

"What's your favorite?"

"Hands down. *Phantom*."

Trisha shook her head. "No, no. Hands down, *Les Mis*."

He squinted, apparently thinking it over. "It's a close second."

Her eyebrows raised. "You're making me question your judgment."

Rusty laughed out loud. Then he changed the

subject, pointing to her ring. "So when's the big day, and who's the lucky guy?"

"June twenty-eighth. It's fast approaching. Grant Ramsey is his name."

"And tell me about Grant Ramsey."

"Grant's a financial planner with Linden Company. He's working hard to build his clientele."

"That tells me his occupation. Tell me about him. What do you two enjoy doing?"

What do we enjoy? Trisha had to search her mind. *We go to dinner every Saturday.*

"Well, life's been pretty busy for both of us. Right now, we just manage a Saturday dinner and planning a wedding."

He nodded as though he understood. It sounded pretty lame. Trisha decided she needed to remedy that as soon as they were married.

Rusty took his last mouthful of coffee. "Let me take these trays up and then we better get to work."

~*~

Trisha waited as Rusty logged on to his laptop and connected to the café's WiFi. He opened his notebook, sat back, and looked up. Trisha's earlier apprehension had faded with the small talk.

"You know you're studying for the bar right now?"

"Good. I hope this doubles for bar prep because I'm not finding much study time."

Rusty was suddenly all business. "Some ground work. We're not looking at intellectual property since Adda wasn't the songwriter. If that were the case, this would be a copyright dispute and filed in federal court. Instead, it's a contract concept, so we'll file in civil court. So, Counselor, where would you start?"

Trisha propped her elbow and rested her chin on her hand. She squinted, feeling the wrinkles form along her forehead. "I'm thinking we need to rule out gender or racial discrimination. Haven Records had other women and other minorities. Unless there's a trail of repeated discrimination, which I doubt, that wouldn't be an argument."

Rusty nodded his agreement.

"Maybe," she continued, "meeting of the minds? Both parties need to fully understand the terms, and Adda did not."

Rusty nodded. "Good thought. We don't see much of it, but let's not rule it out. If we use that argument, we're saying Adda wasn't capable of understanding the terms. Problem is, we can't just say she *didn't* understand. We'd have to prove something *interfered* with Adda's ability to understand unless the language is so vague it's rendered incomprehensible. I'll know better when I get a copy. That may not be the best fit here."

Trisha's pink-tipped fingers tapped a rhythm on the table. "What are you thinking?"

Rusty leaned back in his chair, head tilted upward, lips pursed. After a moment, he sat forward. "Let's look at undue influence or undue duress. What's the difference?"

Trisha laughed. "You certainly are making me study."

His blue eyes filled with mischief. "You gotta know these things. Nothing better than on-the-job practice."

"OK. How's this? Undue duress would be using force or blackmail. Some type of psychological pressure. Undue influence would be one party holding more power and using it to pressure the other."

He nodded. "Keep going."

"Here's my question. Where's the distinction in situations involving artistic people trying to break into cut-throat careers? Agents, producers, publishers— they always have more power, and people are looking for that big break."

"Good question. Undue influence indicates one party had mental, moral, or physical domination over someone with weaknesses, making that party more susceptible to persuasion. In typical cases, a musician may choose to start with a less-than-stellar contract to break into the industry. That doesn't mean the producer imposed unfair power. The artist still made a calculated choice."

Trisha nodded. "That may be our best argument."

"Agreed. And easier to support than trying to prove her mental capabilities from fifty years ago."

Rusty and Trisha mapped out some preliminary plans and cleared their table. The lunch crowd would be starting in before too long. They walked outside to Trisha's car. She had agreed to look into some case studies, noting anything applicable.

Rusty handed her a folder with some websites. "I wish I could set you up with space at the firm. I can't do that since you're not an official intern. Do you have a good place to work?"

"My place is pretty small, but I'll work at Pap's house. It's peaceful when there aren't construction workers. When they're working, I'll use the summer room. Nothing's being remodeled there yet."

"I love old houses. Is it a place we could meet when we need to regroup and discuss strategy?"

"Sure is. I'll bring you the address when we meet with Adda."

Rusty's gaze held hers, a slight grin on his lips. He opened her car door and held it as she slipped into the driver's seat. "See you Monday at six thirty at the Mendino."

As Trisha backed out of her parking space, she glanced back to see Rusty gazing at her. As she pulled into traffic, she managed one more look. He still stood there watching.

~*~

The caterer escorted them to a table and pulled a chair out to seat Trisha. Grant took his place across from her. A table had been set with linen, fine china, and wine glasses. The caterers had prepared five menus in small sample proportions. Trisha and Grant would choose which ones would be offered to their guests. The caterer recommended they have three choices for the sit-down dinner.

Each meal included a green salad, rolls, and butter in small, sampling quantities. The first items presented were Mediterranean chicken with artichokes, rosemary roasted new potatoes, and sugar snap peas. This was followed with a selection of Beef Wellington, garlic whipped potatoes, and broccoli.

Trisha thought back to the last wedding she'd attended. The bride was the daughter of Gram and Pap's friend from church. A buffet line loaded with fried chicken, stuffed cabbage, and an array of sides and salads filled the serving tables in the multi-purpose room of the church. She remembered people talking, laughing, and hugging. The casual, relaxed atmosphere would have suited Trisha well, but that would never do for Grant's family.

The caterer delivered each plate with beautiful presentation. The attendant, looking formal in his dark suit, described each selection with great detail. The pecan-crusted halibut came with rice pilaf and a squash medley. Stuffed pork loin with sausage stuffing and portabella mushrooms, green beans amandine, and saffron risotto in small portions were placed before them. Although each bite proved to be mouth-watering and delicious, Trisha was full way before they'd sampled everything.

Grant appeared to relish each spoonful, assessing the possibilities and commenting on the flavor, the texture, the presentation. The final meal was grilled salmon with mango salsa, julienne carrots, and an orzo vegetable blend.

As the wait staff removed the last plate, the caterer refilled their wine glasses and gave them some privacy to make their decision.

Trisha put her fork down and smiled. "I love this restaurant. Let's come back here every week."

Grant grinned. "And it's free."

Trisha laughed. "What would they do if we decided to use another caterer after they wined and dined us?"

He shook his head. "Oh, they didn't wine and dine us until I placed a deposit."

Trisha's eyebrows shot upward. "You already booked them?"

Grant gave her a nonchalant look. "Just a deposit.

Not enough to worry about if you weren't satisfied."

She nodded and flashed a conspiratorial grin. "Maybe we should tell them we can't decide. We'll need to do this again next week."

"I think next week we'd get the hot dog and burger sampling."

They made their three choices for wedding guests. Menu selections would be inserted into the invitation and returned to the caterer. They'd track them and take it from there. No work or worry for Trisha or Grant.

As they walked toward the car, Trisha hooked her arm through Grant's. "How about if I find something different for next weekend? Maybe a play or musical?"

"I fall asleep at those. Dinner keeps me awake. Dinner and looking across the table at you." He squeezed her arm.

"How about this? I'll pack us a meal and we could hike. There are beautiful trails through these Blue Ridge Mountains."

Grant shot her a look like she had lost her mind. "I can see it now. You walking down the aisle with a cast on your arm, meeting me with my crutches."

She mocked a shoulder punch. "We're not that clumsy."

"And we're not accustomed to hiking."

"Grant!" She turned and put her hands on her hips. "You can't get accustomed to anything until you start. No one's an expert without first being a beginner."

"Honey, I don't want to be an expert hiker. Not my thing. If you're tired of eating out, I'll bring dinner over and we can rent a movie."

~*~

Trisha arrived at Adda's by six Monday evening. She wanted to have some time to talk before Rusty arrived at six thirty.

"Adda, are you OK? You look tired today." Trisha reached for her hand and gave it a gentle squeeze. Adda grasped her hand and held it.

"I ain't had nobody fussing over me in a long time. Why you care about this old lady, Trisha Mills?"

Because you're a human being? Because you sing like an angel? Because you remind me of Pap? She thought through her words. "When I got to know you, I made a friend. Why do you care about me?" Trisha grinned as she turned the question back to her.

"I don't got no kin, leastwise that know me. I know they're out there somewhere. You might be the closest I got to having kin."

Trisha looked at their joined hands. Her pale skin enfolded with Adda's wrinkled brown hands. "Well, that's something else we have in common. I have no family except an uncle who doesn't seem to care about having a niece. Adda, with all of your brothers and sisters, why didn't you go home when you stopped singing?"

Adda released her hand. "I told you if you wanna hear my story, you gotta wait for each part to come. That one's a'coming."

Trisha stifled a smile. "I'll try to be patient. I've asked Rusty Bergstrom to join us tonight. He's the attorney that will help you get your fair share of money from Haven Records. He'll be here in a few minutes."

Adda wrinkled her brow. "He coming here?"

"Yes, I hope that's all right. I didn't know if you

would want to go somewhere else. We can go across the street to the restaurant if you'd rather."

She pressed her lips together and glanced around the closet space. "Guess it'll be all right since you already done it."

"He's rather nice, Adda. You'll like him. I'm going to go out and wait for him. I said I'd meet him near the door. I'll be back in a few minutes."

Trisha walked toward the entrance of the Mendino. Traffic whizzed by on the busy street. She found Rusty waiting on a bench near the entrance. When he saw Trisha, he picked up his briefcase and walked to meet her. "Are we all set? Is she OK with meeting here?"

"She's a little skeptical. I assured her she would like you. Be gentle on the legal parts for now." They walked along the side of the building to the storage room. Trisha tapped on the door then opened it. "I'm back, Adda."

"Ain't nothing wrong with my eyes."

"Adda, this is Rusty Bergstrom."

Rusty walked toward Adda and put his hand out. Adda eyed it for a moment then placed hers out for a brief shake.

"So why you be wanting to help some old lady you don't even know?"

The forthright disposition brought a grin. "Because you're a friend of Trisha's. And because, from what she's told me, Haven Records didn't treat you well."

"Humph. They said they treated me real fine. But that was before time started wearing me out—me and my voice."

Rusty motioned for Trisha to take the one chair in

the room. But she scooted over and pointed to the space beside Adda on the air mattress.

"May I?" she asked Adda.

"Come on and sit, child. And you can get sitting, too." She pointed Rusty toward the chair. When he sat, she took charge again. "I ain't wanting no court trial."

"It's unlikely it would ever reach that point. That's bad publicity for a record company. And people know your music. They know how gifted you are. It would look terrible for Haven Records if people knew they cheated you."

"So how's this work? You just go to Ernie's kid and ask for what should'a been mine?"

Rusty appeared to suppress a grin. "Not quite that simple. I file a legal document questioning the legality of your contract. Once filed, I'll be able to check things like your record sales and how much you would have received in royalties if you had the same contract as other singers."

"You meaning mine was different?"

He nodded. "Yes, Adda. It was different. Were you ever paid for live performances?"

"You meaning concerts where I sung? I was paid in my paycheck. If I sung an hour, Wanda Jean said they added it to my pay that week."

Rusty and Trisha exchanged glances. Her eyebrows raised, and he shook his head in disbelief.

"What I need now is to see your contract." He tapped his briefcase. "If it's OK, I have a machine in here that will let me copy it. I'll read all of the fine print and see how we can force them to give you royalties."

"So you can read all the mumbo jumbo?"

His grin brought a gleam to the blue eyes. "We learn mumbo jumbo our first year in law school."

Adda reached for the box on the floor. She lifted the lid and pulled out the contract. "Now this ain't leaving this room. It's for my remembering box."

Rusty put his hand up. "Scout's honor. I won't take it from this room."

He took the envelope and went to the electrical outlet, pulled out his portable copier, and copied all four pages of the contract. He placed Adda's copy back in the envelope, turned and showed her that all the contents had been returned, and handed it back.

"Next, I'll read through this contract, and with Trisha's help, we'll write a Complaint against Haven Records. Then, Frank Gillen will be served a summons. That lets him know about the lawsuit. He can either agree or disagree. If he agrees, he writes you a check for the amount we request. That's not likely to happen.

"If he disagrees, which we're sure he will, then we ask for some evidence. That means we'll get your sales record, talk with other artists or anyone else who would be able to support our case. We can track the concerts you performed, how many people attended, and how much money other recording artists received for similar concerts. At some point in this process, we're hopeful to agree on a deal."

Adda looked at Trisha for approval.

Trisha nodded. "All right, but Frank Gillen ain't gonna give me nothing he don't have to."

Rusty glanced at her. "That's why you have me and Trish to help you. I have a paper that'll need your signature before I can start. I'm going to ask Trisha to read it through for you."

Rusty retrieved a folder from his briefcase and pulled out one sheet of paper. He handed it to Trisha.

Trisha held it up and read it out loud while finger

scanning the words so Adda could follow along.

"It's a retainer for pro bono assistance. This part says Rusty is the attorney. It has his full name listed as Russell Bergstrom. This line says you are the plaintiff."

Adda nodded. "I see my name printed there."

"This next section says 'Attorney will assist plaintiff with a contract concept dispute against Haven Records.' Then this is the part about no fees." Trisha pointed so Adda would be sure to follow along. "Attorney will not charge Plaintiff for attorney fees. The attorney will absorb all costs and expenses incurred. This last line is for your signature."

Adda wrinkled her brow and looked at Trisha. "And you think I should do this?"

"I do, Adda. I think this is the right thing."

"Then fetch me a pen."

Adda signed the paper and handed the pen back. "I guess we're ready for a mêlée."

12

Adda lifted the lid on the top box. "Well, you might as well stay for the remembering. We getting to all the stuff about the record company."

Trisha turned to Rusty. "Adda has been showing me things from her memory box. It tells the story of her life. We do a few pieces each night we meet."

"I'd be honored to stay for part of your story."

Adda reached in and pulled two items from the remembering box. She held out the first item—a bus ticket stub. "Them record people who comed into the nightclub where I sang, they bought me a bus ticket to Nashville. Said someone named Wanda Jean would be meeting me. My mama, she was real happy for me, but cried when I left. That's when I went and took the blanket.

"The record men fetched me and took me to the bus station, waiting 'til I got on and took my seat. First time I got on a bus that wasn't for school." She held the ticket up to show the uneven creases where it had been crushed and smoothed open again. "I was a'feared 'cause I heard of bus troubles. I just kept my head down and walked on to the back. Kept holding on tight to the ticket so everyone'd know it was paid for." Adda shuddered at the memory of walking down that long row of seats, passing all those white faces. She took the ticket and placed it beside her.

"This is where the contract should be showed, but you already looked it over. When I got to Nashville, Wanda Jean stood there waiting. They must'a told her how to know me 'cause she came right on over when I stepped off that bus. Took me to a room to get cleaned up. She already had some fine clothes waiting and someone there to fix my hair and my face. Took her halfway through the afternoon, but when they got done, I didn't know the person who looked at me through the mirror. It didn't look like the Adda Mae Marsh my mama raised. I looked...special."

Adda glanced down at the small box in her hands. "They said I was perfect, and ready to meet Ernie. That made Ernie sound real important for them to be fixing me up so special before meeting him."

She looked past Rusty to the far end of the room. The walls disappeared and she was back there again, looking into that mirror. "Ernie, he looked at me like I was some real, first-rate lady. Like he didn't know I was a little poor girl from down in Mississippi. He looked at me from my head on down to my feet and then back on up again."

Adda grew pensive, remembering that moment, how her skin burned from the look in Ernie's eye. "'She's a looker, but can she sing?' He talked to Wanda Jean, not to me. Then they took me to a room with lots of music-making stuff and put on a song. I didn't know it, so they asked me what I wanted to sing. I told them, 'Love is a Many Splendored Thing.' I sang that one at the club. They put the music on, and I sang from this little room where they could see me."

Adda looked back, glancing first at Rusty then at Trisha. "Ernie, he come running toward me when I walked outta that room, grabbed me in a big bear hug, and kissed me full on the cheek. He said, 'Adaline, you're extraordinary.' I told him I was just Adda, and he said, 'No my dear. A beautiful girl needs a beautiful name. From now on, you're Adaline.' So I became Adaline."

Adda stifled a yawn, and Trisha reached over to pat her arm. "Adda, do you want to stop tonight? You look tired."

"I'm tired, but one more thing." She started to open the box but changed her mind. She held it close and told her story before revealing its contents.

"Ernie, he comed to see me every day. I knew he had the stirrin's just like old Mr. Gordon had. But Ernie wasn't rough or pushing me around. He loved on me, rubbing my shoulders, touching my face, telling me I was the most beautiful thing he ever saw. Said he loved me and gave me this." She held the box open. "I never had a diamond in my life and didn't spect I ever would. But Ernie said beautiful women should wear jewelry that shines."

Trisha and Rusty leaned in to look at the necklace with the huge stone. Adda placed the lid on top and tucked it away.

"I wore shiny jewelry when I went places to sing, but it weren't mine. I just wore it, and Wanda Jean took it back. But this one belonged to me for keeping. I had some hard times over the years where I thought I might have to sell it, but I couldn't do it. I ain't never had nothing like it. And Ernie, I knew it was wrong to let him be loving on me that way, but figured, after all Mr. Gordon done to me, couldn't matter none. Leastways, Ernie loved me. We just couldn't let no one know. He said it wouldn't do since I worked for him.

Said if people knew, I'd have to stop singing, or he'd have to stop being boss of the company. That's why I wrote him my song, 'Just Call Me Baby.' I just wanted him to be able to let folks know I was his lady."

Trisha jumped up. "You wrote that?"

"Sure enough. Wrote it and sang it just for him the first time. Then it got to be his favorite, and he had me singing it everywhere I went. It almost won me a big award."

"Adda, that was your biggest hit. And it's been remade by at least three people."

Adda had been shocked the first time she heard someone else singing it on the radio. It didn't seem right that someone else could sing her song to Ernie. She shook her head just thinking about it.

"Yeah, I heard it sung by some others. It felt right strange to hear my words to Ernie coming outta the radio with somebody else saying them."

"Adda, do you have any proof you wrote that song?" Rusty asked.

"What kinda proof would you be meaning?"

"Did they give you credit on the labels, like putting your name there as songwriter?"

Adda tilted her head, confused. "I don't know nothing about that. Alls I have is the song I wrote. I kept me a copy."

"Can we see it?"

"Mr. Rusty, I'm gonna show you 'cause it's next in the remembering, but don't be getting ahead of me." She turned to the box and pulled out a piece of lined tablet paper. "I don't know nothing about writing the music notes part, but I knew the sound of it in my head when I wrote these words down."

Trisha took the paper and Rusty stood beside her

to read it. "I know it ain't the best spelling, but all of the words are there."

Trisha brushed her finger over some printed corrections. "Adda, did someone help you?"

"I wrote it all myself, but Wanda Jean fixed a few words for me."

Trisha took her seat and put her arm on Adda's shoulder. "Adda, can we make a copy of this also?"

"Don't see why not. It's been sung by everybody else. Words ain't no secret."

Rusty pulled his copier out and took the original from Trisha's outstretched hand.

"We better leave you tonight. You need to get some rest." Trisha reached over to hug her. Rusty handed her the original of the song. "Is there anything I can get for you before we go?"

"No, sir. Just need me some sleep."

Rusty gave Adda's shoulder a tender squeeze. "Thank you for sharing your story. Sleep well." As they reached the door, he turned. "And Miss Adda, you're still a beautiful lady."

~*~

Trisha and Rusty sat on the bench in front of the Mendino. He turned to face her.

With each step of Adda's story, Trisha grew more determined that they needed to help. "What do you think?"

"She's an interesting lady. Sweet and cantankerous at the same time. What's with that stuff about Mr. Gordon?"

Trisha told him the memories Adda had shared,

including her little Enam Job. Rusty shook his head. "Unbelievable. That sounds like something from slave years, not from this generation."

Trisha felt him staring at her. "You're amazing for getting this involved with her. Not many people would take the time."

She brushed off the compliment. "Oh no. I've been so blessed by her friendship. I loved her music as a teenager. My pap used to dance with me, right in the living room. Adaline would sing, and he'd twirl me around and dip me at the end 'til we both laughed." Her throat ached with the loss, her next words thick with emotion. "Adda brings back good memories of Pap."

They sat, each quiet in their own thoughts.

Rusty shook his head. "You know that necklace isn't a diamond?"

"I suspected as much. Could you tell for sure?"

"Oh yeah. No question about it. It had a scratch on the side. Diamonds don't scratch. It looked clear, no facets cut to radiate the light. Cubic zirconia at best. I see no reason to tell her the truth."

Trisha sighed. "No, neither do I."

Rusty lifted Trisha's left hand and examined her ring. "Now, this is the real deal."

Trisha nodded. "No doubt. Grant would have nothing less."

"But—is he the real deal?"

She jerked her gaze to his. Why would he ask that question? "Grant? He's a good man."

Rusty set her hand back on her knee. "So, back to Adda. What are you thinking?"

"She was so young and naïve. I don't think Adda ever realized how beautiful she was. Or how talented.

She just tried to get by." Trisha clenched her jaw and shook her head. "It makes me so mad, what people have done to her. That evil landowner, her mom for letting it happen, then the record company."

"Trish, you realize she could be looking at millions? The concerts alone would generate that. And this song? It could be a game changer. If the contract dispute isn't enough, the copyright may be the tipping point."

"Good grief. Don't tell her that. It will scare her silly to think of those numbers."

He shifted toward her. "What's more important, it will scare Haven Records silly. They'll be much more likely to want to settle."

"Does this mean we file in federal court?"

"If we go after the copyright."

Her eyes narrowed. "Why shouldn't we?"

"A few considerations. First, if they didn't credit her as songwriter, we'd need proof that she wrote it. This paper alone won't be enough. A lot of time has passed, so it may be difficult to find anyone to support her claim. Next, let's consider the goal here. We want Adda to have the means to live with comfort in a timely manner. It's not going to help her if we're tied up in the system for five years. What's going to be the quickest and surest approach? Federal may move slower. I'm hesitant to go after the copyright. I don't think we need it."

Trisha nodded, her eyes filled with questions.

"In case you're wondering, I'd say the same thing if this wasn't pro bono—if I were getting a percentage."

Her hand flew to her chest. "That's not what I thought."

"I just wanted you to know. She's seventy-five. If this is to have any purpose at all, we've got to get it done."

"And we can settle. Adda won't need much at her age. Just enough to be comfortable and safe. Speaking of comfortable and safe, I'd better be going. I have a morning class."

"Dr. Samuels?"

"Yep. Can't be late."

"Say hello for me. Come on. I'll walk you to your car."

"You don't need..." He silenced her with an outstretched hand.

"Safe. Remember?"

They reached her car, and Trisha hit her remote to unlock it.

"So Trish, what does a photographer say to a group of lawyers before he snaps the picture?"

Trisha tipped her chin and smirked. "I don't know. What does he say?"

"Everyone, say 'Fees!'"

Trisha mocked a shoulder punch. "That's your honored profession you're making fun of."

Rusty opened her car door, his hand on her shoulder.

She slid behind the wheel. "A needed moment of levity. Thank you for your help and for caring about an old lady." Before he closed the door, she reached into her handbag. "Oh, here's the address to my Pap's house. I'll be over there working on the case studies tomorrow afternoon. Let me know when we need to get together.

Trisha eased her car out of the parking space and exited the garage. When she arrived back at her apartment, she went to the box with the vinyls and pulled out the three for Adaline. Two of the three had the song, "Just Call Me Baby", the original cut and a greatest hits album. The album cover listed all tracks including title, playtime, and songwriter in parenthesis. *Just Call Me Baby, 4:39 (E.Gillen, Haven Records)*. Ernie had taken credit for writing Adda's song.

13

Trisha saw Jimmy's pickup truck when she reached the top of Pap's driveway. She called out as she entered the back door. "Hey, Jimmy. You're here again?"

"Hi, Trish. Just checking out the work. These are pretty good guys, but sometimes they get young fellows working for them that don't have the same eye for quality. Gotta keep watch."

"I'm going to be doing some work because it's easier to spread out here than in my tiny apartment. Will I be in anyone's way if I work in the summer room?"

"It's your house, Trish. Don't be worrying about that."

Grandma had always called it the summer room, but in truth, it was a screened porch off the kitchen. It may have been built as a sleeping porch. Many older southern homes had them to offer a cool place when the hot weather made it difficult to sleep. Grandma and Pap always used it as the main entrance once the front porch worsened. It lacked the beauty the name indicated. Trisha considered it a mud room, overflow pantry, and excess storage. Someday she would make it a real summer room.

"Great progress on the front. Looks like they'll be finished within the week."

"Should be." Jimmy scanned the kitchen cabinets. "Hey, do you have some time to talk about this kitchen?"

Trisha glanced around. "It's sure dated, isn't it?"

"Yep, but I see potential."

Trisha shook her head. "I'm not going to have the funds if I need siding. If I don't, I can either talk about the windows or the kitchen."

"Let's just brainstorm this for a minute, even if it's a project you want to put off for a while. I see all of the makings for an authentic farmhouse kitchen with the charm and convenience of today. I think it can be done for a surprisingly low cost."

Trisha ran her hands over the stained laminate counters. Was there such a thing as surprisingly cheap granite? Everything in this room was old and run down. "Talk to me. I'm just seeing old."

"For starters, it's a great size. You could fit a big, old family-sized table in here. The paneling's in good shape, and we're seeing it installed in new farmhouse kitchens today. A little patch and paint would be all the walls need."

Trisha opened a drawer front that never slid smoothly. "But look at these cabinets. They need replacing, and there's a ton of them."

"If this were mine, I'd strip these cabinets down and paint them white. It would brighten this up a lot. It's easy to change the tracking so they operate better. We could even install soft closures and pull out-shelves. Change some hardware, build an island, and you have a new kitchen. Might not cost as much as you think."

Trisha paused to examine the wood. It was awfully dark. And an island would be nice. A slow smile began to form. "White would sure make an immediate difference."

"Your big expense would be countertops if you want a stone finish, and this." Jimmy walked over and tapped the top of the six-burner gas range. "If you like the look, I could keep my eye peeled for a bargain. They sell new six-burners that would fit right in here. Both of those things can wait until you have funds."

"And this?" Trisha walked to the old apron sink. "It's so discolored and nicked. Grandma scoured the finish right off of it." She ran her hand over the pitted surface, yellowed from age.

Jimmy joined her at the sink. He opened the cabinet door and dropped down to look inside, twisting his head to see up under the sink. He pulled his head out and stood up.

"If you want my opinion, I'd try to keep the apron sink. They're popular now even in new homes. The character of this kitchen is perfect for one. You could have this one refinished. That's the cheapest option. If you want to replace it with a newer one, they have more modern features."

He turned the water on hot, switched to cold, examined the faucet base, and then tested the side sprayer.

"You have the basics, so we wouldn't have to retrofit a new one. They can weigh upward of three hundred pounds. You have a strong metal rod underneath and a solid base to support it."

Trisha bounced around the kitchen looking at every feature. Her eyes lit with the new possibilities and she beamed. "Will you get me a price for stripping and painting these cabinets? May as well price the new tracks and soft closures at the same time. I'll stop there for now, but maybe look at the sink and counters after I reassess my finances. Once I get a job, I can take out a home equity to finish the remodel."

"I'm on it. And I think you got yourself some company." Jimmy pointed toward the driveway.

Trisha glanced at the car parked beside hers. Rusty stepped out, stopping a moment to scan the mountains behind the house and the fields to the right. Trisha swung the door open and stepped outside into the bright sunshine.

"Don't you have any other clients?" she teased.

His blue eyes twinkled with amusement. "You're not my client, remember?"

"You know what I mean—other cases?" Trisha held the door wide open for him to enter.

"Just boring ones. Writing wills, filing them, writing business contracts filled with legalese."

"You mean filled with mumbo jumbo?"

"That about sums it up." He stole another glance at the landscape. "This place is incredible."

Trisha held the door open. "The inside's going through some remodeling. I've been working here in the summer room."

Trisha apologized as Rusty stepped inside the cluttered space. "Everything gets pushed out here while the workers are in there. Come on in, and I'll show you around."

Rusty's gaze darted all around. "Look at this place. What a great old home."

Trisha was filled with a new sense of pride. It was a great old house. She had failed to appreciate it when she lived here. "We were just talking about what to do with this kitchen." She peeked into the living room. "Jimmy, got a sec?"

Jimmy Wallace came back to the kitchen, and Trisha introduced Rusty. The two men shook hands. "Jimmy's been organizing the renovations."

"Looks great." Rusty peeked into the living room. "I love seeing old houses restored. They have such character."

"I'm just helping Trisha out. Let me show you what we've done."

Jimmy took over the tour, and Trisha tagged along.

"Trish called me when she started thinking about doing some upgrades. I'm just helping where I can. She's some special girl." He flashed her a grin.

"No argument here. We're working on a case together."

"Glad to hear that." He turned toward Trisha. "That'll give you good experience."

They walked upstairs to see the bathroom with a claw-footed tub and three huge bedrooms. Jimmy showed it off with pride. "Don't see big bedrooms like these anymore. You can fit a little sitting area in each one."

Rusty ran his hand over the dark mahogany door frames and touched the crystal knobs.

Jimmy opened a closet door. "One shortcoming of these old houses. Never enough closet space."

When they returned to the first floor, Rusty walked toward the wall where framed pictures still hung. Trisha watched him examining the photographs. Her high school picture. Her grandparents. Uncle Brendan. He stopped when he came to a picture of Trisha with her mom and dad. She was ten when the photograph had been taken. Dark waves of hair framed her face. She typically tied it back, but her mom wanted it loose for the picture.

Jimmy moved beside him for a better view. "Her mother grew up in our church. Sad, sad day when we lost her. Trisha was a tall, leggy colt when she came to live here. We've been loving on her since then."

Trisha turned so they wouldn't see her eyes, bright with unshed tears. She retreated to the summer room as the men made their way back to the kitchen. Their conversation returned to remodeling. Trisha heard snippets of it until their voices went low. The distinct change in tones peaked Trisha's curiosity, and she stopped shuffling papers so she could hear, but she only heard muffled tones.

Trisha turned her attention back to the legal documents. She looked up from the brief as Rusty came back through the door. "I'm finding a few things."

He joined her on the glider, and she moved some documents between them so he could read along. "Looks like there are many spousal cases using undue influence as an argument, but that's not really a contract dispute."

Rusty tapped the page. "Oh, make no mistake— marriage is a contract. Don't enter it lightly."

She pointed her pen toward him. "I know. I'm headed to family law, remember?"

Turning to the next page, she shifted it so Rusty could read. "In this case, a mentally handicapped man entered a contract to purchase property. He had a trust fund, so money was available. However, the seller misrepresented the property description. The attorney on file used an undue influence argument because the seller pressured him into a limited time frame and the client didn't know to have the property appraised.

They won the case. No compensatory settlement, but the contract was negated, his funds returned."

"Good work, counselor. See, you're studying for the bar."

"I guess I am."

"Here's the Complaint I have ready to file. Read it over and tell me what you think." He handed her the legal document.

Trisha took her time reading it. "You're aware I've only read these from textbooks. This is the first real one I've held in my hand. I'm not the best person to give you an opinion."

"You know the case. Just wanted you to check my wording, see if you thought I missed anything."

She skimmed it and read some phrasing aloud. "The Complaint of the Plaintiff, Adda Mae Marsh, respectfully alleges...marginalized due to limited knowledge of recording contracts...defendant failed to explain in comprehensible terms...legal language was written with abstruseness designed to obscure understanding..." As Trisha reached the end of the document, her mouth fell open. With wide eyes, she looked up. "You're asking for 1.5 million?" A rush of adrenaline sent her heart racing.

"That's a gross underestimate and still leaves room to negotiate. I kept it low, hoping for a quick settlement. I would think an agreement of $500,000 could be reached. That should provide for her needs from this point on. It's more apt to happen faster at that level."

"I had no expectation of that much money." Nor would Adda. She'd be shocked if they received anything close to that amount.

"How much do you think she'd have made for one

concert appearance?" Trisha shrugged. "Have you heard of Rick Maltic?"

"No."

"He's a crooner. Rather unknown but climbing. Cost a cool fifteen thou to book him, and he's not a big name. Take that times...maybe twenty appearances a year over a twenty-five-year span. You're over seven million. And Adaline's name was more famous. Add to that record sales. One and a half million's a bargain."

She shook her head. "Wow. I had no idea."

"I'll file it tomorrow. Then the games begin." His eyes beamed.

"When will Haven Records know?" Her stomach knotted with the thought of setting this in motion.

"Within the week."

She could imagine Frank's expression when they handed him the summons. "You think they'll settle?" Or would Ernie's son be as greedy as he'd been?

"I do, but not the first round."

Trisha handed the brief back to Rusty. Things were really happening. Maybe they would actually help Adda. "So, what are we working on now?"

He sat back and rubbed his chin. He grinned, his blue eyes teasing. "That's a good question. What are we working on?"

Trisha pursed her lips and narrowed her eyes. "I'm not sure what you mean."

Rusty shrugged his shoulders. "Never mind." He seemed to be thinking. "Favorites. What's your favorite...movie?"

He did spontaneity well. "Hmm. *Gone with the Wind*. And yours?"

"*To Kill a Mockingbird*. I want to be Atticus Finch. Your favorite book?"

Trisha laughed. "*Gone with the Wind*. And yours?"

"Guess?"

"Must be *To Kill a Mockingbird*?"

"Nope. *A Time to Kill*. Good legal thriller."

She poked his arm. "You tricked me."

He rubbed his arm feigning an injury. "How did I trick you?"

She folded her arms. "Do I need to state the obvious?"

"OK. Truce. I have to go to do the boring things that pay bills." He stood up and held out his hand to help her to her feet. But when she stood, he held it for a long moment before releasing it, his blue eyes drilling hers. When he freed her hand, she exhaled. Those eyes were hypnotic, and she hadn't realized she'd been holding her breath.

"I'll file this tomorrow and then prepare a summons. It will be served to Frank Gillen by the end of the week. It requires their answer within thirty days. I'm working on a list of items we'll request for discovery. Then we'll be ready to meet with Adda again. Will you be seeing her before that?"

"Oh, yes. I try to see her every couple of days. We'll be doing more of her memory box later this week. Do you think you should be there?"

"I can be. Why don't you see what she wants and let me know? I'd like to know her better but want to respect her wishes. I don't want her feeling uncomfortable, like I'm stealing her best friend." He gently bumped shoulders with her.

"I'll ask her and let you know."

Trisha walked with him to the door where he hesitated and then gave her a quick hug. Were they actually becoming…friends?

She had to work on Grant, lighten him up a little. They never had playful conversations. Trisha thought back to her breakfast with Rusty. He said she was serious. Could that be what attracted Grant to her? Both serious personalities. A memory sprang to her mind. Her mother doing dishes and saying something silly. Her dad hip-bumped her. She swatted him, and they both laughed. Maybe she didn't want to be serious.

14

A ding alerted Trisha to an incoming e-mail. She hit the icon on her phone. It was from Rusty.

What's the difference between a lawyer and a herd of buffalo?

The lawyer charges more.

Hope you're laughing. Filed suit this morning. Time to pray. Can you keep Friday evening open?

Trisha hit reply. Her fingers flew over the keys.

I'm laughing. And praying, And yes to Friday. What will we be doing?

Another ding sounded to alert her of a reply.

Working, of course. Did you think I was asking you out?

Heat rose to Trisha's cheeks. Thankfully, he couldn't see. He was probably grinning at his computer as he typed, those blue eyes sparkling with amusement. She clicked reply.

I know that, silly. What kind of work?

Trisha waited for her e-mail to deliver his response.

Investigation. Did you talk with Adda?

It was time to end this cyber talk. She sat on the sofa and pulled her legs up under her before pushing the button she had programed for Rusty. He answered on the first ring.

"Good morning, Miss Mills."

"I hate virtual talk."

"Ah. And I thought you just liked the sound of my voice."

Was he flirting? "Rusty! Can you be serious for one minute?"

"I'll try my best. I get a little high when I file a suit for which I get no money but will put in more hours than a dissertation requires."

Trisha sat up straighter. "Oh. Are you sorry you started this?"

"Not at all. Did you talk with Adda? Does she want me to come with you for the next...what does she call it...remembering?"

"Yes, it's called remembering. No, I haven't spoken with her. I'm going at lunch today. I try to have lunch with her twice a week. I'll ask her then. Her memory box has to be in the evening since she sings all day. I figured to go over Thursday evening. What do you have in mind for Friday?"

"Just a little outing. Trust me."

~*~

Adda sat at the café table where Trisha had lunch laid out. It was sure good to be tasting all the different foods she brought. Adda would've liked some fried okra and collard greens but didn't want to ask. If Mr. Rusty got her some of that money, she'd get herself a whole meal of them.

Trisha pulled out something round and all curled up. She called them wraps, but they were sandwiches without bread, all curled inside a flatbread like a crepe. Vegetables and some curly pasta mixed up together to make a salad. It wasn't fried okra, but it was pretty tasty.

"Mr. Rusty get that law stuff to young Frank Gillen yet?"

"He filed it in court, and Haven Records will know soon. You feeling OK about this, Adda?"

"Mr. Rusty, he sure is a charmer. Telling me I'm still beautiful. Got himself some big, blue, shining eyes."

Trisha smiled. "Yes, they are the prettiest blues I've seen."

"Them blue eyes be looking you over, girl."

"Rusty? No, Adda. He knows I'm getting married. We're just colleagues—business partners."

Adda gave her a squint-eyed nod.

"Speaking of Rusty, do you want him to come with me tomorrow evening? He can be there unless you'd rather him not."

"You bring that man around. He's needing to know the story."

~*~

Adda expected Trisha and Rusty at six-thirty, so she was surprised to hear a knock on her door at six o'clock. She had used Trisha's slow cooker to heat up some soup. She pushed the soup back on the top box and stood slowly.

Another loud knock was followed by a man's voice. "Adda, it's Rusty."

"Hold your horses. I'm a'coming."

Adda opened the door and put her hands on her hips. "I can tell time. Ain't time yet or I'd 'a had the door unlocked."

"Sorry, Adda. I hoped to talk with you for a few minutes."

"Come on in." The crock to the slow cooker soaked in the utility sink with soapy water. "I'm still finishing up my evening meal."

Rusty sat across from her. "You just go on and finish. Mind if I talk while you eat?"

She tipped her eyes over the cup of soup. "You ain't the one eating. No reason you can't be talking."

Rusty reached into his pocket and pulled out some dollar bills. They were folded so Adda couldn't see the amount. He dropped the money into the box that she set out every day when she sang.

"I'm putting this in so you can take tomorrow off. I have a little surprise."

She eyed him with suspicion. "What kinda surprise you thinking of?"

"Just a little birthday surprise. I thought we might do a little shopping."

"But it ain't my birthday 'til August."

"Well, we'll call it an early birthday gift."

A knock sounded. A glance at the clock showed six fifteen. Adda shook her head. "Can't nobody tell time anymore?"

Adda called for Trisha to come in. Trisha seemed surprised to see Mr. Rusty, but then she took her seat on the mattress and waited. Adda carried her soup bowl and placed it in the utility sink. She'd have to clean that later since everybody decided to come early.

She moved back to her mattress and pulled the next items out of the box.

"After Ernie got me that diamond necklace and said no one could be knowing about me being his lady, that song got real important. Every place I went singing, they wanted to hear it. The folks would all hoot and holler and clap when it started." Adda closed her eyes. She was back on that stage, holding the microphone for the cheering crowd, saying "Thank you," 'cause that was the only thing she was allowed to say.

"Pretty soon, I got this piece of paper delivered to me. It came real special-like with a delivery man bringing it right to my door."

She held up the paper, and Trish read it aloud. "Congratulations! You have been nominated for Female Vocalist of the Year for your recording of "Just Call Me Baby". Your presence is requested at the Grammy Award Ceremony in Los Angeles, California."

Adda handed Trisha the next item—an airline ticket stub.

"I was a'feared to get in that plane, but Ernie was so excited that I couldn't disappoint him. I got in and held the seat, praying 'til my knuckles ached. Only time I was ever in one of them was going there and coming back. I don't aim to ever be in one again." Adda shuddered, recalling the bumps that made her think they would fall from the sky. Every time that big plane bounced, her hand squeezed Ernie's arm.

"Wanda Jean brought me a fancy dress to wear, and Ernie looked at me real proud. But I didn't win the award. Went to Ella Fitzgerald, a real fine lady from what I could see."

Adda sighed and put the ticket stub with the nomination announcement.

"Ernie, he was powerful disappointed. I got on that airplane to come home and didn't even have him sitting beside me. Wanda Jean took that seat. I was mighty feared about disappointing him."

With her eyes downcast, Adda shook her head, wanting to shake away the memory. She didn't say anything as an explanation to the next item, simply handed it to Trisha who read it to herself before handing it to Rusty. Trisha stretched her arm around Adda's shoulder.

After Rusty read the engagement announcement with a picture of Ernie's big smile and his arm around a beautiful blonde, he placed it face down on the other items.

"Turned out his new wife became his next singing star. Didn't matter none that he was the boss." Adda's chest still burned with the memory. How could she have been that foolish? "I never saw Ernie again 'cepting once when he walked through the studio while I recorded. Oh, they still had me singing 'cause folks still bought my music. I still weren't allowed no fried food or stuff that would stop me from looking good. They still brung me pretty dresses to wear, but it weren't the same without Ernie."

Trisha squeezed her shoulder. "Do you want to stop now? Maybe that's enough for one night."

Adda reached for the next item. "No, ma'am. I got one more." She shook off the despair and continued.

"I never heard from my family 'cause I didn't get no mail or have no phone. Guess they didn't know how to get word to me, so they sent it to the record company. Wanda Jean brung me this note."

Again, she handed it to Trisha who read it aloud. "Mama's real sick. She's wanting to see you." Trisha handed it back. "Were you able to go, Adda?"

"Oh yeah. Wanda Jean got me a bus ticket, and I

went, but I was too late. They put her in the ground before I got there." Adda had stood and cried over the fresh dirt where her mama lay—right next to Enam Job. "I stayed mad at her for a long time for not helping me. But I knew Mama had some hard times of her own. Don't take much figuring when you look at the picture."

"What do you mean?" Trisha questioned her.

Adda's brows arched. "My mama and daddy had skin dark as a midnight sky, just like six of my brothers and sisters. Three of us, well we was golden brown. Don't take much figuring to know that Mama had her share of troubles. She always feared us losing our home."

Adda glanced at Rusty who had been silent. Those big, blue eyes looked sad as an abandoned dog. "That's enough remembering for tonight." Adda stood, holding on to the side of the bed until she had her footing.

Rusty and Trisha stood to leave. Trisha hugged Adda, holding her close for a long time. "Sleep well, sweet lady. I'll see you soon."

"I aim to sleep well. Got me a big day tomorrow."

Trisha raised her eyes in question. Adda ignored them and turned toward Rusty.

Rusty stepped in to hug her, but Adda held out her hand to halt him. "I be needing a private minute with you, Mr. Rusty."

"With me? Umm, OK, but let me walk Trisha to her car first."

"I'm fine, Rusty. It's still light out."

"You go getting this girl safe to her car and come on back."

Adda left the door unlocked so she wouldn't have

to stand up to let him in. She would have liked to get some water after all the talking, but then she'd be crossing that street in the middle of the night to visit her bathroom. She just sat back down and waited.

~*~

Rusty and Trisha stepped outside and closed the door. Trisha looked up with questions on her face.

Rusty shrugged his shoulders. "I haven't a clue."

"And that comment about having a big day tomorrow?"

Rusty looked at the street traffic. "Maybe Fridays have a lot of people passing by here." He hit the button to change the light to walk. They crossed over to the parking garage and stopped for a car making its exit. As the driver motioned for them to pass, Rusty put a gentle hand on Trisha's shoulder.

"You don't have to take me in. My car's on the third level."

Rusty ignored the suggestion and kept walking.

"Don't forget tomorrow night."

He glanced her way, detecting a slight blush rising to her cheeks.

"You never did tell me what we're doing."

"Sure I did."

She stopped walking. "You didn't. You just said 'investigating.' Investigating what?"

"This case, of course." He was straight-faced, but his eyes revealed a smile.

"You're impossible. Where should I meet you?" The elevator opened, and they stepped on. Rusty pushed the number three and the doors closed.

"Adda's."

"We're coming here again? Don't you think that's too much for her—two nights in a row? It drains me. I can't imagine the toll it takes on her."

They exited the elevator on the third level. At Trisha's car, Rusty stood facing her and took her hand in his. "It'll be fine. Didn't I say to trust me?"

His eyes held hers. "All right. You're the boss. Let me know what she wants to talk to you about."

He grinned. "I believe I heard her say 'private.'" He hugged her and opened the car door.

She slid behind the wheel. "Get in. No sense you walking back two blocks."

Trisha dropped him off in front of the building.

~*~

Adda heard a low knock and then Rusty walked in. He took his seat across from her.

"So what can I do for you, Adda?"

Her eyes bore into his blue ones. "Ain't nobody gonna be hurting Miss Trisha."

Rusty's eyes widened as he careened back in his seat.

He leaned forward, returning her gaze. "Adda, I would never hurt her. What made you think that?"

Her eyes drilled his. "I see the way you looking at her. I know when a man's thinking on those things."

Rusty sat back and rubbed his hands over his face. "I promise you," he said crossing his heart, "I'll never hurt Trish."

"But you's having the stirrins?"

"That doesn't mean I'd hurt her. Not every man is

135

like Ernie or Mr. Gordon."

Adda squinted, eyes still glued to his. "You fixing to steal her from that man of hers?"

"Well…" He searched for a response. "Let's just say I wouldn't be disappointed if that happened."

"So you fixing to try?"

Rusty crossed his leg, ankle resting on his knee. "What would you think of that, Adda?"

She flashed a smile. "I think you best be hurrying. Her wedding be here a'fore you know it."

15

Trisha peeked out the window to see Julie's car before opening the door, anxious to see her reaction to the changes. The wide front steps led to a beautiful veranda that wrapped around the house. The front door had been painted forest green to match the shutters, a stunning difference from the dilapidated porch with the rotting wood.

Julie's mouth gaped open as she walked up the steps.

Trisha's eyes sparkled with delight. "What do you think?"

"Unbelievable! I thought I had the wrong address when I saw the front of the house. You did this?"

"Well, I picked the design."

"All I can say is…wow."

"Jimmy suggested the wrap-around, and I love it." She stepped toward the corner and pointed to the new French doors. "We changed the double window in the dining room to this. Did you notice the steps? I asked the workers to widen them."

"Amazing. You've got to keep this place."

Trisha shrugged her shoulders. "We'll see."

They walked where the exposed hardwood floors awaited refinishing. Trisha led Julie to the dining room table where she pulled out the wedding folder. She'd created it when they returned from New York and set the date. It started with a checklist, followed by a page for each category.

"All the girls have been in for their fittings. I expect the dresses to be ready in three weeks. Here's the band we secured." She flipped through the pages. "Here's our menu."

Julie grabbed the folder and read it out loud. "Awesome. And I can only pick one?"

Trisha laughed. "You can have mine, too. I'll be too nervous to eat."

Continuing through the folder, she pulled out a picture of the table centerpieces. The wide base allowed votive candles to rest on the glass, while the vase began as a narrow vessel, widening as it reached eighteen inches tall. Pale-pink tea roses formed a tight circle with strings of tiny pearls woven throughout before cascading down the sides.

"I would never have spent the money for this. Grant's mother fell in love with these and asked if she could purchase them for us. Then, when we talked with the bakery, she sent them the picture of the centerpieces and...ta da!" Trisha flipped to the next page, where the picture of the cake matched the pale-pink tea roses with faux pearls scalloping the edges.

"Classy. Too bad you didn't pick the pink for our dresses."

Trisha closed the folder. "That's all I have. We still need a few decisions for the ceremony. Jules, I want to do something, but I'm a little nervous about it."

"And that is?" Julie drew her feet up and sat cross-legged on the chair.

"I want to have Adda sing at the ceremony."

"Awesome. Why would that make you nervous?"

"Grant's not happy about my friendship with her.

And, well, she might feel out of place. She wouldn't know anyone and...how do I say this kindly...her level of literacy is evident in her speech. I don't care, but I wouldn't want her to feel uncomfortable."

"So what are you going to do?"

Trisha shook her head. "It would be so special, almost like having Grandma and Pap with me."

"You could have that lawyer come with her. He's met her, hasn't he?"

"Oh, yes. But I couldn't ask him to do that."

"Well, you'd better decide soon, girl. Otherwise, Grant will have the opera lady he likes so much. Her high soprano will pierce our eardrums."

"Maybe I'll brave the subject at dinner Saturday.

~*~

Trisha wore jeans and a long-sleeved UNC T-shirt, left over from her undergrad days. Asheville enjoyed beautiful weather in May, but evenings could be cool. Rusty said to meet at six, a little earlier than usual.

Trisha knocked and called in. "It's Trisha." She heard Rusty's voice calling back. "It's open. Come on in."

Trisha opened the door and saw him seated in the canvas folding chair. She then glanced at Adda, seated on the side of her bed. Trisha's mouth dropped open. Wide-eyed, she started to speak but struggled to get the words out. "Adda, you...what did you do? You look incredible."

Adda's grin stretched the width of her face. African braids adorned her head. The twisted ropes of hair were pulled back against her scalp and then cascaded down her back. Her face shone from more than the smile. The understated makeup evened out her skin tones, adding a blush to her cheeks and a gloss to her lips. Trisha had never seen the clothes she wore. Straight-leg dress slacks with a crisp crease in a soft taupe and an ivory-toned top under a blazer matching the slacks. Trisha stood and gaped at her. She caught the movement of Adda's foot tapping to draw attention to the shoes. She wore brown flats designed to slip on with ease, adorned by a decorative bow.

Her foot continued to tap, a smile pasted on her face. "Me and Mr. Rusty had a little outing today. I got me a real shower at the YMCA and then went to a place that fixed up my hair and my skin just like Wanda Jean used to have her lady do. 'Course Wanda Jean never done this." She tapped her braids and they bounced. "I had a mind to have her cut it to look like it did on that record cover, but the lady thought that weren't the best with my face being fuller. So we done it this way. Ain't all mine, you know. They weave in some extra to make it long."

"It's gorgeous." Trisha stared at her, stunned.

"Then we went and done us a little shopping. Mr. Rusty said it was my birthday gift. I told him my birthday ain't coming 'til August."

Trisha turned her gaze toward Rusty, her mouth still opened in shock. "You did this?"

"Of course not. I can't braid hair. I'm just the one who took her."

Always skirting around the surface. "But you arranged it."

He grinned. "You think I can't arrange a little surprise every now and then?"

Trisha looked from one to the other, and then she

walked over and embraced Adda. "You're so beautiful! Better than your album cover."

Adda just flipped her hand down in disregard. "Can't cover up old." But she still smiled.

Rusty feigned offense. "No hug for the one who organized it?"

Trisha walked over and stood before him. In a whisper-soft voice, she said, "You're amazing."

While they hugged, he whispered back. "Glad you finally see that."

She pinched him. "And you're impossible."

Flecks of light danced in his cornflower eyes. "Are you ready?"

Adda stepped toward the door. "Yes sir."

Trisha looked at her and then turned questioning eyes to Rusty.

"We're going out. Are you ready?"

"Where?" She scanned her casual attire, but relaxed when she took a closer look at Rusty's. Khaki cargo shorts, an army green T-shirt layered with an unbuttoned plaid shirt swinging loose, sandals, and sunglasses perched atop his head.

He shook his head. "You ask too many questions, Counselor."

~*~

When they stepped from the parked car, the rhythm of drums filled the whole area. Trisha exited from her side while Rusty opened Adda's door.

"Give me a minute." He went to the back and opened his trunk. There was a clattering sound as he lifted something from it.

"Need help?"

"Nope. All in one neat package." He came around to their door pulling a luggage-sized pack on wheels. Unlike a suitcase, the backs of the folding chairs stuck up.

"Neat. You can wheel your chairs in."

Rusty just smiled, his arm around Adda's shoulder. "Let's go."

Trisha fell into step beside them. "Is this the drum circle? I've heard of it but never saw it."

"You live a sheltered life, my dear."

She frowned. "I was raised by old people, remember? We seldom ventured into town."

He lifted one eye in question. "And Grant?"

Trisha didn't answer. She just kept walking. *Why did he look so smug?*

The crowd came into view. People sat in a haphazard circle, all forms of rhythm instruments sounding. Bongo drums, snare drums, tambourines, kettle drums, rhythm sticks, wrist bells. People danced inside the circle, even children, an eclectic, multi-cultural jam session. Trisha's eyes spanned the crowd. It seemed to organize itself, with no discernable melody, just free-form rhythm.

She thought a seat outside the circle with a view would be nice, but Rusty walked right inside, found a free space, and proceeded to open his pack. He pulled out two chairs, a collapsible stool, and drums. A set of two connected bongos and another free-standing drum.

He opened the chairs and motioned to Adda and Trisha. Then he placed the stool, forming a little semi-circle for the three of them with the drums inside.

Trisha's eyes widened and filled with unease.

Rusty winked at her. "Let's jam."

The unease turned to alarm. "Rusty, I don't play. I don't know how."

His hand swept over the crowd. "You don't have to know how. You just play. Just feel it."

Beside her, Adda had already gotten into the beat, tapping it out with gentle fingertips. Rusty joined her. Trisha sat in between them looking from side to side. Then she placed a hesitant hand on the bongo drum and met the beat. After a few moments, she fell into the rhythm and found her foot tapping along.

Adda moved in full swing, drumming, swaying, her braids swinging with the beat. Trisha's chest filled and expanded with the music, just as it had when she was a teen listening to Adaline reach the fullness of sound. It filled her and surrounded her until nothing remained but the music.

Then she caught the movement as Rusty stood, walked to Adda, and extended his hand. She took it, and they danced. Not like she had danced with Pap, but arm in arm, swinging, turning, moving to the beating drums. Adda laughed like a school girl until she put her hands up in a "stop" motion and collapsed onto her chair.

Rusty extended his hand to Trisha. Once again, her face filled with panic. He leaned in close to her and whispered, "Trust me."

She stood and he took her hand, tucking it in the crook of his arm. "Just feel it." And they danced. They twirled. They turned. When they returned to the drums laughing, both joined the rhythm chorus again.

Trisha had no idea how long they had been there, but eventually, Rusty stopped beating and sat back, a smile lighting his azure eyes.

"You know, they'll go all night. I think maybe we should get this lady home."

Trisha just smiled and nodded. Satisfied, she breathed in the wonder of the evening. Rusty handed her his keys. "You take her to the car. I'll pack this up."

Trisha hooked arms with Adda and walked to the parking lot.

When Rusty arrived back at his car, the ladies both sat in the backseat. He poked his head in the open window. "Your chauffeur has arrived."

Trisha wore a satisfied smile. "Hope you don't mind. We're talking girl talk." They rested their heads together in contentment.

"At your service, ladies."

Rusty found a parking space on the street near the Mendino. Trisha and Rusty walked Adda back to her room. After Trisha hugged her, Adda reached for Rusty's arm. She pierced him with her eyes. "You be remembering my words, Mr. Rusty."

"Adda, Adda. You've got to drop the mister. I'm just plain old Rusty."

"Well then, plain old Rusty, you best be hurrying."

They closed the door before Trisha asked, "What was that about? And what did she want last night?"

"Attorney client confidentiality. Let's get ice cream." He motioned to the small shop with the sidewalk tables.

When they had ordered and picked up their ice cream, they sat at a petite round table.

"Did I say thank you for tonight?"

Rusty licked his ice cream cone. "Don't need to."

Trisha held her dish of ice cream. "I want to."

"Well then, you're welcome."

Trisha looked up at him. "It was special. For Adda

and for me."

They ate, content with the silence and watching the city move around them.

Trisha finished and set her cardboard dish beside her. "You did lie to me, you know."

Rusty put his hand on his chest. "Me? Lie?"

"Yes, indeed. You said we would be investigating."

"And so we were."

"You said investigating the case."

"And so we were." He repeated.

She squinted one eye. "Really? And what did our investigation discover?"

He shook his head and shot her a frown as though he questioned her judgement. "Come on, Counselor, think. We now know that if we get to trial, Adda will have the stamina for a whole day in court. And, if they question her musical ability, we've discovered she has rhythm. And sometimes in court, you have something unexpected thrown at you. We learned how to dance around the issues like any good lawyer. Do I need more?"

She laughed. "You're impossible," she said for the second time that evening.

"But don't forget, I'm also amazing." His eyes remained fixed on her.

Trisha held his gaze until it suddenly felt too personal. She bit the inside of her lower lip and looked away. "I better go. It's getting late."

He stood and reached for her dish to put it in the trash. "So, what's on your agenda tomorrow?"

"A day in Charlotte with my friend, Julie. I have shopping to do for the wedding. Then I'll have dinner with Grant."

Rusty's eyes dimmed. What had she said that made him sad?

16

Trisha awoke from her short nap on the sofa. The shopping trip in Charlotte wore her out. It was hard to keep up with Julie's energy. Her phone alarm sounded at five o'clock. She set it so she could get changed before Grant came. They had played phone tag and never connected. The last message said he'd be bringing dinner, so she chilled some wine and moved her school clutter from the coffee table. One more week 'til graduation.

Grant arrived at five thirty with Chinese take-out. One carton with General Tso's and the other with Sweet and Sour Chicken, along with myriad containers filled with rice, sauces, and fortune cookies. Trisha poured the Riesling.

"So what's our movie?" Trisha spooned a little from each carton onto her plate.

"An old one I found. *Bang the Drum Slowly*."

Trisha felt the color rise to her face. Did he know about last night? And why should she feel guilty? She'd done nothing wrong. She took a bite and tried to act normal. "What's it about?"

"Honestly, I'm not sure. Something to do with baseball. It just had good ratings, so I thought we'd try it."

Over dinner, her mind focused on wedding and graduation talk. Grant's parents planned to come to town for the graduation next week. But as soon as the movie began, Trisha relived the night before. She heard the beating of the drums, saw Adda spinning and laughing, felt Rusty's arm linked with hers. She saw herself spiraling and laughing as though someone removed from the scene observed it. What would Grant think if he saw her dancing in a public park, laughing freely, letting her reserve down?

Trisha never engaged with the movie and fell asleep to the distant beat of drums in her head. She woke as the credits scrolled.

"Hey, sleepyhead. You missed the whole thing."

She yawned and stretched her arms. "Sorry. I couldn't keep my eyes open."

Grant reached behind her and massaged her shoulders. "How's that feel?"

"Divine. I crammed too much shopping into one morning."

Grant continued kneading the muscles in her shoulders. "Who's Russell Bergstrom?"

Trisha swung around and faced him. "Why do you ask? How do you know him?"

"I don't." He moved his hands from her shoulders and sat beside her. "You were sleeping, and I wanted to check the time. Your phone was closer than mine. I noticed quite a few calls to and from him." He arched his brow. "Should I be worried?" He poked her bare foot with his and flashed a mock sneer.

Trisha pulled her foot back from his reach and snatched her phone from the coffee table, sliding it into her pocket. "You don't see the phone calls when looking at the time." She shot an accusing glare in his direction. "Rusty's a colleague. We're working on something together."

"I thought you wrapped up your projects."

Trisha clenched her jaw. "He's not a student. He's an attorney and I'm helping him with a case."

"An internship?" His tone perked up.

"Unofficially. Professor Samuels connected us. It's good experience for me."

"Honey, that's great. Why didn't you tell me?"

She heaved a sigh. "You're always complaining that I'm taking on too much. I thought you'd fuss about it."

"Not at all. Nothing like authentic experience. What's the case?"

"I'm not able to talk about that. It's a contract dispute."

His eyes brightened. "Corporate? Maybe you'll like it and forget about family law."

The whole conversation about practical experience seemed to energize him. Maybe this was the best time to ask her question.

"Hey, I've been thinking of something." She rested her arm on his. "What would you think of having Adda sing at our wedding? It would—"

"Absolutely not." He pulled back from her, hands on his hips. "What are you thinking?"

"Grant, you didn't even hear me out. Let me finish my sentence, please."

He crossed his arms. "Finish your sentence."

"It would bring such a connection for me, remembering Grandma and Pap. I have no one but a few friends and Uncle Brendan, if he even comes. It would make me feel like my grandparents were a part of my wedding."

"Trisha, I'm sorry you lost your grandparents, but this is my wedding, too. I'm not having some woman that sings on the streets provide the music."

After their last conversation, Trisha had known this would be a battle. She gave her best argument. "She's not only a street singer. We would use the name Adaline. She was quite famous. People would be impressed." That should reach the Ramsey ego.

He stood and gathered up their glasses. "No one remembers her. People would think you brought your maid. This isn't going to happen."

Trisha's mouth dropped. "That's a terrible thing to say. I can't believe that just came out of your mouth."

"You want someone famous, we'll hire someone famous." He turned and walked into the kitchen with the glasses.

When he came back, he reached for his jacket. "I'd better get going. Love you, Trish." He left without as much as a kiss good night.

Trisha stood in place near the sofa. Grant cared about appearances and affluence, but bigoted? She had never seen that before.

~*~

When Trisha walked through the summer room, she saw the wood-grained doors first. They had been removed from the kitchen cabinets and taken to the summer room. A folding table groaned with the weight of all the dishes, pots, and pans.

She hurried to the kitchen. The cabinets had been stripped down to bare wood, the doors removed. The kitchen table was crammed full of her pantry foods. Trisha looked around in dismay. She'd asked Jimmy to get prices first, but he must have forgotten. Well, too late now. She'd just have to pay for it when the bill came. That meant putting off any window or siding work until she saw how her funds held up. It was unexpected, but she wouldn't say anything to Jimmy and make him feel bad, not after all he'd done. In the future, she'd have to be careful to clarify everything so he didn't get ahead of her.

Trisha made a cup of tea and sat in Pap's recliner. The house was silent, just the way she wanted it right now. She hadn't been able to shed the melancholy feelings since Grant left last night. They seemed to spar every time they were together. Had it always been like this? No, it hadn't.

They'd been together three years. He'd charmed her when they met. She'd attended a Christmas party with some friends, and he'd asked one of them about her. When they were introduced, Trisha had never seen a more handsome man. His fascination with her equaled her attraction to him. He invited her out for New Year's Eve, and they'd been together ever since.

They had been happy. The busyness of life stole their joy. She kept telling herself things would be better after they married. But why? What would make it better? He would still be an aggressive high-achiever building his clientele. She would be the same perfectionist starting a law career worrying about failure.

She had never seen Grant as incensed about anything as he had been about Adda. *Why?* He claimed that he worried about her time and safety, but was that really it? Or could it be a deeper prejudice?

Rusty had treated Adda with such gentle respect. It was difficult not to compare him with Grant. Rusty saw her as more than a colleague. Adda had suggested it, and Trisha denied it. But she knew.

Was this compromising her relationship with Grant? Trisha closed her eyes and rubbed her temples. She hadn't crossed any line of propriety, or had she? Allowing a subtly flirtatious relationship to grow provided a foothold for trouble to enter. It was the demise of marriages. She wouldn't allow it. She would not let her marriage fail before it began. From this point, she would keep her relationship with Rusty professional.

So why did she keep thinking about him? He made her laugh, but it was more than that. An excitement bubbled up from deep inside her each time she saw him. He uncovered something repressed, a joy she hadn't experienced since tragedy expunged it from her life at twelve years old.

He treated both her and Adda with a genuine respect. He was sad when he heard of Adda's heartaches. Yet joy still managed to flourish. An envious joy that Trisha coveted. Could she find that with Grant?

Trisha's phone buzzed in her lap with the arrival of a text message.

A man saw a lawyer and asked, "How much would you charge for answering three questions?" The lawyer said, "A thousand dollars." The man asked, "Isn't that a little expensive?" and the lawyer answered, "Yes, it is. Now what's your third question?"

Have a happy Sunday. I'll see you tomorrow at Adda's.

Trisha read the message. Then she reread it and smiled through tears.

~*~

Trisha had missed a call from Rusty.

She called him back when she got out of class. "Hi. I saw that I missed your call. Everything OK?"

"Yes. We heard from Haven. They didn't bother to utilize their thirty days."

Trisha walked across campus while she talked. "I suppose they refuted everything."

"As expected. That was no surprise."

Rusty read her the response. They accepted no liability, stating that she was *disentitled to recovery due to delay.* "That's good news because they didn't deny wrongdoing, just faulted her for delay in pursuing. It's time to start discovery. We'll request record sales and concert appearances. We'll have to find comparable artists. Tonight, we need to talk to Adda and gather names of people that worked for Haven during the time of her employ, people she worked with, anyone who can vouch for their treatment of her, anyone who might verify that she wrote the song."

Trisha reached her car and slipped inside. "Obviously Wanda Jean can. Adda said she corrected some of the spelling. We need to do that first. Once Adda's shared from the box, her emotions are drained."

"My thoughts exactly. Can you arrive about fifteen minutes early? Meet me outside. She about bit my head off the last time I went early."

"Sure. And Rusty, I have a favor to ask. I'll see her tonight and Wednesday. Then I have graduation on Friday night. Grant's parents are coming in from Raleigh, and I'll be tied up for a few days. Will you check on her? It might be five days before I can go, and that's a long time without a good meal."

A heavy silence hung between them before Rusty spoke. "It's coming fast. Graduation then the wedding. Of course. I'll take care of Adda."

17

Trisha was determined to keep all interactions with Rusty on a professional level. He was a hugger, but she would keep that light. After all, she hugged Jimmy and some other friends from Pap's church. Quick and superficial. She looked through her phone messages while she waited for him on the bench outside of the Mendino.

When he stepped into her view, she did a double take. She had said professional, and that's how he looked.

"Wow, what's with the suit and tie? I've never seen you like that."

He shook his head. "Big meeting. No time to change. Sorry I'm running late. It ran longer than expected." He motioned toward his suit. "Hope it doesn't make Adda nervous."

Trisha took in the dark suit, striped tie, and dress shoes buffed to a burnished glow. "Ha. After last Friday, she's wrapped around your finger."

He reached a hand out to Trisha, but she pretended she hadn't seen it. She stood and fell into step beside him. They walked to Adda's door and knocked.

"Come on in. It's open even though it ain't time yet."

When they walked in the door, Adda looked at

Rusty, a grin forming at the corners of her mouth. Trisha caught the nod and conspiratorial wink she sent his way. Some unspoken language had formed between them.

Rusty reached down to hug her shoulder. "Long meeting. I didn't have time to change."

"Well, you looking mighty handsome in that fine suit. You'll have all the ladies smitten with you." She turned to Trisha. "Don't he look mighty fine?"

Trisha chuckled.

Adda appeared quite smitten herself.

"Yes, Adda, he looks mighty fine." She glanced his way as he set his briefcase on an overturned bucket. He did look good. Keep it professional.

Trisha scooted up on the air mattress beside Adda. Rusty removed his jacket and looped it across the back of the canvas folding chair. He sat down with no apparent notice of the stark contrast between the dingy, frayed chair and his sophisticated suit coat.

Rusty opened his notebook. "Adda, we came a little early because I'd like to get some information before you share more of your story. We heard back from Haven Records, and as we expected, they denied our request. Now, we start gathering all of our information. I'd like to talk with people who knew you when you worked with Haven. Did you have any close friendships, anyone who worked with you except for Ernie? How about the men who met you in Mississippi?"

"Them men's probably dead. They was near my daddy's age when they first heard me sing. Wanda Jean, she was a little older than me, might be dead too."

Rusty wrote down names with a fluid movement

of his hands. He had long fingers, clean fingernails, yet there were scrapes and nicks, indication of physical work, perhaps landscaping. Or maybe from hiking.

"How about friends?" His question to Adda jolted Trisha from her fascination with his hands. He didn't multi-task. He wrote and then turned his eyes back to Adda, making eye contact with her when he spoke.

"Ernie and Wanda Jean didn't want me going no place. Like I said, they knew my poor schooling would show, so they kept me away from people where I'd get to talking. Didn't have no close friends. There were two ladies. They came to the studio to sing what they called backup. Made it sound real nice having those extra voices in between mine."

"Do you remember their names? And do you have a last name for Wanda Jean?"

"Wanda Jean's name was Marshall. The two ladies was Helen and Marcella. Never heard no last names for them. They talked real polite to me in between working when we would stop for the sound men to check everything out."

Rusty wrote and then turned back to Adda. "About how old were those ladies? Older than you, younger than you?"

"Helen and Marcella? They was pretty close to my age."

"Is there anything else you can think of that would help us?"

"No, sir. I weren't allowed to have no girlfriends. Only Wanda Jean and them extra singers."

He grinned. "How about men friends?"

Adda put one hand on her hip, holding the other to her air mattress. "Now, Mr. Rusty, what you saying?"

"Just teasing you, my dear. That's all I need for now. So, what do you want to share with us today?"

~*~

Adda stepped from the side of the bed and reached into her "things to remember" box. She pulled out the items she had selected, setting them beside her on the air mattress.

"So, I told you that I went home when my mama died. It'd been five years, and there were children everywhere. I didn't know who went with who. There was tiny babies to teenagers. I knowed some of the teenagers when they was little, but couldn't recognize them since they growed." Everyone had been staring at Adda like she was a stranger in her own home. If she'd have stayed instead of leaving for Nashville, she'd be knowing all those new faces.

"Minny's little Edith was about four, the one in Minny's belly last I saw her. Everyone could tell that Edith was touched. She talked to herself and didn't make no sense. Sometimes she just rocked back and forth. Minny didn't have no man so she and Edith stayed with Daddy."

Adda reached for the first item—a child's scribble in red crayon. "Edith, she took a liking to me and sometimes she would make me carry her around, which weren't easy at her age. That surprised Minny since Edith didn't go to nobody but her. I kept that picture of scribble and would pull it out just remembering the way that child's arms felt clinging to my neck." When Edith had clung to her, Adda wondered what Enam Job's arms would've felt like holding on to his mama, what his sweet face would've looked like in that crowd.

Adda set the picture back down beside the other items.

"My daddy and all my kin thought that I had lots of money. They see'd me coming on that big bus and wearing nice clothes. They thought I comed to help them outta being poor. Every one came telling me 'bout hard times, but I told them I didn't have no money. No one believed me but Minny. My daddy said he never thought one of his own would be so selfish and said I weren't his daughter no more if I wouldn't be helping my own kin. I tried to get Minny to come back with me. Wanda Jean could send a ticket for her and Edith, but she wouldn't leave Daddy alone. Said it wouldn't be right so quick after he lost Mama."

Adda stopped and reached for the next thing on her stack, a thread-worn towel wrapped around to protect it. Just seeing it wrapped up brought back the awful feeling of being all alone. She could still feel the ache of packing her suitcase to leave, knowing she'd never see them again.

"You remember that I stole that blanket that my mama made? Well Berta saw it and tried to steal it back."

The scene flashed so clear in Adda's mind. Opening the suitcase with the quilt folded on top, no bigger than a baby-sized blanket. Berta took one look and lunged across the room. Adda could still hear the sound as the precious fabric tore in half.

"I grabbed it from her, but she held on. By now all the threads was getting thin and I heard that blanket rip in two. Berta, she jumped at me and started hitting me with her fists when Daddy came in and stopped it.

He told me time had come for me to be a'going."

Adda stopped and took a sip from a water bottle that Trisha had given her.

"When I packed up my suitcase, I knew I wouldn't never see my family again, 'cepting maybe Minny. I went into the drawer where Mama kept that old family picture. I slid it into my suitcase under the ripped piece of the blanket. Figured I deserved it since it's all I'd see of them whilst they still had each other to be seeing."

I called Wanda Jean, and she called a hotel and they let me stay there cause my bus weren't returning 'til the next day."

Adda looked down at the item in her hand. "In that room, I was mighty sorrowful 'cause I knew I wouldn't never see my family again. Then I did a real evil thing. I stole again."

She unwrapped the towel to reveal a Bible.

"I had my little Jesus book that Mama read to me, but I never had me a copy of the real Good Book. I can't read too good, but I can read some. I just kept crying and reading, crying and reading. I knew I needed my own Good Book. After I done that evil thing, I felt real bad 'cause I could've asked Wanda Jean, and she would'a got me one. I had me a little spending money from time to time, and one day I just put a few of them dollar bills in an envelope and wrote the name of that hotel. I didn't say who sent it or why, just sent some money to pay for that Bible. I don't expect that God likes stealing, but 'specially stealing a Bible."

Rusty leaned forward, taking Adda's hand. "Adda, I don't think God likes stealing either. But I think it made Him real happy that you wanted His book. And the people who buy those books, the

Gideons, I think they would have wanted you to have it."

"You got a Good Book, Mr. Rusty?"

He smiled. "Yes, Adda. I have a Good Book, and I read it every day. If there are parts that are hard for you to read, I'll be happy to come over and read them to you."

Adda remembered the sound of the preacher's voice when she was a youngster sitting on her daddy's knee. No one had ever read to her except him and her mama reading that little golden book. "That'd be right nice."

~*~

Tears stung Trisha's eyes. Rusty reading scripture to Adda. The beauty of that image overwhelmed her. She tried to dab the tears without notice. Adda scooted closer and reached her arm around Trisha's shoulder. She leaned close to Trisha and whispered, "He's a mighty fine man, ain't he?"

Trisha nodded, her eyes swimming with unshed tears. Hopefully, Rusty hadn't noticed. "Is there anything else, Adda?"

"I told Wanda Jean I needed to be getting my own mail. I figured I didn't have no kin left but Minny and Edith 'cause they all thought I kept money to myself. But I told Minny that I'd write to her and get a place to be getting my own mail. Wanda Jean got me my own box down in the post office, and she brought me my mail every week."

Adda lifted a stack of envelopes with a rubber band around them.

"These was letters from Minny. I got letters for years, and most times Edith had something tucked in there. Even though she was touched, she learned to write her letters. Minny got herself a man and got married. She said he took real good care of Edith and got her some schooling for kids that didn't learn good. He got work here in Asheville and moved Minny and Edith up here."

"They live here?" Trisha gasped.

Adda pinched her lips together. "Don't you be hurrying my story."

"Sorry." Trisha slumped like a scolded child.

One envelope stuck out, loosened from the rubber band. Adda had pulled it free for tonight.

"Got me this letter from Minny about ten years after I left home and my daddy disowned me.

She looked from Trisha to Rusty and then handed the letter to him.

"You can read it out loud."

He removed the letter from the envelope and unfolded it with care.

"Dear Adda, I hope you are doing well in Nashville. I have some sad news to tell you. Daddy's dead. He just fell over whilst working in the field and died right there. He's already buried, so there's no reason to go back home. No one left living in that little shack. I hope they tear it down. I love you, sister. Please try to visit me. Love, Minny."

Rusty handed the letter to Trisha. She looked at it and handed it back to Adda.

When Adda tucked her items back into the box, Trisha and Rusty stood to leave. Rusty reached for the lid and covered the box. "What can I get for you, Adda?"

"I got all I be needing. You seeing Trisha to her car?"

"I sure will. Good night. Sleep well."

Rusty hugged Adda. He closed his eyes and silently moved his lips.

He's praying for her. Trisha wanted to capture that picture and hold it close to her heart.

They walked toward the parking garage, Rusty's hand across her back. When they stepped into the elevator, Trisha observed what he was wearing. She felt disheveled in her jeans and T-shirt next to him. The suit looked as crisp and fresh as ever.

"Do you think they're still here, Minny and Edith?"

His eyes shone with amusement. "I thought you learned your lesson. Don't get ahead of the story."

She nodded but had no energy for a grin.

"You look sad tonight. We've had harder nights than this one with Adda."

He was right. This didn't hold the same heart-wrenching parts like losing her son. Her melancholy had nothing to do with Adda, but she couldn't share that. "I guess the whole picture, as it all comes together, it's just sad."

"Her story's not done yet. As long as we have breath, our story has another chapter. Adda, you, me. Our stories aren't done."

His eyes held hers. The intensity of his stare brought heat to Trisha's cheeks. Had she ever felt this vulnerable with Grant? The elevator door opened, and he motioned for her to go before him. At her car, he hugged her. She had forgotten about her resolve to keep it professional. Did he close his eyes and send God a silent prayer for her?

18

Adda could have had a day or two off after what Rusty put in her box. That was a whole week's worth of what she got. But the sun was shining bright and that always made people stop and spend some time listening. Most people dropped something in the box if they stood there a while.

She was back from her lunch break when she saw him. Frank Gillen. Oh, he looked older, too, but he'd taken real good care of himself. He wore sunglasses, so Adda couldn't see his eyes. But she knew. He sat listening to her music for near an hour, but he never came over to speak. Adda needed another break and told folks she'd be back in a little while. That's when Frank walked right up to her. As she wrapped up her equipment, he stood before her and pulled his sunglasses off.

Adda spoke without looking up. "Them sunglasses didn't keep me from knowing who you was. Ain't no mistaken cause you look like your daddy."

He stepped closer, invading her space. "So Adaline, you're suing me."

Adda never stopped her packing up. Frank was a bully when he was little and, from the way he glared at her, that hadn't changed. "You come all the way from Nashville to tell me what I already know?" She finished wrapping up the cord and folded the chair. "I best be going." She began to walk away.

Frank grabbed her arm and turned her around. "Don't you walk away from me."

With one foot, he shoved her wheeled cart out of her reach as he clutched her arm. Panic jolted through her. She tried to twist her arm away from him but couldn't match his strength.

"If you know what's good for you, you'll drop that suit right now." He leaned close to her face, squeezing her arm. "You're not—"

"Take your hands off of her before I call the police."

Relief surged through Adda when she saw Rusty. She'd never seen his face mad or heard his voice that loud. She was no match for Frank, but Rusty might give him a scare.

Frank swung around.

"And who might you be?"

"The one who's going to put you in jail if you don't get your hands off of her."

Frank loosened his grasp, and Adda squirreled out of it. "Rusty, this here's Frank Gillen."

Frank glared at him. "Rusty. As in Russell Bergstrom? So you're the gold digger that convinced her to sue. Do you chase ambulances, too?"

Rusty placed himself between Frank and Adda. "Touch her again, and we'll file assault charges."

Frank slowly placed his sunglasses back on his face. He stretched his neck around Rusty to see Adda. "Drop it, Adaline." Then he turned to walk away.

Rusty picked up the chair and reached for the wheeled cart. Shifting them both to one arm, he put his other around Adda.

"Let's get you inside. No more singing today."

~*~

Trisha's lease was up at the end of May. She would move back into the farmhouse for a month. That left another week to move all of her things. She started packing and taking things over a little each day. As she carried the first of her boxes in through the summer room, the cabinet doors lay in the same place they had been. Jimmy's truck was in the driveway, so she called to him.

"Jimmy, it's Trish." She walked in the kitchen and set the box down. The walls had been patched in a few rough spots, and a fresh coat of paint covered two walls.

"Don't step in here. Floors aren't ready."

Trisha walked to the doorway and peered in. The gossamer shine on the floors was vivid. If she didn't know better, she would have thought they were new hardwoods.

"They're beautiful. I'm…I'm speechless. How much is done?" She craned her neck to see the entry and stairs from her vantage point.

"They're all done but the kitchen. We'll finish up the work in there before they finish the floors." It would have been the perfect opportunity to remind him that she hadn't agreed to the kitchen yet, but she wouldn't do that to Jimmy.

"Upstairs?"

"All done. Floors are done, and we did a little patch up and painting."

She opened her mouth to speak

"All in the price I gave you," he assured.

Trisha gazed at the ceiling beams, cleaned and shiny, the mahogany wood a striking contrast to the white paint. Whoever refinished the wood had quite a job working that high. The fireplace showcased the room with the stunning tiger-eye grain that Jimmy had buffed to life. And now the floors had returned to their original glory. How could she sell this place? It was always home, but now it was hers. She looked around with a newfound pride. Did she dare broach the subject with Grant?

Jimmy went out the front door and walked around the house, coming in through the kitchen. "Floors are dry, but I'd give them another day. Then just your socks for about a week."

"I'm moving some things in. My lease is up, and I'll stay here until the wedding. What's left for the workers?"

"Just the kitchen. Then we'll take a break until you're ready for more. No hurry."

Trisha continued to scan the room. "The sad thing is, these changes should have been made years ago. Grandma and Pap could have enjoyed them. But then, you know what pack rats they were." She shook her head with the memory of it.

Jimmy looked around, admiring the details. "So what's your plan? Are you and Grant going to live here?"

"I wish. I'm not sure I can convince him."

"Can't blame him if he hasn't seen it. Bring him around. Let the house speak for itself." There was truth in those words. She had been frustrated with Grant, tired of arguing. But he hadn't seen it. Maybe that would make the difference.

~*~

Trisha called Grant to see if he'd help her move some things to the farmhouse. It was so rare for her to call him at work, and even more rare for her to ask for help. He immediately agreed.

Trisha held her breath as they started up the long driveway. Jimmy had delivered a new layer of gravel last week.

Grant slowed his car. "Well, at least it's not a dustbowl anymore."

As they turned the bend and the house came into view, Trisha turned her gaze toward Grant, hoping to catch his expression. He raised his eyebrows when he saw it but made no comment.

She rested her hand on his shoulder. "What do you think of the porch?"

"Very nice. Makes a big difference. Is that a wrap-around?"

"Yes. There's a great view of the mountains from that side. We can go in the front so we don't have to carry these so far. No more rotted wood."

It might have been easier to store the boxes in the summer room for now, but Trisha wanted the wow effect that the kitchen didn't have. At least not yet.

She unlocked the front door while Grant went back for another box. The entry way had a stone floor that could be walked on. Trisha wanted no clutter when Grant entered, so she left the boxes on the porch.

"Just set that there for a few minutes and come on inside." She held her breath while he stepped in.

His eyes widened. "Whoa. Are we in the right

house? Trish, this is remarkable. You did all of this?"

"Well, I had it done. We need to take our shoes off. The floors are still pretty fresh."

They kicked off their shoes and walked around in socks. Trisha showed him the mantel, the beams, the gleaming handrail and newel post. Bright sunshine flooded the rooms, accentuating the glowing wood. She opened the new French doors in the dining room and stretched her hand toward the view of the mountains.

"The kitchen isn't ready. I'd like to do more to it but have to space the work out."

Grant pulled her into an embrace "Honey, this is incredible. Forgive me for doubting you. Have you had it reappraised?"

Of course Grant would think of that. "No, why would I do that?"

"Well, obviously it's worth a lot more now. You can raise your asking price significantly."

Trisha didn't answer. She turned and went to the porch for the boxes and began setting them at the bottom of the staircase.

"Jimmy said to leave all of my things here. He'll have some workers over this weekend, and they'll carry them all upstairs."

"Good. I wasn't looking forward to that."

Grant made multiple trips to the car. When all of the boxes were stacked, Trisha took his hand. "Can we sit outside for a little while?"

They walked out to the porch and went around the corner. The sun was shining on the mountains in the distance, bathing them in shades of blues and purples. The stained glass above the dining room windows cast a prism of colors on the floor boards.

Two Adirondack rockers were waiting.

They sat and enjoyed the view. Trisha squeezed Grant's hand. "This is so peaceful."

He rested their joined hands on the armrest of Trisha's chair. "It really is. It feels removed from the world. It might be a great option for a bed and breakfast. Maybe it could be marketed with that suggestion."

A knot hardened in Trisha's stomach as she formed the words in her mind. "Grant, I don't want to sell this place. I want us to live here."

"Trish…"

"Hear me out, please." She turned pleading eyes toward him. "I've only touched the surface of what can be done here. This place has so much potential, and it's so peaceful. It would be the perfect place to raise a family. Please don't keep seeing it as it was. See it for all that it could be."

He turned his rocker and took her hand. "Honey. You've done an incredible job. I am seeing it for what it could be. I just don't want it. I don't want an old house. They come with old furnaces, old plumbing, old roofs. And look at this." He waved his hand around the acres. "I don't want this job. It's non-stop mowing and raking."

"We could hire someone to do that."

"And it's still old. I'll build you something new. You can have fun planning and designing our own house."

"Will you at least think about it?"

"Trisha, look at the commute I'd have. And probably you as well. You're not likely to land a job in this rural area."

"Thirty minutes, Grant. That's all it took us to get

here."

He shook his head. "That's an hour every day. Then back into town if we want to go anyplace decent for dinner or an evening out. There's nothing in this backwoods area."

They sat silently rocking on the porch, looking at the mountains.

When Trisha spoke, her voice was low and cracking with emotion. "Why is it always your way?"

He sighed deeply. "It's not. We have to compromise. You're not thinking this through."

She removed her hand from his and stared at the distant mountains. The silence stretched between them.

Trisha turned back toward Grant, sadness etched on her face. "When did we ever compromise that it didn't end up your way?"

His eyes drilled hers. "I don't see you moving into my place."

"That's a temporary situation. If this house is sold, that's permanent." Trisha stood from her rocker, wishing she had her car here. "Will you take me home now?"

19

Adda settled into the canvas chair, thankful that Rusty came along when he did.

"Adda, what did he say to you before I arrived?"

"He just slid those old sunglasses off and looked to see if I remembered him. Looks just like Ernie. Then he told me to stop the suing or I'd be sorry. That's all a'fore you come along. He squeezed real hard." Adda rubbed where he'd hurt her.

Rusty examined her arm. "Do you need to see a doctor?"

"No, just sore. It ain't broke."

Rusty stooped down before her so they would be at eye level. "Adda, listen carefully to me. I'm going to use my phone to take a picture of your arm while I can still see the marks. Then we'll file a complaint and get a restraining order. That means Frank Gillen's not allowed to come anywhere near you again."

Adda held her arm out while Rusty snapped a few photos. He slid his phone back in his pocket. "I have to get back to work. First, I'm going to run across the street and bring you coffee and some lunch. Then I want you to lock this door and don't open it for anyone but me or Trish. I'll be back later, and I'm going to bring you a telephone."

"Ain't no need…."

"Shh. I'll bring you a telephone with my number

and Trish's number programmed in. All you'll have to do is push one button to reach us. I don't think he'll be back. All he wants to do is to scare you. We're not going to let him do that."

"But you forgetting one thing. My bathroom's across the street."

He ran his hand through his hair. "So it is. Just be careful."

Adda pulled her legs up on the air mattress and laid her head down. Her braids fanned across the pillow. "I'm mighty glad you came by."

~*~

Trisha's phone rang. She glanced at the screen and saw Rusty's name. She hit 'silence' and slid it back in her purse. She wouldn't talk with him while she was in Grant's car. When they pulled in front of her apartment, Grant got out of the car.

He reached for her hand. "Why don't you change, and I'll take you to dinner?"

She shrugged away from his touch. "I'm too busy. When do your parents arrive?"

"Not until Friday morning. They'll be here until Monday."

"I'll see you Friday for the graduation."

"Not before then? I thought with classes being over I might find you and a home-cooked meal waiting for me."

Trisha had opened her apartment door and swept her hand toward the boxes. "I'm a little busy here. I'll see you Friday." She was giving him a cold shoulder, but she couldn't help herself. It broke her heart to think of selling the house.

It was the following morning before Trisha realized that she had not turned her phone back on. When she looked at the screen, she had two missed calls and three text messages from Rusty. Something must be wrong.

She phoned him but got no answer, so she also left a text message. After an hour passed without hearing anything, Trisha called his office.

"Brackston Law Firm."

She recognized Brooke's voice. "Brooke, this is Trisha Mills. Is Rusty available?"

"Hello, Trisha. He's not. All of the associates are in a meeting that probably won't end until four o'clock. If it's an emergency, I can take him a message."

Never mind. She'd see him this evening anyway. "No, it's not an emergency, but thank you anyway. I'm sure he'll get my message when he's free."

~*~

Trisha parked and went to the crosswalk. Traffic was heavy for a Wednesday evening. As she waited for the light, she could see Rusty seated on a bench outside of the Mendino. She caught a glimpse of her image reflected in the store window, pushed the hair back off of her face, and straightened her blouse. She needed his light-heartedness tonight. He could always find a way to bring a grin to her face.

His back was to her, and she saw the sandy-blond hair curling at his neck. Her step quickened just thinking of the light that his eyes always held.

With great deliberateness, she stayed out of his

view and walked behind the bench. People were passing all around him so he probably didn't sense anything different. Trisha gently touched a finger to his hair. He reached a hand up and scratched it. She did it a second time, and he swatted as if a bug had landed on him. The third time, she gave him a gentle pinch. He turned around then, and she burst out laughing.

Reaching for her hand, he led her around to sit.

"You're not going to pinch me back, are you?"

"Not yet. I'll wait until you're not expecting it. Hey, we need to talk before we see Adda."

"I know we were playing phone tag. I'm sorry I missed you."

His eyes weren't smiling.

"Something's wrong. What is it?"

"Frank Gillen paid a visit to Adda. He tried to intimidate her into dropping the suit."

Trisha gaped. "He's not allowed to do that."

"Of course not, but obviously he's not going to play by the rules. He bruised her arm pretty good."

"No… Is she all right."

"Yeah, she's spunky. But I'm worried. I took pictures and will file a restraining order. I wanted to get it done today, but it'll have to wait until tomorrow. Technically, we could have charged him with assault."

"So you were here?"

"I ran over at lunchtime and was just arriving when I saw him. He grabbed her arm, and I sprinted toward them."

Trisha put her hand on his arm. "Thank God you were there. Rusty, maybe I should take her home with me. Do you think that's a good idea?"

He sat back and rested his head, looking skyward.

"I don't know. Let me think about that. At least here, there's plenty of people around."

Trisha resisted the urge to reach up and touch his face.

"I know you have a busy few days. I'll be here as much as I can, but I need to go to Nashville next week. I hope two days will do it."

"I'll be here. I just need the weekend, and then I can come as much as needed."

He clearly didn't have the same hesitation because he reached up and smoothed a lock of loose hair off of her face. "I was hoping you might come with me. Selecting witnesses is a whole different level of experience. But I suppose it's better for you to be with Adda."

"You'll be taking their statements?"

"Informally. Right now, I'm just trying to gather witnesses. If we subpoena them, they'll be formally interviewed, and it'll be recorded."

Trisha would have loved being part of that process. But Adda's safety was more important.

"No matter what, neither of us can be here twenty-four seven. And I already worry that she crosses this street alone at night. Think about the farmhouse. I'll be moving back there in a few days."

"Really? I didn't know that."

"My lease is up. I'll stay there until the wedding."

He looked away and rubbed the back of his neck. Then he dropped his elbows to his knees and rested his forehead in his hands.

Trisha had never seen him this way. She rubbed his back. "It'll be OK. We'll take care of her. Even if I need to stay here with her."

He sat up abruptly. "Let's go see her. She said this

will be the last night of remembering. It's all she has to show us."

~*~

Adda took the last items from her box. Trisha came in, took hold of her arm, and looked at the marks. Then she hugged her.

"Don't go fretting over a little bruise. Sit on down. I told Rusty that this will be the last night we'll be remembering. I'm coming to the end of my story."

"The end of your story so far," Rusty corrected her. "We'll be adding to that remembering box for years to come. Your story isn't over."

Rusty and Trisha took their typical places.

"I lost track of the years, so I don't rightly know how old I was when I could tell that my voice weren't as strong. When I was recording, they made me do things over and over. That was about the same time I got this letter from Minny." She handed it to Trisha.

Trisha read it aloud. *"Sister, I know it's hard to get away, but if you can manage a visit, it would be a blessing to see you. I haven't been well. I'll tell you more about it when you come."*

Adda took the letter back and folded it, returned it to the envelope, and set it aside.

"I been to Minny's two times before. She had a right nice little house. She had a little more learning than me and fit right in with that neighborhood. Her man, Cecil was his name, he treated her and Edith real good. So I told Wanda Jean that I need to see my sister 'cause she was ailing. She bought me a bus ticket, but she didn't get me no ticket that was bringing me back to Nashville. She said she'd be in touch. She knowed Minny's phone number."

Adda shook her head back and forth, three or four times. She'd been so worried about Minny that she didn't think to question why. And even after all those years, buses still made her nervous.

"Minny was real bad off when I got there. They said it was the cancer what got her. I ain't never seen nobody so thin. When she saw me, I could look at the bones in her face. But her eyes looked real happy that I was there. Edith was all growed up, but she was still touched. All she done was cry for her mama." Adda could still hear the sound of Edith wailing. She could still see Cecil pacing around, not knowing what to do. "Cecil let me stay with them for two weeks 'til Minny passed into the everlasting. They had a nice church with lots of folks crying and cooking." Adda had been surprised to see the hundreds of people who came out for Minny's memorial. Loneliness gripped her. She'd had only Minny in her life. Now she had no one.

"Minny got a place in the cemetery right by the church. I was thinking how much better it would be to get buried in the church instead of back behind the fields like my mama. Sort of like God watching over your resting place."

Rusty reached over and took Adda's hands in his. "But remember, Minny and your mama were already standing in the presence of God."

Adda nodded. "I know that, but the church was real comforting to see right there beside her. I stayed two more days before I called Wanda Jean for my ticket. That's when she told me I weren't needed no more. My singing for money was done." Adda had thought nothing could get worse after putting Minny in her grave. Then she made that phone call to Wanda Jean. She had no family except Edith, no job, and nowhere to live. When she hung up that phone, her legs didn't want to hold her up. They'd buckled beneath her, and Cecil had to help her to a chair.

Adda shook off the memory and reached for the next item from her box.

"A few days later, a box was delivered to Minny's house with all my stuff from the room in Nashville. This letter came with it. You might be needing to make yourself one of them copies." She handed it to Rusty.

He scanned it and glanced at Trisha. "A termination letter. Yes, Adda, I will be needing a copy, but I didn't bring my copier. I'll have to come back for one tomorrow."

Adda flapped her hand. "You can take it and make your copy. It ain't one of the things that I'm treasuring. And now I know you coming back."

Rusty carefully placed it in his folder.

"Cecil was a real good man, but it wasn't fittin' for me to stay there with Minny gone. But I didn't have no money but the few dollars that came with that letter from Wanda Jean. She said it was the last of my earnings. Well Cecil said he couldn't see no kin of Minny's in trouble so he helped me get a place to live. Got me a little apartment here in Asheville and moved me in. He paid for three months of my living money. I told him I'd get me some singing money somewhere. Singing's all I know how to do. But I didn't want to be Adaline no more. I wanted to have my given name."

Adda pulled out the last item that she had to show us. It was a paystub.

"I got me a real job singing in a place that gived me a pay every week. I didn't know how to do all that banking stuff so Cecil helped me. Pretty soon, I was going into that bank on my own and trading that paper check for real money. I was right proud of myself."

Adda placed the items back in the box like she was finished. Trisha's mouth gaped open but Rusty sat there patiently.

"I know I ain't got nothing in here to tell the rest, but ain't much to tell. Cecil found himself a new wife and moved. Edith needed help with regular living stuff and he found a place that gives her a room of her own and folks live there to take care of her. I went to see her a couple'a times, but then she stopped knowing me. Don't remember nothing from one day to the next. That place I was working? Well, they went and sold that business, and I didn't have money for my apartment, so I got this place. It works real nice cause I can get me singing money right here where I live."

Everyone was quiet. The story had ended without the drama of the beginning.

"You said that the story ain't done yet. I'd sure be liking something in my remembering box that tells about both of you."

Rusty opened his folder. "I'll give you this. It's your copy of our agreement. But I'd like to give you something way more interesting than that. Let me think about it." He looked at Trisha. "And you?"

"I, um…" She stuttered. "Give me a little time to think. I'd love to have something in that box. But I want something happy. There's enough sad in there already."

They stood to leave, but Rusty had one more thing. He pulled a phone from his pocket.

"As promised. It's fully charged. Keep this plug handy and every time one of us is here, we'll get it charged."

Adda stood up, hands on hips. "I ain't the best at reading and writing, but I know how to put a plug in."

Trisha and Rusty exchanged an amused glance.

"Sorry, Adda. Plug it in every day, and it will stay charged. This button is to call Trish. This button will call me. Call anytime you need us, day or night. When we finish a call, make sure you push this button. It ends the call."

"Whatever happened to just hanging up?"

"Well, we'll call this the hang-up button."

20

Trisha had put the call off long enough. Her Uncle Brendan was the closest relative she had. In fact, he was the only living relative other than a few second cousins on her father's side whom she had never met. They didn't have a bad relationship, just had no relationship at all. He seemed relieved when her grandparents took her in. Even at twelve, she recognized she had freed him from the responsibilities of worrying about them. Trisha once overheard her mother talking about him. "Brendan's just an odd duck. He's married to his work."

The phone rang without answer. She could call his office, but that might not make him happy. She left a message on his cell.

"Uncle Brendan, It's Trisha. I'm sorry I missed you. I just wanted to chat and give you some updates on the wedding plans. My graduation is tomorrow, and then the bar exam will be coming up soon. Call me sometime when you can talk."

She'd done her part. If he cared at all, he'd call.

Trisha went to her closet and began unloading some of her clothes into suitcases to move them back to the farmhouse. Her car was already filled with boxes from the kitchen. Pretty soon, this place would be empty. She planned to stay at the farmhouse tonight but then return to the apartment through Monday. She needed to be close when Grant's parents came to town. Monday evening, she and Chester would move back to the farmhouse.

Trisha left in time to beat the Thursday rush hour. As she turned the bend on the driveway, her heart still fluttered just looking at the dignified picture the new front porch created.

There was so little left of her past. Her mother had played in this yard as a child. She ran up and down those stairs when she was a teenager. Probably slammed the bedroom door a time or two just as Trisha had done. How could she give this up?

What would Grant do if I just put my foot down?

The boxes and suitcases made it as far as the bottom of the stairs. She'd carry one up every time she made a trip. Loading and unloading the car was enough for today. Trisha slipped her shoes off and slid into a pair of soft slippers. She took an unhurried walk through the rooms, admiring the radiant shine on her floors. Only the kitchen remained in disarray. Picking up her briefcase, she went through the new dining room doors to the veranda. She had decided to call it a veranda rather than a porch. It had earned the gracious title. Trisha sat down with her bar exam prep book and began reading.

The gravel driveway alerted her to an approaching car before it came into view. As it turned the bend, Trisha's pulse quickened. She hadn't expected to see Rusty until he returned from Nashville late next week. The side of the veranda was less visible, so she walked to the front and waved.

He closed the car door and jaunted up the walk to the stairs. In a few short steps, he stood before her.

"Rusty, Why...? I didn't expect you." Why did she

always get tongue-tied?

"I was hoping you were here. I wanted to review a few things before I leave next week." He glanced at the book she still held. "If you have time."

"Oh, this? Yes, I'm happy to put it down for a while."

"But you are taking the test, right?"

"Probably. Why is everyone so worried about me and this test?"

He left her question unanswered. "Want to sit out here?"

A wide grin filled her face. "After I show you something. But you'll have to slip your shoes off."

Rusty followed her to the front door where he slid out of his shoes. He could see the floors from the entry way.

"Wow." His face lit with excitement. "This is gorgeous. Whoever did this knows his stuff. Are they all finished?"

"All but the kitchen. It still has some work being done."

Rusty walked around and shook his head in disbelief. "Tell me you're not selling this place."

Trisha didn't respond. How could she when she didn't know? They walked through the kitchen to the summer room.

"The cabinets have been sanded and aren't finished yet. At some point, I hope to replace the countertops and sink. And Jimmy's keeping his eye peeled for a bargain on a new six-burner range. We had a little miscommunication about the kitchen. I thought he was getting me prices, and I guess he thought I wanted him to have it done. It'll be fine. May drain me a little further than I wanted, but I can still pay. He's saved me a bundle already."

Rusty ran his hands over the cabinets, his back to Trisha. "Someone did a real nice job of sanding these."

When he turned, he wore an amused smile. "Let's go talk about interviews."

Rusty had a list of people he wanted to talk with. Helen and Marcella were still living in Nashville. He hadn't been able to locate Wanda Jean but hoped to learn her whereabouts from others involved with Haven. He and Trisha worked to compile useful questions. When they finished, the sun was setting. They walked outside to the back of the house for a view of the mountains bathed in hues that spanned the spectrum. The colors seemed to change before their eyes.

Rusty rested his arms against the fence and looked up. "I bet you never get tired of this. God's quite an artist."

Trisha nodded, although he couldn't see. "I didn't appreciate it until I was grown. When I was a young girl, this didn't mean much to me. I was so angry when I came—mad at my parents for leaving me. I know that's irrational."

Rusty turned and leaned his back against the fence, looking at Trisha. "Irrational, but quite common." His features softened. "Did you say it was a car accident?"

"Yes, they were together on their way to work. Brilliant morning sunshine caused a multicar accident." The memory of that day was like a vise squeezing her chest. "I argued with my mother that morning. She told me to change my skirt, that it was getting too short." Trisha had loved the skirt. Loved its herringbone pattern, the feel of the stitches, the pleat in the front. But at twelve, she had grown tall and leggy. Her mom acquiesced, weary of the battle. "My mother gave in but told me that if I was called to the office, she couldn't leave work to bring me other clothes. When the intercom called me to the office, I was sure the principal had seen my skirt. I walked to the office, tugging at the hem, trying to get as much length as possible. But it wasn't about my skirt. One look at Pap, and I knew something was wrong." Trisha didn't tell Rusty about the day she took scissors and cut the skirt to shreds. She'd never worn herringbone again.

It had been so long since she'd talked about that day. Rusty was a good listener. His eyes held compassion.

"After that, I just missed them so much that nothing would bring me joy. Grandma would hold me, and we'd cry together. I always thought about what I lost. I never gave much consideration that Grandma had lost a daughter. They were so patient with me. They loved me back to health."

"I wish I could have known them."

Trisha tilted her head. "Why?"

"I'd thank them for showing you how to live. How to find joy again."

She shrugged. "Me? I always feel like I'm living with hurried chaos instead of joy."

Rusty reached his hand to her. She looked at it, unsure. Then reached and placed her hand in his.

"There's an inner joy and a sense of justice. I see it in the way you love Adda. Speaking of Adda, I have a surprise for you. Let's go inside."

Trisha started toward the veranda. A peacefulness flowed as she walked the grounds beside Rusty. Meandering back, they stopped to look at the butterfly bush, a baby blue hydrangea, and pink, downy phlox.

Rusty bent to examine the blanket of color formed by the phlox. "Their bloom is so short-lived you have to delight in the moment."

He stood and continued toward the front. When they reached the stairs, he started toward his car. "I'll be right back."

Trisha went inside and stood at the door. She watched him stroll to the car, reach inside for something, and turn to come back, his carefree gait growing so familiar. As he bounded up the three steps, he held something behind his back. Trisha craned her neck to see, but he kept it concealed.

"Have a seat in the living room."

They kicked their shoes off and stepped on the luminous floor.

Trisha sat on the sofa and watched his back, unable to see what he was doing. Before he turned around, she heard the music. It was Adaline, but nothing like she'd ever heard before. The brilliant sound echoed with a clarity that reverberated throughout the room. Her mouth dropped open.

"How...? What...?" She couldn't get the words out.

"Simple. Digital music and a wireless speaker. Sit back and close your eyes."

She obeyed, captivated as she heard the old music in a new way. She felt the movement as Rusty sat beside her. They listened in companionable silence. The song ended, caught a breath, and went into the next on the playlist, one slightly more spirited.

Trisha opened her eyes as the tune changed and Rusty stood. He extended his hand, and Trisha took it as she stood. She expected he would turn the music off and say good night. Instead, he drew her into a dance hold.

"Let's dance." It wasn't phrased as a question.

Trisha was stabbed with traitorous panic. "I shouldn't."

He continued to sway with the music. "Pretend you're a teenager dancing with your pap."

Trisha tentatively lifted her hand to his shoulder. His other hand cloaked her cold one in its warmth, like a velvet wrap. Stepping back with the beat, he held their hands high, twirling her beneath them. Then he twirled her to the side and back again until she smiled. His movements were graceful, fluid. He was no stranger to the dance floor.

She returned to the circle of his arms as the music slowed. His embrace was closer than Pap's had ever been, causing her arm to naturally rest around his neck.

As the music swelled, he drew her closer, resting his cheek against her hair. She breathed in the scent of him, a musky scent of outdoors, the scent of fresh cut grass and woods. The pulse of her heart pounded and she wondered if it penetrated all the way to his own. Every cell in her body was heightened as never before.

He breathed her name against her ear. "Trish." She turned toward the sound and their lips found each other. She was powerless to pull away. He released her hand from the dance hold and wrapped his arm around her. She buried her free hand in his hair and returned his kiss with eagerness.

The music peaked, the cadence swelling to the conclusion. When Adaline's eternal last note ended, the breath of silence broke the spell. Trisha pulled back.

Her voice was rich with emotion. "Rusty, I can't. I can't do this. I'm so sorry."

He rested his forehead on hers as they stood focused on each breath inhaled and exhaled. He tipped her chin up and held it, touching her face.

"Trish, we have something here. Something special. I know you feel it, too."

She shook her head and stepped back. "This can't happen. I'm getting married."

He cupped her face with his hands. "Don't, Trish. Don't make the biggest mistake of your life."

Trisha reached for his hands and moved them from her face. She held them in front of her. "This was a mistake, Rusty. I'm so sorry."

He tightened his grip on her hands. "Why, Trish? Why are you getting married?"

Her chin began to tremble. "Why? What kind of question is that?"

"A question for you to ask yourself. Why are you marrying him?"

She inhaled deeply and let it out slowly. "We're a month away. Our plans are all in place. Invitations have gone out. Dresses are ready. I've been with Grant for three years."

"Sweetheart, listen to what you just told me," he spoke gently. "Do you hear what you didn't say?"

Trisha realized her omission. "I love him. I do. He's a good man."

"But is he the right man for you? I don't think he is, Trish. I watch you when you mention him. And I know how you are with me. You can't tell me you don't feel the difference."

She wouldn't deny it. There was no sense trying. "I can't let this happen. I won't do that to him."

"Honey, you never talk about him unless I ask you something. Don't you think if he were the most important person in your world, you'd be anxious to mention him? Instead, I see your face tense every time his name comes up."

His arms slid around her waist, and he drew her closer again. "From the moment you walked into my office, I knew. I denied it when I saw the ring, but I can't deny it any more. We only have once in a lifetime to find a soulmate."

She gave him a weak smile. "That's a clichéd term."

His eyes disarmed her. "Maybe, until you find yours. We exchange glances and know what we're both thinking. You finish my sentences. I can't imagine not being with you. You're my first thought every morning. That's a soulmate."

Trisha tasted the salt and realized she was crying. "Rusty, I can't. I'm sorry."

"Is your relationship with Grant healthy?" he persisted. "Does he bring you joy? Do you share the same interests? Convictions? Dreams?"

Trisha knew the answer to all of those questions was no. "I can fix this after we're married. We're both just stressed right now."

"You won't fix it. Trust me. You'll just manage the dysfunction and learn to live with it. Is that what you want?"

She shook her head and took a step back, her eyes downcast.

"Does he know you? Really know you?"

Trisha raised her eyes, stopping short of rolling them. "Of course he does. I told you, it's been three years."

Rusty recaptured her hands and drew her forward. "That doesn't mean he knows you. We've been together six weeks, and here's what I know. I know you have a compassionate heart that hates injustice, a heart that hurts when others hurt. I know you long for a heritage that defines you. You cling to the pieces of your past. I know you're sensitive and cry easily, except that you try to hold the tears back because you think they make you weak."

"They do, and I can't afford to be weak."

"No, sweetheart. Tears are a cleansing gift from God. They're natural and healthy. Even Jesus wept, and there's no weakness in Him." Rusty took a breath and continued, "I know you're spunky and will fight for what's right. You're loyal to a fault, even at your own expense. I know you're afraid to fail, but I think you're learning that failure is a part of growing. See Trish, you can learn a lot about a person if you care. Ask him. Who does he say you are? What has he learned in three years?"

Trisha turned her head away. "I can't think right now. You're confusing me."

Rusty tipped her chin up, turning her back. "If you were in love with him, no words would confuse you. You'll betray yourself for the sake of loyalty. Don't spend the rest of your life with the wrong person because you don't have the courage to make the change."

She stepped back out of his reach. "Rusty, you need to go."

"The thing about soulmates is—it has to be both ways, or you aren't actually soulmates," he continued as if she hadn't spoken. "Either one person is mistaken, or one person is in denial. And, Trish, when you stand before God and the church and make those vows, all other possibilities end."

Trisha walked to the front door and held it open. She felt a burning in her stomach as his shoulders slumped in defeat. At the door, he leaned in and kissed her cheek and then walked across the porch. Before he stepped down, he turned and looked back. Their gaze held.

"Does he dance with you?" Without waiting for an answer, he walked to his car, slid in, and drove away.

21

When Rusty's car pulled away, Trisha locked the door. Back in the living room, she saw his electronic device and wireless speaker. She walked over and found the file with Adaline's music. With shaking hands, she set it to play through the full playlist. She curled her knees up on the sofa and cried herself to sleep to the mournful voice of Adaline.

She woke on the sofa at one thirty in the morning, one dim light casting shadows on the ceiling. The speaker was silent, but the red light glowed like a laser point, alerting her that it hadn't been turned off.

Trisha walked over, hit the button, and watched the red fade and disappear. She checked the locks and lights before going to bed. As she walked through the dining room, she saw the wedding folder on the table. Trisha pulled out a chair and flipped through it page by page. So much work and money put into this one day.

She flipped to the guest list and seating chart. Her eyes scanned the names looking for guests that were her friends and relatives. Most of the names were unknown to her, invited by Grant and his parents. Twenty-five tables of twelve and only one round table represented Trisha. She had planned to let Pap invite some of his friends, but when he died, she scratched their names.

She closed the folder and trudged the stairs to her old bedroom, unable to shake Rusty's words from her mind.

~*~

Even though Trisha needed to be at the ceremony an hour before it began, Grant insisted on picking her up. "I don't want to have two cars there afterwards. I told my parents we'd all go out for a celebration. Maybe a cheese plate and wine."

Grant knocked, but then he entered with his key. Trish walked out wearing a simple black dress, her heels in her hand. She glanced around the small room.

"You're early. Where are your parents?"

He pulled her into his arms and kissed her. "I'll drop you off and then run back to my place to pick them up. I wanted a few minutes to tell you how proud I am of you." He kissed her again.

Trisha leaned into him and rested her head on his shoulder. "Thank you. I needed that."

Grant stroked her hair. "Nervous?"

Her shoulders shrugged. "Maybe weary would be a better word."

"Almost done, honey." He pulled back and reached into his pocket, retrieving a small box from a jeweler. "This is a little graduation gift." Grant's eyes beamed.

Trisha opened it with care, pulling the gold ribbon from one side and then unknotting it with a pink fingernail. She lifted the lid. A necklace—the initials TLR formed in diamonds, surrounded by a border of gold dangled from a fine gold chain. Her breath caught in her throat.

Her gaze shot up from the box to Grant, questions etched in her brain.

His eyes danced with pleasure. "Your new initials. I know you have a month, but this is a special day. I wanted you to have something special to go with it."

He leaned in and kissed her.

He's so excited, I can't tell him. It should be an A. Trisha Ann.

Grant wanted her to wear it with her black dress, but she convinced him she shouldn't wear it until her name was Ramsey. It would never be Trisha Lynn. She supposed that's what he was thinking. Lynn had been her mother's name. She once told him her mother thought about giving Trisha her own name for the middle but didn't like the sound of it. She thought Trisha Ann had a better flow. Maybe she could just wear it in remembrance of her mom.

Grant dropped her outside of the school, and she went in to join her classmates. The number of graduates was small. Garlington Law School limited acceptance to fifty new students each year. A few always dropped before completion. Trisha was among forty-six graduates. A celebratory atmosphere filled the holding room where they pulled on caps and gowns, talked, laughed, and hugged each other. Trisha had a few closer friends in the mix, but Rusty's words returned to her. She was serious. She hadn't allowed herself to be lighthearted or to join them for evenings out just for fun. Instead, she crammed for every test, poured her heart into every assignment, afraid of failure. Rusty read her well.

They lined up in the assigned order, and the cue rang out to begin the procession. Trisha sighted the top of Grant's head through the crowd. As she drew closer, she saw his parents. They turned to watch the graduates and smiled when they saw her.

She waited through all the regalia of a commencement: music, honors, valedictorian and salutatorian speeches, and the keynote. Finally, the time arrived to call each graduate for their earned degree, ending the tedium. One by one, each received their coveted certificate. On cue, they stood in unison, turned, and the exit march began. She saw Grant but kept her eyes forward to match the decorum. As she passed the place where he was seated, her gaze was jarred by the familiarity of a man in the back of the auditorium. Rusty stood, leaning against the wall, his eyes fixed on her. As she got closer, she made out the slightest hint of a grin. He did a brief thumb's up.

Trisha broke eye contact with Rusty and looked straight ahead while the graduates continued toward the room where their guests would meet up with them. Trisha's muscles tensed just thinking of Grant and Rusty in the same room. Would Grant look at her and know? Her emotions must be engraved all over her face.

She tried to still her shaking hand as she watched the doorway and each person who entered. Grant, who had been seated near the front of the auditorium, was one of the last to reach the hall. Rusty hadn't stayed. Trisha breathed with relief.

Her future in-laws hugged her. Her mother-in-law leaned close. "Grant's so proud of you, dear. He loves to tell everyone he's marrying an attorney."

~*~

Trisha and Grant walked hand-in-hand as they left the graduation. Grant's mother walked on his other side. "The trip in from Raleigh exhausted me. Just drop us off at your townhouse and you can have some time with Trisha."

Trisha was tired, so the change in plans didn't disappoint her. She and Grant returned to her apartment alone.

Grant held the door as they walked in. "Can I pour some wine for us?"

She plopped onto the sofa, overcome by fatigue. "Yes, please. That sounds nice."

Balancing two wine glasses, Grant handed one to Trisha. He swirled, sniffed, and sipped his own.

Trisha reached for his hand. "Thank you for everything. I didn't want to walk for graduation, but I'm glad you talked me into it."

"You deserved it. You worked so hard."

Trisha turned so she faced him. "If someone didn't know me, and asked you to tell them about your future wife, what would you say?"

Grant gleamed, a seductive smile on his face. "I'd tell them you're beautiful, smart, and that you've worked hard to become an attorney. I'd tell them you'll be the best attorney this city has ever seen."

Trisha was solemn. "But what about me—about who I am, not just what I do?"

Grant reached for her hair and tangled his fingers inside the waves. Then he stroked her cheek. "I guess I'd say you have a gorgeous mane of hair surrounding this incredible face. Big beautiful eyes. I could mention some other attributes, but you might not want me to do that."

His eyes lowered to her chest. She tipped his chin up with a finger. "That's not who I am. That's what I look like."

Grant rubbed his temples. "Trisha, I'm giving you compliments. What is it you want?"

Her shoulder slouched, and she exhaled. "Nothing. I guess I'm just wondering, do you want to marry me so you can say your wife's an attorney and show me off when we go places? I don't want to be a trophy wife."

Grant crossed his arms and stiffened. "Where's this coming from? All because I said I'm proud of you? Sometimes I don't get you."

She put her hand on his arm. "I'm sorry. I guess I'm too tired."

Grant stood and reached to help her up. "I'll be going. I'll pick you up at six tomorrow night. We have dinner reservations at The Whitmore. I thought you'd like that."

~*~

Trisha pulled on her nightshirt and brushed her teeth. She reached for her laptop and thought about Rusty's tablet over at the farmhouse. She'd have to get it back to him before he left for Nashville. She closed her eyes and saw him standing against the back wall, giving her a grin and a thumb's up.

Trisha knew what she needed to do. She needed to distance herself from Rusty. It was the only sure way to save her relationship with Grant. Yet Adda connected them until the suit ended. She couldn't turn her back on Adda.

That's what she'd see if she practiced family law. Two people who once loved each other enough to marry, forever connected by a child. A jolt of panic gripped her chest. Could that someday be her? No one married expecting the road to lead them to divorce. *No.* She would never allow her marriage to fail.

Curling up in bed, Trisha opened her e-mail. Rusty's name jumped out at her, obscuring all others. She clicked on the link.

Saw Adda today, and all is well.

Isn't it a shame how 99% of lawyers give the profession a bad name? Well done! Welcome to the 1%. Hope you're laughing. Does he make you laugh?"

22

Adda went to her markings on the cardboard. The last one was F, making today Saturday. She marked her S before slipping into her flat shoes and walking across the street. At least she didn't have to worry about her hair. Her braids bounced as she walked. The donation box had been good, so she bought herself a nice breakfast biscuit with ham and eggs. Adda suspected Rusty kept her donation box a little fuller. Maybe she'd only sing 'til lunchtime today.

Adda ate and cleaned up in her sink before pulling her equipment out to the front. Saturdays always had less people, but the ones who passed seemed to have more time to stop and listen. Most times when people stopped to listen, they pulled something out of their wallet for the box.

Adda only sang two songs before she saw him. Frank sauntered on in there and sat down. He didn't say anything, just glared at her. His gaze stayed on Adda for over an hour, and he scowled the whole time. Adda's voice quavered, and she forgot the words a time or two.

Her throat was starting to scratch, and she needed to walk across the street for the bathroom. But she feared Frank would try to talk to her, maybe rough her up again. She announced her break and started wrapping up her equipment. He never left his bench, and his eyes didn't leave her.

She walked her equipment to the storage closet and went around back of the building. There was a public restroom she could go to in the lobby if they didn't lock the back door. She peeked over her shoulder. Frank hadn't followed.

When Adda returned to her room, she checked the secret place where she kept money from the week's donations. She counted $38.00. That would have to be enough. She wouldn't be singing again today.

~*~

Trisha turned the bend on the gravel driveway, not expecting anyone to be at the house. Jimmy's truck sat in the driveway and what looked like a car beside it, mostly hidden by the truck. As she drove closer, her pulse began a rapid beat. Rusty. He must have come to pick up his tablet and speaker. If Jimmy hadn't been here, he'd have been locked out. Trisha gave a momentary thought to turning around. *No. This is my house. He can pick up his things and leave.*

Trisha opened the door. From inside came the sounds of George Strait singing about Amarillo. She walked through the summer room to the kitchen.

Her mouth dropped open and hands went to her hips. "What in the world are you doing?"

Rusty sat on the top step of a ladder, paintbrush in hand. Jimmy was kneeling in front of a base cabinet screwing hinges to replace the doors. He looked up at Rusty.

"Uh-oh. Busted."

"Jimmy, you told me you'd get me a price. I don't

want you doing this."

He pulled himself up off the floor, brushing wood shavings from his jeans. "Trish, would you rather me sit in the rocking chair staring at the TV? You know me. I gotta be doing something."

Trisha's exhale came out in a big sigh. She looked up at Rusty on the ladder. "And you? Don't even think of telling me you had nothing better to do."

His eyes held the gleam that had become so endearing. "Oh, I had things to do, but nothing better I wanted to do. I'm learning a lot from Jimmy."

Jimmy piped in. "He's pretty handy with a sander. I've seen lots worse on jobsites."

Trisha swung back around to face Rusty. "You sanded these? Why didn't you tell me?"

"Can't I have some surprises?"

Trisha shook her head and walked away. This must be what all their whispering was about. Why would Rusty do this? At the entrance to the living room, she slipped her shoes off before stepping on the hardwood. A rush of adrenaline hit her as she stood there remembering the dance. The dance and the kiss. She passed through the room to the entry and saw that all of her boxes were gone. They had carried them upstairs. The same boxes that Grant hadn't wanted to carry.

Footsteps followed her. She expected to see Rusty but turned to find Jimmy behind her.

"Trishie, you're not upset, are you? If you don't like it, I can make some changes."

She was an emotional mess, but none of it had to do with the kitchen or Jimmy Wallace. He was the embodiment of kindness.

She reached to hug his shoulder. "I love it. I just

don't want you to think you have to do all of this. You've done so much for me already."

"I promise I won't overdo it, and I won't do anything I don't want to. Rusty offered. We've had a good time working together. Nice fellow."

She nodded. "Yes, he is." *Too nice.*

"Come on back in the kitchen. Let me show you something."

They returned to the kitchen where Rusty painted away, singing with the radio. Jimmy reached for a folder in one of the cabinets. He leafed through it until he found the page he wanted, turning it so Trisha could see. The drawing showed a built-in wine rack, a series of diagonal strips formed diamond shapes where the wine bottles would be stored.

"This little space right here," he pointed, "is pretty useless. Something like this might dress it up. Add a little something special."

"I like it. That would break the monotony and give me nice storage."

"We think alike. Rusty's idea. We sketched it out this morning."

Trisha looked up, but Rusty never turned. He just kept painting.

"Rusty?" He turned at her voice, raising his eyebrows in question. "Thank you. For this and for coming last night." She turned back to Jimmy. "I feel bad leaving you, but I just came to pick something up. I have dinner plans in town."

"You go on and git. We're fine."

Rusty's phone rang, and he retrieved it from his pocket. Trisha heard only one side of the conversation but knew something was wrong. Rusty descended the ladder and walked to the summer room. When Trisha heard Adda's name, she followed him.

"Listen, this is what I want you to do. Keep your door locked and don't answer it for anyone but me. I'm on my way, but it will take me close to an hour. If you have to go out for any reason at all, call me first and I'll stay on the phone with you."

Rusty appeared calm, but his words alarmed her. "What's wrong? Is she OK?"

He slid his phone away. "Yeah but Frank showed up. She only did one hour because he sat staring at her the whole time. She went back to her room and stayed there. After a few hours, someone knocked. She didn't answer, they tried the doorknob. It unnerved her and she's flustered. Could have been the manager or anyone, but she's nervous. I'm going in to calm her."

"Should I come? I can change plans." She imagined Adda alone and frightened.

He took her hands in his. "Don't worry. I'm just going to talk to her. He wants her scared."

"What about the restraining order?

"Just filed it yesterday. He must not have received it. If they couldn't locate him, they couldn't serve it."

"We can still bring her here." Trisha looked around at the disarray.

"Not until you're living here."

Rusty still held onto her hands. Trisha needed to keep him at arms' length. She freed one hand, then the other. She gave his arm a gentle squeeze, thanked him, and withdrew her hand. The light left his eyes, and she fought the urge to embrace him.

Rusty took a step back, his shoulders slack. "She'll be fine, honey. You go have a nice dinner."

~*~

Grant picked up Trisha at the apartment. She wore a floral skirt with a green scoop-neck top. He walked over and touched the fine chain necklace she wore. With his lips pressed together, he hissed. "It would have looked nice on this." He dropped his hand and turned toward the door. "You ready?"

"I'll wear it after the wedding. It doesn't seem right until then."

He stiffened as he opened the door. "Well, we'll just wait. I'm getting used to it."

Grant's parents had been seated at the Whitmore. They ordered wine and were looking at the menu when Grant and Trisha arrived.

Grant's father stood and held the chair for Trisha. Trisha had always loved the Whitmore. It had casual elegance and excellent food. She would enjoy the evening if she weren't seated across from her future in-laws. She had only met them a handful of times over the past three years. They treated her with courtesy but never relaxed their reserve.

Mr. Ramsey wore the practiced smile of a politician. "You look lovely tonight. You're going to be a beautiful bride."

She flashed a polite smile. "Thank you."

Grant looked at his menu. "The filet is their specialty. But Mother, I imagine you want the Chilean sea bass."

"I certainly do." She smiled smugly at Trisha. "He knows me well."

"And Trisha, I suppose you'll want the salmon?"

She had the menu opened, reading it. "Perhaps, but I'm looking."

Grant's head tilted toward her. "Although I can't

imagine why you'd want salmon when you could have sea bass."

Trisha didn't respond but ordered blackened salmon with crawfish creole sauce.

Once they ordered, Grant's mother turned to Trisha, patting her hand. "Let's talk about the wedding, dear. I know you have that girl as your maid-of-honor."

"Julie," Trisha interjected.

"Yes, that's right. But I'm thinking, either Jennifer or Stephanie would be best to say a few words. They know Grant better, and of course they'll be your future sisters-in-law. Philip and one of the girls could stand together for the toast. Do you have a preference who you would like to ask?"

"Julie's going to do it. I've already asked her."

"I'm sure she'll understand when you explain. Our guests won't even know her. Jennifer and Stephanie are both well spoken. We're not sure Julie could...present herself in the same manner."

It took a moment for Trisha to understand what she'd heard. Julie had her own manner of speech. She had a tendency toward hyperbole and exaggerated emotion. They couldn't know that unless Grant had told them. Had they prepared this conversation ahead of time?

Trisha pulled her shoulders back and lifted her chin. Making direct eye contact, she answered her future mother-in-law with a slow, determined voice, "Julie will be doing the toast."

"But dear, don't you think ..."

She leaned forward. "I want Julie to do it."

The waiter arrived with a basket of bread for the table. Trisha sat back but watched Mrs. Ramsey, her eyes steel flints.

Mr. Ramsey broke the silence. "I hear you're interning on a civil suit. How's that going?" He took a warm slice of crusty bread and passed her the basket.

"It's progressing. I'm not able to talk about it." She passed on the bread and handed the basket to Grant.

"Of course, my dear. But are you enjoying the work?"

Am I enjoying it? Working with Rusty? Worrying about Adda?

"I'm learning so much. The practical experience is helpful."

"Grant said you might be switching from family law to corporate? That provides many more opportunities for advancement."

Trisha shot a look at Grant. He refused to meet her eyes.

"No, sir. I'm better suited for family law. The experience from this suit is applicable in many ways."

Salads arrived. Trisha said a silent prayer of thanks and a plea for help getting through this dinner. Mrs. Ramsey still seethed but broached the topic of the wedding once again.

"We're so sorry about your grandfather. Who will be walking you down the aisle?"

Trisha glanced in Grant's direction. "That's something I've been thinking about. I have some ideas but want to talk with Grant about them."

Mrs. Ramsey looked confused and turned from Trisha to Grant. "Well, can't we talk about them now? This seems like the perfect time since we're here together."

Heat rose to Trisha's face.

Grant pulled at his collar and looked down at his

salad.

Trisha jabbed her fork into her own salad. "I'm still collecting my thoughts. I'm not quite ready."

"Well Trisha, that's where the term *brainstorming* comes in. Four heads are better than one. I think it would be nice if Philip walked you down the aisle."

Trisha set her fork down and dabbed at her mouth with the linen napkin. "I'll take that into consideration and let you all know when I decide."

I'll decide since Grant's a coward.

~*~

Trisha kicked her shoes off back at her apartment. They had both remained silent during the ride home.

Grant's jaw was set. "Did you have to be so snippy with my mother?"

Trisha swung around. "Your mother already had her wedding. This is mine!"

He ran his hands through his hair. "They've been a big help to us, and you're starting off on the wrong foot. You've got to learn a little give and take."

Trisha stepped toward him. "And you need to have a little backbone. Do you always cower to her?"

He narrowed his eyes. "I don't cower to her. I try to keep the peace. A lesson you obviously haven't learned."

"Go home. I'm tired." Right now, all Trisha wanted was to be alone.

Grant's hands went to his hips. "Who is walking you down the aisle?"

"No one. I'm walking alone."

His arms flailed out, chest height. "You can't do

that."

Arms crossed, Trisha drilled him with her eyes. If he shrank before his mother's steely eyes, she'd give him a dose of hers. "I can, and I will."

Grant turned and slammed the door behind him. Trisha walked over and flipped the lock.

Fine. She need to check on Adda anyway. She glanced at the clock. Nine thirty. After taking a series of deep breaths, she hit the button set for Rusty.

"Hi." He would know it was her from his caller ID.

"How's Adda?"

"She's OK. Sleeping now," he whispered.

"Rusty, where are you?"

"I'm at Adda's. She talked until she exhausted herself. The door locks from the inside or with a key. I can't leave and have the door unlocked. I don't want to wake her."

Trisha pictured the tiny, windowless space with nothing but a canvas folding chair. Rusty couldn't even rest his head on the back of it. "How about if I come, and you can go home to rest. I'll bring myself something more comfortable to sit in."

"No, I'll be fine. I've slept in worse places. How was your evening?"

At that moment, Trisha felt no sense of loyalty. "Painful. And don't gloat."

"Me? Gloat?"

Trisha could almost see the playful light in those blue eyes. "His mother tried to bully me. But I was spunky. You'd be proud of me."

"I always am."

A warmth filled her, unlike the heat that rose with anger earlier in the evening. "Are you staying there all night?"

"Maybe. She's out pretty soundly."

"Good night, Rusty."

"Good night, sweetheart."

They hung up, and Trisha curled her legs up on the sofa. The thought of Rusty trying to sleep in that small chair played on her mind. He couldn't even stretch out on the floor. All of a sudden, an idea came to her.

Trisha folded the lounge chair from her patio and loaded it in the back of her car. When she reached the Mendino at ten, she had no plan on how to get it in there. She didn't want to go to the parking garage and walk alone at night. Pulling her car to the curb in front of the Mendino, close to Adda's door, she called Rusty.

"Hi, again."

"I didn't wake you, did I?"

"No, is something wrong?"

She smiled to herself. "No, but would you step out of Adda's for just a moment. I'm out front."

"Why?"

"Just come." Excitement bubbled up with her surprise.

He hung up, and she saw him open the door. He sprinted over to her, standing behind her car. "What are you doing here this late?"

She lifted the trunk and pulled out the chair and a blanket.

He took the chair from her. His eyes softened, his head tilted.

"You did this for me?"

In answer, Trisha leaned forward, brushed the hair back from his face, and placed a soft kiss on his cheek.

"Good night, Rusty." She got back in her car while

he stood watching.

Halfway home, Trisha ignored a text message while driving. At home, she locked the door behind her and opened her phone to see the text.

I'm lying here warm and cozy. Thank you. By the way, you'd love my mother. She defines kindness. Sleep well.

23

Trisha arrived home from church and checked her phone. She'd accidentally left it behind, and after several hours it had accumulated a missed call from Grant and two texts from Rusty.

The first text contained a picture—a selfie of Rusty and Adda leaving church. Her pulse caught in her throat when she saw their smiling faces. Under the picture, Rusty wrote, *I had delightful company at church today*.

Trisha closed it and opened the next text. *Did you?*

She frowned and hit the message button to make it disappear. *Why did he always do that?* She switched to her phone icon and returned Grant's call. No answer. Trisha looked around the apartment at all that needed to be moved. She would make a run to the farmhouse. She should be back in time to connect with Grant and his parents.

She filled her trunk and backseat with boxes. A laundry basket filled with books waited, but when she went to move it, she couldn't budge it. Emptying half of them, she carried the basket out to the car and then brought the rest of the stack in two trips. On the road to the farmhouse, the phone tucked deep in her handbag began ringing. Trisha glanced at the vibrating purse but decided against digging it out. Once she reached the house and began unloading the car, she forgot all about the call.

One final walk-through to see what Jimmy had finished, and she'd be on her way. When she passed through the dining room, she saw a gift basket, tied with green gingham cloth and gathered with ribbon at the top. A card with her name peeked out, its corner tucked inside the ribbon. Trisha flipped the light on and sat at the table, pulling it closer. Freeing the card from the top, she slid it from its envelope. It had no signature, but there was no mistaking the sender. *Congratulations. Well done, Counselor.*

Each item nestled in mint green tissue. One by one, she opened them until the basket was empty. A box of ginger tea bags and a jar of raw honey. A mug with a scripture she loved. *The LORD your God is in your midst, a mighty one who will save. He will rejoice over you with gladness; He will quiet you by His love; He will exult over you with loud singing. Zephaniah 3:17.* How had he known she loved that scripture?

As she unwrapped the next piece of tissue, the scent of lavender tickled her nostrils. Lavender soap and a scented candle. She'd once told him lavender was great for stress relief.

Beneath the soap and candle, green tissue paper folded around a DVD. *Gone with the Wind.* She laughed when she opened a miniature replica of a bongo drum. A little note on top said, "Remember the music." A CD of Adaline's Greatest Hits rested near the bottom.

Pressing her fingers along the next item, Trisha couldn't venture a guess. She unfolded the paper to find two magnets, each about four inches long. Holding the pair of magnetic flip flops, she tried to get the connection. When she turned them over, she saw the writing on each. "Soulmates." One had her name, the other had his.

The last item was in an envelope. She opened it and pulled out a certificate for two tickets to *Les Misérables* at the Charlotte Theatre. The enclosed card had a phone number and confirmation number. "Tickets on hold. Call to schedule your date. If he won't go, you know how to reach me. Does he know your favorite things?"

The necklace with the wrong initials forged from gold and diamonds. Grant didn't know her taste in jewelry. He didn't even know her middle name.

Trisha pulled the phone from her purse. Only then did she remember the missed call. It was Grant. Let him wait. She would call Rusty first to thank him.

"Hey Trish. How's the visit going?"

Warmth filled her at the sound of his voice. "I haven't seen them today. I'm at the farmhouse. Rusty, thank you for my surprises. How did you remember all of those things?"

"Like I said, you can learn a lot when you care enough to watch."

Trisha began placing each item back in the basket. She held the cup and turned it in her hand.

"I get most of it, things I mentioned or we talked about. But I never mentioned the Zephaniah scripture. How did you know I love that? And don't say lucky guess."

He laughed. "No luck at all. Just careful observation."

She laid it gently in the basket. "Observing what? Where?"

"Save the questions for court. Did you remember I'm leaving in the morning?"

"Yes, I plan to spend time with Adda. Is she OK?

She's not frightened?"

"No, she's fine. We had a good day today. Went to church and then out to lunch. She should be home napping."

"Use the term 'home' lightly. I hope you get some good leads in Nashville. When you're back, we need to talk about getting her out of there."

"Short trip. Just an overnight."

Trisha inhaled the aroma of the candle before setting it in the basket. "Call me if there's anything to report."

"I'll do that."

She lingered for a moment, not wanting to hang up, yet they both had places to be.

"I'd better go. Thank you again. Be safe."

They hung up and Trisha looked at her phone and the missed call from Grant. She slid it back in her purse. She'd call him from the apartment.

~*~

When Trisha returned to her apartment, she discovered Grant pacing her floor.

He bolted across the room to meet her, the corded muscles of his neck revealing his anger. "And where have you been all day? I've been waiting here over an hour."

Trisha startled. "Grant, you scared the daylights out of me. I didn't see your car. What are you doing here? Where are your parents?"

"They decided to go home since you had no interest in spending time with them."

They now stood face to face. "That's not true. I

planned to see them this evening."

"What about brunch? We tried to reach you."

"You never invited me to brunch. You said 'we're going into town for brunch.' That didn't include me."

"You're splitting hairs here, Trisha. You know that included you." His voice rose with each word.

"No I did not. I thought you were taking your parents out. Otherwise, you'd have asked me."

Grant ran his hands through his hair and sat down.

Trisha sat on the arm of the sofa. "I'm sorry. Did they really leave?"

"Of course they did. You weren't exactly welcoming."

"I said I'm sorry. Grant, your mother, she's so...controlling. How can you take that?"

He rubbed his eyes, and then he shook his head.

"I don't know, Trish. It's all I've known. And she's my mother. I just keep the peace."

Trisha walked around and joined him on the sofa. "You know, a peacemaker is better than a peacekeeper."

"Sounds the same to me." Grant laid his head back and rubbed his temples.

Trisha saw his struggle. He tried to walk a fine line with his parents. She reached her hand to his and held it. "No, a peacekeeper just lets it happen, stays quiet so the boat doesn't rock. A peacemaker will work the problem in a kind, compassionate manner. Talk to her. Tell her you're grateful for her involvement but there are some things you want to work through on your own, you and me. Be gentle but firm."

When he sat up, he picked Trisha's hand up and kissed it. "How'd you get so smart?"

She shrugged her shoulders. "I guess it's my blue-collar background."

He caught her hand again, rubbing his thumb over the silky skin. "I know last night was hard. Let me make it up to you. Where would you like to go?"

"Right now, I just need a shower. I've been moving boxes. Let me get cleaned up and then we'll talk."

Trisha went into the shower and Grant hit the power button on the TV remote.

Ten minutes later, Trisha called out to him. "Almost ready. Five more minutes."

"Hey, you had a missed call from that attorney you're working with, and a text message. You want me to read it for you? It says, 'Trisha, please call me…'"

Trisha bolted from the bedroom, her eyes wide as she grabbed the phone from his hand. "I've asked you to leave my phone alone."

His hands flew up in a surrender motion. "Just trying to help. I saw the first few words and it said *important*. I thought you'd need the message."

"And I've told you there are confidential things I can't discuss. That's going to be the case all of our lives. So please don't touch my phone." She took it and turned on her heel toward the bedroom. Was she going to have to hide her phone? How would Grant react if she started reading his text messages?

Trisha slammed her bedroom door and opened the message. *Trisha, please call me as soon as you get this. Someone broke into Adda's room and trashed it. She's inconsolable.*

Trisha rushed to get her shoes while hitting the return call. "Rusty, what happened? Is she all right?"

"Long story. Right now, I've got to get her out of

here."

"Bring her to the farmhouse. I'll meet you there."

Trisha opened the door to find Grant's eavesdropping posture leaning toward it.

"Sorry. An emergency with the case. I've got to go."

"Whoa, hold on. Who are you taking to the farmhouse?"

"I can't talk. I'm sorry, but I need to go."

Trisha found her purse and grabbed her keys.

Grant caught her and turned her toward him. "Honey, if someone's in trouble, you can't have them at the farmhouse. That's not safe. You'll be living there tomorrow."

"It's not unsafe. Trust my judgment for once." She shook his hands off and ran out the door.

24

It was illogical to hurry. Trisha would arrive before Rusty and Adda. Yet the adrenaline surging through her body went right to the gas pedal. Someone had been in Adda's closet and trashed it. Rusty couldn't console her. That's all she knew. Adda wailed in the background throughout the phone call.

At the farmhouse, Trisha paced around without purpose. She should be getting space ready for Adda, but she couldn't focus. Could Adda walk the stairs? She'd have to. Trisha had no first-floor bathroom, a problem she hoped to remedy when she lived there. If she lived there.

The tires on the gravel driveway came sooner than expected. Trisha ran to the door, her heart sinking when she saw Grant's car parking. She took in a deep breath and then exhaled slowly, stepping outside to meet him. "Grant, what are you doing here?"

"If you hadn't sped off, I'd have offered to drive you. I need to know that you're all right."

He mounted the three steps up to the porch. Trisha reached her arms to him, and he embraced her. "I'm sorry I hurried out." She had been apologizing way too much. She just needed to have this lawsuit end. It was shaking her to the core. The lawsuit and Rusty Bergstrom.

"Grant, please trust me on this. I'm not in any

danger. I promise you. Just a temporary move to help a plaintiff." She needed to appease him and get him out of here fast. He stepped back, still holding her hand. "Trish, don't you see how unprofessional this is? Attorneys don't bring clients to their home. If this person needs a place to stay, her attorney—not you, but the one representing her—should find something appropriate."

Trisha refused to step near the door. Once inside, it would be harder to make him leave.

"I know you're right, but this is an emergency. Something will be worked out soon. Please go so she'll have some...some identity protection. I'll walk with you." She started down the steps, thankful when he followed.

They reached his car only to hear the gravel of an approaching vehicle. One last attempt.

"Go, Grant." But it was too late. As soon as Rusty's car parked, Adda rushed out. Her braids flew as she hurried to Trisha. Wrapping her in an embrace, Adda wailed once again. She clutched an envelope tight in her fist. Trisha tried to loosen the grip Adda had on her neck.

Adda moaned, repeating the same words and grasping the envelope. "My Enam Job. My Enam Job."

"Shhh. Everything's OK now. Let's get you inside." In her peripheral vision, Trisha saw Rusty approach Grant. He reached his arm out and introduced himself. With Adda still clinging to her, Trisha shimmied her stance so she could see them.

Mrs. Ramsey's steel flints looked out of Grant's eyes. "Is that the homeless singer?" He spit the words with disdain.

"That's Adda Marsh, and yes, she's a singer,"

Rusty responded.

Grant smacked the side of his leg. "I told Trisha not to get involved with that woman. She never listens to me. Is that what this case is about?"

Rusty became rigid, red blotching his neck. His words contained controlled anger. "That lady needed help. Trisha isn't a child. She listens to her heart." He turned away from Grant and came over to pry Adda's arms from Trisha.

"Come on inside, Adda. We're going to take care of you." He walked her up the three steps and into the house. Trisha walked behind them and turned toward Grant.

"I'll call you tomorrow."

Trisha didn't anticipate his heightened level of rage. He bounded the steps and grabbed her arm, turning her toward him. "You lied to me, telling me you were helping with a case."

"I did not lie. I am helping."

"Lie of omission. You're the one who led this charge. And this is why you've been impossible to live with for the last month." He pointed his finger in her face.

Trisha swatted his hand. "Don't point at me, and don't yell. They'll hear you."

"I don't care what they hear. And I don't care for that man's attitude. She can't stay here. You need to tell them now."

Trisha gaped at him. "You're telling me who can stay at my house?"

He stepped closer, apparently attempting intimidation. "I'm not kidding Trisha. This has gone too far."

She would not be intimidated. Standing tall, she

leaned forward into the narrow space left. "Someone needs to leave my house right now, and it's not her."

His jaw tightened and he pointed again. "You need to start acting like a Ramsey."

Trisha stepped back. "Is that what it is? Acting?" With that, she turned on her heel and started toward the house.

Grant reached for her arm, jabbing his index finger in her face. "This isn't over."

Her eyes pooled with tears. "Oh, it's so over."

Grant stormed to his car. The tires spewed gravel as he sped away.

Trisha's tears turned to sobs. She stepped down from the veranda hoping no one would hear. Walking around to the side of the house, Trisha leaned her back against the fence and slid to the ground. With her face buried in her hands, she wept until she cried herself out. She remembered Rusty's words—tears were a cleansing gift from God. She'd have to take that on faith. She felt no cleansing, no healing, just emptiness. Trisha looked up. Rusty was watching her from the summer room window. She stood and went inside through the back door to where he stood.

Rusty enfolded her in his arms and stroked her back. "I wanted to come out to you, but I was afraid to leave her." He pointed toward the living room. "She's in there on the sofa."

Trisha gave a tearful grin. "A man's worst nightmare—two crying women." She pulled back and looked at him. "I'm sorry you had to hear that."

He touched the puffy space below her eyes. "I'm sorry I didn't deck him. I couldn't afford the lawsuit."

"Or the publicity."

"Oh, I can see the headlines now." He scrolled his

hand through the empty space. "Wannabe Suitor Attacks Fiancée."

He kissed her forehead and motioned for them to go back to Adda.

Trisha joined her on the sofa, sliding her arm across her back. Adda had calmed down but still clutched the envelope with Enam Job's lock of hair.

"Fill in the missing details for me. Where was Adda when this happened?" Trisha spoke to Rusty so she'd get more clarity. Adda had a singular focus on the envelope she had almost lost.

"Adda stayed in and kept the door locked like I asked her to. When she needed to go across the street, she locked the door behind her. She was gone fifteen minutes. That meant someone was watching and waiting. They picked the lock and made no secret that they'd been there, spilling and scattering everything in the room. The bed was slashed, the slow cooker shattered…"

Adda buried her face on Trisha's shoulder.

"I called the police," Rusty continued. "They came and filed a report. Once the police finished their photos, we searched for the memory box items and found almost everything. The contract and song were missing."

"What about the restraining order? Shouldn't he be arrested for breaking in?"

"They never served it. They couldn't locate him. And we have no proof that it was him."

"It had to be him. Who else would do this?"

"Yes, but we have no proof. He's got to go home sometime. It'll be served when he does. He may be headed back to Nashville now. I'm sure he knows the police were there. I suspect he watched from some vantage point."

"What about her things? Is it still in disarray?"

"The building manager came out, infuriated when he found out Adda was using the room for more than storage. Her connection with the Mendino is over. He's giving me a few hours to get back there and clean it out."

Trisha turned to Adda who sat up again. "You don't need to worry, Adda. I have lots of space here."

Rusty leaned forward. "Just for tonight. I'll find another place."

"No." Trisha negated the idea. "She needs to be with someone. I'm the logical person." She would not allow Grant to dictate who stayed in her house.

Adda's voice broke through their discussion. "You all are talking about me like I ain't here. I ain't staying and putting Trisha out. I been taking care of myself for a long time."

Trisha reached for her hand. "You aren't putting me out, Adda. I have lots of space here." She swept her hand around the room.

Rusty apologized. "I'm sorry. We should have included you. If you could live anyplace you want, where would it be?"

"Anyplace I want?"

"Anyplace. I'm not saying it can happen, but just if…"

"Last time I saw my Edith, I was looking at all the buildings they got. Edith's building got nurses that take care of people 'cause they ain't fit to look after themselves. But there's other buildings, like one where older folks live and they have stuff folks can do, like movies and painting and singing. Somebody cooks, and you all come into a big room and eat together so's you ain't eating alone. Always thought that would be right nice."

Rusty nodded. "A senior living community. You'd like that?"

Adda's slight smile lightened the heaviness of the day. "I'm thinking I'd like that, and maybe some of them folks might even want me to sing from time to time. But I wouldn't take no money."

Rusty nodded. "Can't do it yet, Adda, but we just might get Frank Gillen to pay for a place like that."

Trisha turned toward her. "Until then, will you stay here with me? I'd be grateful for your company."

"Let me be thinking on that for a day or two. Mr. Rusty, are you getting me my stuff?"

"I am, and I better get to it before they set it on the sidewalk. OK if I hold onto it until I'm back here in a few days?"

He stood, and Trisha rose to join him. "Of course."

Rusty's voice lowered to a whisper. "I was careful to make sure no one followed me. No one could have hidden once we hit these rural roads. Will you two be all right if I still head to Nashville in the morning?"

"We'll be fine. Don't worry. Will you be meeting with Gillen and his attorney tomorrow?"

"I hope so. I want to talk with some potential witnesses and hope to have something worthy of requesting a settlement. Are we in agreement that enough money to set her up in her senior living community, good health care, and a little extra will suffice?"

"Yes, she doesn't ask for much. That would make her happy."

Rusty reached for Trisha's hand. "I'm so sorry for today. You sure you're OK?"

His hand brushed over the ring.

Trisha gave him a weak smile. "I have a lot to think about."

Rusty kissed her cheek. "I'll be praying about that." As he left, he turned and pointed at the door. "Lock this."

25

Trisha walked behind Adda as they climbed the stairs to the second-floor bedroom and bath. "Lordy, I gotta climb these stairs every time I need the bathroom? I might as well be keeping myself up there."

"Sorry, Adda. I wish I had a first-floor bathroom. I hope to have one put in, but that will be after I get a job. I can fix an extra bedroom for a little living area if you'd like. I'll spend time upstairs with you. But it's so beautiful here, and I know you'll want to come down to sit outside sometimes. Maybe we can try to keep the stairs down to twice a day. Can you handle them?"

"Oh, I can handle them. Legs are strong enough. It's just the rheumatoid in my old knees. That's what my daddy called it."

Trisha moved Adda into her Grandma and Pap's room. It was the largest bedroom and close to the bathroom. Adda ran her hand over the comforter and pushed down on the pillow to test it. "This is real fine. Real fine."

Her pap couldn't bear to clean out Gram's clothes, and Trisha hadn't tackled the task yet. She pulled open the closet door and looked in a few drawers.

"I think there are things here that will fit you. They're all clean, so just help yourself to anything you like. I'll be right back."

Trisha went into the bathroom and opened the old medicine cabinet. At least eight unopened toothbrushes filled the first shelf. Freebies from the dentist. Trisha gathered toiletries, a towel, and a washcloth and took them to Adda.

Adda fingered the clothes in the closet. She wouldn't find anything fancy. Her grandmother was a simple woman.

"These all for one person?" Adda looked amazed. "Growing up, we shared a few shirts and britches among us young'uns. Then, when the record people took care of me, they brung me stuff to wear when I was singing, but they weren't for keeping. I ain't never had this many clothes all my own."

"Anything you like is yours. Just take it. Rusty will bring your box of clothes in a few days." Trisha pulled open a dresser drawer. "Here are some nightgowns. They'll be more comfortable for sleeping."

A shadow passed Adda's face. "I had me some fancy ones when Ernie courted me. Most times I just sleep in these old clothes."

"Tonight, you get comfortable and rest. I'll show you around tomorrow. You're going to like the view of the mountains."

Adda had a pained expression. "I'm right sorry about your man. He don't like me being here. I ain't wanting to cause no trouble between you."

Trisha let a sad smile cross her face. "You aren't the problem, Adda. Please don't worry about it."

Adda's eyes locked with Trisha's. "That Rusty sure gonna make someone a good husband. Some girl's gonna be powerful lucky to get him."

Trisha suppressed a laugh. "You're right. He's a wonderful man. Good night, Adda."

~*~

Trisha rose early to watch the sunrise. The air was cool, but she loved sitting on her veranda. She held her Zephaniah mug filled with ginger tea. The words faced toward her. *He will quiet you with His love. He will exult over you with singing.*

Trisha sat drinking in the beauty of the morning with a peace in stark contrast to yesterday. No matter what happened with Grant, God exulted over her with singing, a concept too amazing to comprehend. She had decisions to make, hard decisions. Grant. Rusty. Her whole future. Yet God quieted her with His love. This morning, that was enough.

When the sun rose and bird song was at its peak, Trisha went up to check on Adda and heard the snoring. She eased the door closed and tiptoed back downstairs. Jimmy arrived around nine.

"Morning, Trish. I gotta remember to start knocking now that you're living here. I have all the pieces cut for the wine rack. OK if I put it in this morning?"

"Yes. I can't wait to see it. The kitchen looks so bright and cheery. All those years with curtains blocking the light and those old, dingy cabinets."

"I have this sanded and painted. Won't take me any time to install."

"I should tell you, I have a house guest. A friend is staying here for a few days. She's upstairs sleeping."

"You want me to wait so I don't wake her?"

"No. She's sleeping like a winter bear. You do what you have to do. One question—if you were going to put in a first-floor powder room, where would be the best place?"

"I thought about that when we first started talking. I'm thinking you'd want to take this space," he walked back toward the summer room, "and have your bathroom door round the corner coming from the hallway, far end of the entry. You'd lose a little summer room and a few feet here at the doorway to the kitchen. But it could be kept to a minimum since it's just a powder room. You thinking about doing it?"

"Not yet, but someday. Maybe someday soon." So many decisions to make, but one was becoming crystal clear. She wouldn't sell this house. Not yet.

Jimmy went to work on the wine rack when a text came in to Trisha's phone. "In Nashville. Left at five this morning. Had light traffic 'til around seven. How are my two favorite girls?"

Trisha's fingers flew over the keys. "All is well. Adda still sleeping. Jimmy installing wine rack. Let me know how interviews go."

As soon as she sent the message, her phone rang. Julie's name appeared on the caller ID.

"Morning, Julie."

"Hey. How about coffee. I'll meet you in thirty minutes at The Brewster?"

"I can't, Jules. I need to stick around home today."

"Because?" She stretched the one-word question.

"Just because. How about next weekend? We'll plan something special."

"Just because. Hmm. Just because you're sick? Just because you finally let Grant stay over? Just because you don't want to catch me up on wedding details? I haven't seen you for a while, my friend."

"I know. Jimmy's here doing some work."

"So he's done work without you there before."

"I'm prepping. I'll be sitting for the bar soon, remember." Trisha walked to the dining room to pick up the study book.

"Good-bye. I guess I'll see you at the wedding."

"Julie…" But the phone went dead.

It rang again in fifteen minutes. Julie must have finished stewing and was calling to apologize. She reached for it. *Oh no…Grant's name.* She dropped it back on the table as though it burned her fingers. *I'm not ready to deal with you, Grant Ramsey.*

The day dragged by as she waited to hear from Rusty. There had been no word from him since the morning text. Digging through her grandmother's recipes, Trisha found one labeled, *Graham Cracker Cream Pie.* She scoured the kitchen looking for ingredients. She had all of the staples, if she could only locate graham crackers. Sure enough, she found a box, unopened, on a shelf in the pantry. Trisha turned the box to each side looking for the date. It wouldn't have surprised her to find they had expired five years ago. *Ta-da.* One more month before expiration.

"Adda, let's do a little baking. I owe a pie to the man who's been helping me with the house."

Trisha pulled all of the ingredients to the table. Adda crushed the crackers and ran the rolling pin over them.

"I never learned much cooking from my mama 'cause daddy needed help in the field. By the time I was growed enough to help, most of the boys was gone from the house."

Trisha cleaned two pie pans and pressed the cracker mix to form a crust. "I didn't either. I was too young when my mother lived, and Grandma never took the time to show me. I can follow a recipe, but I'm not the cook that grandma was."

The filling consisted of a home-made pudding with meringue. Trisha added a sprinkling of cracker crumbs on top just like she remembered Grandma doing.

Adda went to the sink and wiped off the rolling pin. "Oh, I remember my mama bringing a big, steaming dish of collard greens and fried okra. Makes my mouth get to watering just thinking about it."

Trisha wore a sad smile. "I can picture my mother standing in our old kitchen cooking, but I can't remember anything special she made. I guess I was too young to pay much attention."

The phone rang three more times. Grant. She ignored each and refused to listen to the voice mail. *Where was Rusty's name? What was happening in Nashville?*

Evening approached, and Trisha sat with Adda on the veranda. Still no word from Rusty. It was so unlike him. After looking at her phone again to check the time, Trisha texted him.

How are things going there? Have you had the interviews?

No answer came back. Trisha locked the house and walked back up the stairs with Adda. She went to her own room to study. The call didn't come until nine thirty.

Trisha grabbed the phone. "Rusty. I've been so worried."

"So sorry. It's been a long day and my phone went dead. Everything all right there?"

"Yes. Tell me about the interviews."

Rusty yawned and she remembered he left at five

a.m. That meant he'd been awake since four.

"You're tired. Do you want this to wait 'til tomorrow?"

"I am tired, but I'll give you the highlights. I met with Helen, Marcella, and Laura. I wasn't expecting her, but they gave me her name, and we managed to connect. Seems everyone but Adda knew Haven Records owned her. She didn't know any better, and didn't know her treatment differed from other musicians. They supplied what she needed—food, clothes, necessities, but kept her isolated and dependent upon them for everything. I'll give you more details when I'm home."

"Were you able to locate Wanda Jean?"

"No. Helen thinks she died, but I haven't been able to confirm that. You can see my notes when I'm back. I have an appointment with Robert Pitney tomorrow. He's the attorney for Haven records."

"Oh. What time?"

"Ten thirty. I'm planning to ask them to offer a fair settlement. I'm optimistic. Even without the copyright, her performances alone could have made her rich. We're not asking for much, and they could stand to lose much more if it goes to trial."

"Except it won't. She's still saying she won't go to trial."

"You and I know that, but they don't."

"You sound exhausted. Go get some rest."

He sounded hesitant but asked the next question. "Have you talked with Grant?"

"No. I'm not ready yet."

"Sorry I asked. Good night, Trish."

Trisha hung up and looked at her missed calls and two voicemails. She hit the speaker and played the first. It simply said, "Call me."

The second voicemail was more in-depth. "Trish, we need to talk about yesterday. I let my temper get the best of me. Can you meet me for dinner?"

She closed the phone. Her eyes began to burn. She rubbed them, determined not to cry again. How could there be any tears left after yesterday?

~*~

Adda slept in the bed for the second night, her envelope with Enam Job's lock of hair under her pillow. She had a bed like this in Nashville. A body could get used to it real quick. She felt the aches spill right out of her muscles when they laid on the softness. But then her mind just rambled on and on.

Now what will happen if Frank won't give over no money? I can't go back to the Mendino? Maybe I should'a never listened to Trisha's ideas thinking I might get something. Maybe I should'a left the good Lord to look after me. At least He gave me singing money.

26

Adda slept through the bright orange sunrise. Trisha held her cup of tea, and it warmed her hands against the morning chill. Just a little too cool, but she also had a beautiful view from the dining room through the new French doors. Trisha moved inside and sat at the table. The wedding folder waited where she had left it.

Pulling it toward her, Trisha flipped page by page. Pap paid for her wedding gown. They had just buried Grandma, and she hated the thought of leaving him. But the date had already been set for June. He told her to pick whatever she wanted—said her Mom, Dad, and Grandma would be watching from heaven, and he wanted them to see her wearing a beautiful dress. Julie had shopped with her, but the other attendants, Grant's sisters, lived too far away. She had tried on at least a dozen dresses and kept coming back to this one. A simple design, but the ivory satin was luxurious. She couldn't take her eyes off of it.

She flipped to the menu she and Grant had chosen, thinking back to the night of their tasting experience. It had been a nice evening, lighthearted with a little laughter. Until she suggested they try hiking. Grant wasted no time shutting down that idea.

Trisha continued through the notebook—the opulent centerpieces and matching cake—showy just like Mrs. Ramsey wanted. The venue—a lavish banquet room far from her budget. The Ramsey's insisted on paying. The guest list belonged to Grant. All Ramsey friends and relatives. She slammed the folder closed.

Her neat, tidy, organized life was unraveling, and she was helpless to hold it together. Without Grant, she had no one—no family and few friends. She and Julie were close, but Julie had a family, a sister and brother, places to go for holidays and vacations, a place she belonged. Trisha hadn't heard anything from Uncle Brendan. Just like Adda, she had family out there who didn't care to know her. Trisha grew weary of trying. That left Grant. Was that enough reason to marry?

Needing a distraction, Trisha looked up Wanda Jean Marshall, trying to find an obituary. Nothing populated on Internet search engines. She hoped Rusty would be successful today, and they wouldn't need to find Wanda Jean.

Adda began moving around upstairs, and Trisha listened for when she would descend the steps. She worried about Adda maneuvering those steep stairs on her own. Trisha pulled out an old jigsaw puzzle. Grandma could often be found searching for pieces to complete the picture. Pap would walk by, scan the scattered parts, and locate it in a snap.

Maybe Adda would enjoy doing a puzzle. Her days were long and empty without anywhere to go. Trisha took her outside each day and tried to keep her walking. But she needed something more. Today they'd try the puzzle. Maybe tomorrow she'd go to a craft store and buy some watercolors.

After breakfast, they opened the puzzle. As they sorted pieces, Trisha asked Adda about Wanda Jean.

"It sounds like she worked for Haven Records for a long time. She worked there when you came up from Mississippi and when they terminated you?"

"Oh, yes ma'am. Wanda Jean was Ernie's helper. He couldn't do nothing without her help. She stuck with him for a long time."

"Did she have a family?"

"She weren't much older than me. Just a single girl when I came. She got her a man and married him, but he left her with a baby girl. She worked all those years with her own mama, helping out raising her little Becky."

"Was her name Marshall before she married or was that her married name?"

Adda laughed. "She was so mad at her man when he left, she quit using his name. She was Marshall before she got hooked up with Hank Tillman. Then she called herself Marshall again."

"But her baby, Becky, her name would have been Tillman?"

"Yeah, but Wanda Jean, she hated it. Made her madder than a wet dog."

"Did you know Becky?"

"I see'd her from time to time, but Wanda Jean kept her away from work. Right pretty little thing. She always had her hair in what she called pigtails."

Ten thirty came and went. Trisha's and Adda's gazes were glued to cardboard bits of the picture. Trisha couldn't keep her mind off of the law office in Nashville. What was happening?

When the phone rang at eleven thirty, Trisha grabbed it without looking at the caller ID. It wasn't Rusty's voice, but Grant's.

"Trisha, I've been trying to reach you. Did you get

my messages?"

Trisha lamented not checking before she answered. But she would have to deal with this at some point.

"I did. I wasn't ready to talk to you." Trisha stood and walked out of the dining room while Adda continued to assemble the puzzle.

"Honey, I'm sorry I lost my temper. I can break away for lunch. Can you meet me? We need to talk this through."

Trisha went into the summer room, out of earshot. "I can't. I'll meet you tomorrow. Eleven at Brewsters?"

Grant sighed. "If you can't meet for lunch, how about dinner?"

"Sorry. It will have to wait until tomorrow."

He persisted. "I can come out there this evening?"

"No, Grant. Tomorrow. Eleven. I need to go."

Trisha hung up without allowing him any further argument. If Rusty wasn't back, it would mean leaving Adda alone. She couldn't even call Julie. She'd be at work. Besides, she hung up mad the last time they talked. Before she stepped back inside, her phone signaled a text message from Rusty.

Leaving Nashville. OK if I stop over tonight? I can fill you in then.

Trisha hit the call button instead of texting.

Rusty picked up right away. "Hi. Everything OK?"

"Yes, I wondered if you'd be back in time for dinner."

"Should be."

"Come hungry. And I have a favor to ask. I need to run some errands tomorrow and hate to leave Adda alone. Do you have any time mid-morning to visit with her?"

"I'll make time. See you around six tonight. No settlement. I'll give you all the details then."

Trisha went back inside. "Adda, let's make a grocery run. Rusty's coming for dinner."

Adda turned, and a smile stretched across her face. "Well we can whip up a mighty fine meal for him."

~*~

Trisha left the jigsaw puzzle at one end of the dining room table and set three places at the other end. Adda answered the door when Rusty arrived.

"Come on in. Trisha made you a real fine dinner. We're just getting it all brought to the table."

"Hi, Rusty." Trisha called as she walked from the kitchen. "Come in and sit down. Everything's ready."

Adda ushered him to the seat at the end between the two ladies. Trisha carried a platter of stuffed pork chops breathing in the rich aroma. As she set it before Rusty, she caught his glance moving from the platter to her left hand where her diamond rested.

Adda turned toward the kitchen. "I'll go fetch that salad. Trisha said it's your favorite."

Rusty's eyes widened. "Waldorf salad?"

"I'm thinking that's what she called it."

"I told her it's one of my favorites."

Adda's smile returned and she shot him a conspiratorial wink. "Well she thought it up, not me."

Trisha laughed. Adda couldn't be more obvious.

When they were seated at the table, Rusty reached for both of their hands. "May I give thanks?"

After Rusty prayed, Trisha asked about Nashville.

"So the trip was unsuccessful?"

"I wouldn't say that. It brought pretty much what I expected, successful in locating three people who each will give a deposition. Unfortunately, we didn't get the settlement. Haven wouldn't budge. But I'll go back there in a week to meet with the witnesses and with Haven's attorney. We'll get their signed statements and record the interviews."

He stopped to taste the salad and butter his roll. "Adda, those ladies had sweet things to say about you. Helen, Marcella, and Laura."

"I forgot about Laura. She was a real quiet one."

"Then I met with Robert Pitney." Rusty stole a glance at Trisha. "He was less than cooperative. Spewed terms like frivolous, ridiculous, unfounded, and my favorite—gold-digger."

He cut into his pork chop. "Everything's delicious. I'm going to owe you both a dinner out."

"Oh, this old lady ain't needing to meddle in. You just go and take Trisha out to a real nice dinner. Just you young'uns."

Trisha lifted her eyes, stopping short of rolling them. Then she shifted the topic. "So, back to the case, what's next?"

"We'll continue with discovery and depositions. After depositions, I'll suggest a settlement again."

"Do you think that will do it?"

"I hope so. I'm gathering numbers from similar artists. It should convince them that making a settlement is more advantageous for Haven than going to trial."

Adda set her fork down. "I ain't going to no trial."

"I know, Adda. We're going to work hard to avoid that."

When dinner ended, they all carried dishes back into the kitchen. Adda sat down by the puzzle.

"I'm real tired tonight, Rusty. Why don't you go on in and help Trisha clean up them dishes?" she said with a sly grin.

"I think I'll do that. Enjoy the puzzle."

Rusty walked over and admired the wine rack. Trisha watched as he ran his fingers over the interlocking pieces. "Nice job routing these. What's next for the house?"

Trisha loaded plates into the dishwasher. "Nothing. I need a job. I don't think I'd do as well as Adda singing on the street."

Rusty put his hands on her shoulders and moved her away from the dishwasher, taking over the task. "You put the food away. I don't know where all the right dishes are."

When they finished the clean-up, Rusty ventured the same question he had asked before.

"So, have you seen Grant?"

Trisha kept her eyes on the counter as she wiped it. "I'll see him tomorrow."

~*~

"Julie, it's Trish. I hate that I missed you, but I'll leave this message. I've had a lot going on, things you aren't aware of. I'm sorry I couldn't see you when you called. Can we meet at noon tomorrow? Please don't be mad at me. Text me and tell me where to meet. I need to talk to you. It's important."

After leaving the message, Trisha went to the drawer, where she put the jewelry box with the

241

necklace. She opened the box and ran her fingers over the diamonds forming the letters TLR. Grant had seemed excited when he'd given it to her. His face filled with expectation. One out of three. Only the letter T fit. She closed the box and placed it in her purse.

27

Trisha parked her car in front of the coffee shop. Grant's car was already parked there. Chimes jingled as she opened the door, and Grant bounded to his feet. She bypassed the counter and went right to his table.

"Trish." He reached to embrace her. Trisha twisted away from his hold and took a seat across from his.

"What would you like? Tea? Or maybe some cappuccino? I'll go get it."

Trisha shook her head. "Nothing for me, thank you."

"Honey…"

Trisha put her hand up to stop him. "I know you're sorry. You told me on the phone. We need to talk but not about Adda." She leaned forward. "Grant, do you see what's happening?"

He nodded. "We're always arguing, but it's because of the stress. It will be better when the wedding's over, and we're walking on the beach."

He reached for her hand, but she withdrew and placed it on her lap. "Why? What makes you think it will be better?"

He smiled. "We'll be more relaxed. No wedding plans. No graduation."

Trisha gave him a sad smile. "No, Grant. There's always a new stressor. You'll still be working hard to build clients. I'll be sitting for the bar and then a job search. I'll have stressful cases. We'll have your mom trying to run our lives. Life has stress. People handle it. That's not the problem."

She watched him stiffen at the mention of his mother.

"Trish, I wanted you to be careful. It's been too much, your grandfather's house, the case for the singer, school. I tried to caution you."

Trisha gazed down at her lap. When she raised her head, tears formed in her eyes. "I have some things to give you, Grant. First, this." She slid a small paper from her pocket.

Grant read the little track with the Love Chapter written on it.

Love is patient. Love is kind. Love does not envy or boast. It is not arrogant or rude. It does not insist on its own way. It is not irritable or resentful. It does not rejoice at wrongdoing, but rejoices with the truth. Love bears all things, believes all things, hopes all things, endures all things. Love never ends. 1 Corinthians 13:4-8

His lips pressed into a thin line. "I know I've been horrible. I already admitted it."

Trisha reached for his hand. "I didn't give you the track as a reprimand. I gave it to you because I want you to know it, to believe it. If that's what love is, then what do we have going on here? Ours doesn't look like that."

"Two ways, Trish. I could be saying this to you."

"I know that. I know I've been resentful and I've kept record of wrongs."

He took her hand in his. "So how do we fix this?"

Her eyes remained downcast as he ran his thumb over the back of her hand and fingered the ring she wore. She pulled her hand back, slid it to her lap, and removed the ring. Her chest ached, no room for any more sadness. Her eyes blurred with tears as she reached for his hand and placed the ring in it.

Grant pulled his hand back, dropping the ring to the table. "No. No Trish." He blew out a puff of air, picked it up, and tried to place it back on her finger. Trisha curled her hand into a fist and pulled back.

"Honey, you're overreacting. Don't do this. Just a few weeks 'til the wedding."

She shook her head. "Then a lifetime to regret it."

"We won't regret it. I promise it will get better."

"I'm sorry, Grant. Truly. I have so much to work through. I love you, I'm just not sure I'm in love with you. I need time to figure that out, to figure out who I am. I have an emptiness deep inside, and I fear I've just grabbed at anything that would fill it. That's not fair to you."

"So don't cancel the wedding, just postpone it. We'll change the date and send out apologizes with a new 'save the date' card."

Trisha shook her head. "And then cancel it later? That would be worse."

Grant ran his hands through his hair. "Do you have any idea how humiliating this is going to be? My father's a prominent official. People all over the state will be talking about it."

Trisha gave a weak smile. "I think you're overestimating the impact." Before he could say anything, she pulled a third item to the table, the jeweler's box with the graduation necklace.

Grant swatted the box back toward her. "That was a gift."

"I can't keep it. Not now."

Grant balled his hands into fists. "What do you

think I'm going to do with it now? Just keep it."

Trisha stood and picked up her purse. She started to walk away when he grabbed her wrist.

"Trish, don't. Please."

Trisha pried her hand free. She turned teary eyes toward him. "Don't make this harder than it already is. And Grant, my name? It's Trisha *Ann* Mills."

She walked out the door and got in her car. As she backed out of the driveway, Grant stood in the doorway and stared as she turned her car and left.

~*~

Her tears made it difficult to talk.

"There won't be a wedding." She held up her unadorned left hand. "We'll be sending a notification to everyone on the guest list."

Julie was never at a loss for words, but today she sat there, apparently stunned. Finally, she said, "Don't send those letters out for a week. Maybe you'll work things out."

"Jules, it's over. It won't be worked out. This wasn't just an argument. I realized it wasn't right." Trisha dabbed at her tears and blew her nose.

Julie walked around to Trisha's side of the booth and hugged her.

"You're the closest I have to a sister. I want you to come meet Adda. She's staying with me. That's why I couldn't leave the other day, but I couldn't tell you about it then. Come over some time and meet her."

~*~

Trisha drove home. She looked in the rearview mirror and was appalled at her swollen, blotchy face. She'd rather not see Rusty this way. She pulled her car over and texted him.

On my way home. I know you have to get in to your office, so please feel free to leave. Adda will be fine. Let her know I'm on my way.

Clicking her phone off, Trisha pulled the visor down for the larger mirror. She touched the puffy clouds under her eyes. They were tender, sending stabs of pain with each touch. As she closed the mirror, Trisha saw the scripture that she always kept there. Zephaniah 13:7. Her keychain. The same scripture dangled from her keys. *You learn a lot when you care enough to watch.*

She reached the driveway and turned the bend. Rusty's car was still there. He and Adda sat on the veranda. Trisha pulled her car as far to the back of the driveway as possible, gave a casual wave, and walked to the summer room.

In a moment, he stood beside her. He reached up and touched the swollen space below her eyes, her hand where the ring had once been, and then he wrapped his arm around her shoulder. She leaned against him, her body shaking with sobs all over again. He held her, rubbing her back, whispering platitudes until the flood of tears stopped and her body stilled.

She gave him a pouty smile. "I wanted you to be gone."

"I know."

She leaned against him again, and his lips brushed her cheek.

"Rusty?" Trisha stepped back and looked at him.

"I'm not ready for another relationship. I need time."

"Take all the time you need. I'll be waiting."

~*~

Adda dozed on the sofa, and Trisha tried to find distractions to keep her mind off of her failure. She did a search for Becky Tillman and wrote down all of the possible responses. Then she searched for Rebecca Tillman. Some of the hits were repeated, but a few new people surfaced in cyber world. She'd start with locations in and around Nashville, spreading the circle out to include surrounding states. There was a physician with that name in Kentucky. Social media showed some in Tennessee, Georgia, and North Carolina. A Rebecca Tillman graduated from Emory in the 70s. Public information websites identified all of the Rebecca Tillmans who had married and provided their married names. Trisha wrote all of the information she could find.

The twang of a text message sounded, and Trisha reached for her phone.

"When you pass through the waters, I will be with you; and through the rivers, they shall not overwhelm you. When you walk through the fire, you shall not be burned, and the flame shall not consume you. Isaiah 43:1"

Trisha typed back. *Thank you for the timely reminder.*

Another text followed. *Do you know how cold it was last winter?*

She smiled as she typed. *How cold was it?*

So cold I saw a lawyer with his hands in his own pockets.

Groan! Is there no end to these?

My dear, I've just touched the surface.

~*~

June in Asheville provided the best of climates. Cool nights and beautiful days. The surrounding mountains somehow tempered the heat. Trisha sat on the ground, pulling weeds from between the spring flowers. She had done this task for years. Grandma had difficulty getting up from the ground, so it became Trisha's chore. She hated it as a teen but grew to appreciate it. There was something satisfying in pulling on the garden gloves, freeing the good growth to stand tall and shine, discarding the parts that threatened the beauty.

Adda sat on the webbed folding chair Trisha carried outside for her. A glass of iced tea sat on the table beside her.

"Adda, tell me about Becky. How old would she have been when you left Haven?"

Adda sipped her tea. "She was growed up, but I never see'd her then, only a few times when she was a young'un."

"Did you ever hear about her, if she married, where she lived, or what kind of work she did?"

"I recollect Wanda Jean talking about her marrying, but I don't know where she lived. She went away somewhere for schooling."

Trisha pulled off the garden gloves and lifted her trowel into a bucket. She sat on the ground with her knees bent, her hands resting on them.

"I'd love to talk to her, see if she can tell us about Wanda Jean. I found some people with the name Becky

Tillman but don't know which might be her. One's a doctor."

"Wanda Jean didn't say nothing 'bout that. Iff'n she was, I think Wanda Jean would be bragging about her baby."

"You're probably right. "Another one I found went to school in Atlanta, to Emory."

"Becky went away for schooling, and I'm thinking she said Atlanta."

"Do you know her husband's name?"

"If I knowed it once, I ain't remembering. Why you wanting to talk to her when Rusty said Wanda Jean's dead?"

"He said 'might be.' We don't know for sure."

"Well I'm guessing the Becky Tillman in Atlanta is her."

After dinner, Trisha looked up marriage licenses filed in Tennessee and Georgia in the 1970s. Two Rebecca Tillmans came up on the search. Becky had married either Raymond Malcolm or Joseph Paradiso. The Paradisos lived in Grand Rapids, Michigan, the Malcolms in Greenville, SC. She'd try Greenville first.

The phone rang and went to voice mail. Trisha hung up. It was too complicated to leave a message, and she didn't want to scare her off before she had a chance to explain. If Wanda Jean was living and they could find her, they'd have an eyewitness to verify Adda's claim as songwriter.

28

Trisha woke the following morning to an e-mail from Rusty. "Next two days are filled with meetings and appointments. We scheduled depositions sooner than expected. I'll leave for Nashville in three days. That means it may be close to a week before I get out there again. Call if you need me, although Brooke won't pull me out unless it's an emergency. Hope you're doing OK. Praying for you and Adda."

Trisha's shoulders dropped. Rusty's absence left an emptiness, more so since there was nothing ahead for her—no wedding plans, no job search until she obtained her license, no more work on the house. Just Adda and hours to fill.

She tried the number for Becky Malcolm and a man answered. "May I speak with Becky please?"

"Who's calling?"

"My name's Trisha. I'm calling for an old friend of her mother's"

Without answering, she heard him holler. "Beck, phone."

A moment later, a lady picked up.

Trisha hesitated. It may not even be the right Becky.

"My name is Trisha Mills. I'm looking for the Becky Tillman, whose mother is Wanda Jean Marshall. Is that you?'

"Yes. How can I help you?"

Trisha hadn't realized she held her breath until she felt the relief of an exhale. "My friend, Adda, once worked with your mother. She performed as Adaline."

"Adaline. I knew her when I was younger. My mother spoke highly of her. She had quite a talent."

Trisha wasn't sure how to phrase her next question.

"Becky, is your mother still living? Adda heard that Wanda Jean had passed on."

"Oh, no. Mother's in a nursing home. She's eighty-two, but she's doing well."

"Is she still in Nashville?"

"No, she's here in Greenville, near me. I convinced her to come about ten years ago. She had a small apartment until she couldn't continue living alone."

"Do you think she would like a visit? I'll be happy to bring Adda to see her."

"I'm sure she would. That would be delightful. She's at the Maplewood Retirement Center"

Trisha thanked her and hung up. She couldn't wait for Adda to wake up.

~*~

Trisha drove on I-26 toward South Carolina. Greenville was less than two hours away, but she decided to make it an adventure. She booked a room in the revitalized downtown area. They would walk the suspension bridge over the Reedy River in Falls Park and check out what performing arts might be scheduled at the Peace Center. Maybe they'd do some shopping and sightseeing. Rusty wasn't the only one with surprises for Adda.

Rusty—She glanced at her phone. No messages. She didn't plan to tell him they were away. It would be better for them to visit Wanda Jean without a male attorney present. Trisha wouldn't pump for information but would guide their conversation. If Rusty went, he would ask direct questions. That might make Wanda Jean apprehensive.

Trisha rolled the suitcase as they checked into their hotel. Adda had selected two outfits from Gram's closet. Her braids still looked fresh and new. The stylist told Adda they would last between six and eight weeks. She should still get another week out of them. Then perhaps Trisha would take her to have them re-done.

Main Street had no shortage of quaint cafes to choose from. They chose one closest to Falls Park. They ordered and sat at an outdoor table watching people walk by. The refreshing sound of the waterfall could be heard in the background. It felt freeing to get away. Away from the memories of Grant's outrage on the evening Adda came. Away from the idleness while waiting. Away from the wedding folder, which only reminded Trisha of her failure. She would shred it when she returned to Asheville.

After lunch, Trisha brought the car around front for Adda. She put the address of the Maplewood Retirement Center in her GPS and headed in that direction. At last she would meet the infamous Wanda Jean.

~*~

Adda was unsettled about making this trip, but Trisha was insistent. So many memories came with thinking of Wanda Jean. Not all of them were bad. But Adda hadn't seen her or talked with her since the phone call, when she said they didn't need her singing any more.

The door at the home didn't open. Trisha pushed a buzzer, and someone spoke out before letting them in. Then they had to sign their name and say who they would be visiting.

Adda craned her neck to look around. It appeared to be a nice place, the kind of place where Adda might live if Frank would give her some of the money she should have. They walked down a long hallway with pictures of oceans, rivers, farms, and mountains. All different, so everyone saw something reminding them of home. There was a reading room where some folks sat in wheelchairs with their books.

When they walked in Wanda Jean's room, she sat in a wheelchair, too. Adda had to look twice to recognize her. Her hair had turned gray and was curled real tight. She appeared tiny with that big chair all around her and a little patch of quilt on her lap. When she looked up and saw her visitors, her mouth opened real wide.

"Well glory be. Is that you, Adaline?" She stretched her arm out for Adda to take her hand.

"Hello, Wanda Jean. I ain't Adaline no more. I use my given name, Adda Marsh."

Wanda Jean smiled when their hands joined. "Well sit down. Pull some chairs over."

Adda grabbed a chair and started moving it.

Trisha stepped in and introduced herself. "I'm Trisha, Adda's friend. She's told me so much about you."

"Well glory be. I hope she didn't make me sound terrible."

Trisha reached out to help Adda with the chair.

"Not at all. She said you treated her well."

"Some of those were hard years. But enough of that. Adda, tell me about yourself. Where are you living? Did you find any more of your family?"

"I'm living in Asheville, close to Edith. I never left there after Minny died, and Ernie sent that letter about not needing my singing no more."

Wanda Jean turned toward Trisha. "Adaline had the most beautiful voice I've ever heard. No one better."

"I know. I listened to her growing up. My pap loved her music and taught me to love it."

They reminisced for close to an hour and heard about Wanda Jean's daughter and grandchildren. Adda told her about the "big old house" in which she was staying.

Trisha started on the questions, which were the real reason for their visit. "Wanda Jean, was it unusual for recording artists to be hired instead of receiving royalties? Adda's songs are still selling, and she doesn't receive any compensation."

Wanda Jean shook her head. "It was awful what they did to you, Adda. I tried to tell Ernie a time or two, but he ruled me with an iron hand. I had to support my Becky, so I kept my mouth shut."

Trisha probed. "In what ways? What do you mean by awful?"

Wanda Jean shot an apologetic look at Adda and then back to Trisha. "Adda couldn't drive. That tied her to the apartment Ernie put her in. He kept a close eye on her and squashed any outside interest or friendship before they could begin. I knew he didn't pay her a living wage. He had me grocery shop every week and take her whatever clothes he wanted her to wear when she made appearances."

"That's criminal."

Adda glanced in Trisha's direction. "She knowed about the song—the one I wrote for Ernie."

"Oh yes. Adda cared for him. The song she wrote for Ernie became her biggest hit, and he stole the credit."

Trisha shook her head. "How could he get away with that?"

"He always did whatever he wanted. No one but Adda and I knew she wrote it. Except Becky. She was young then, but when Ernie died, I told Becky what a scum he was. I told her about him stealing the song."

"How did you know she wrote it? Because Adda told you, or did you see it being written?"

"I not only saw it, I helped her with a few words, repairing some of the spelling."

Trisha leaned forward. "Wanda Jean, if we could prove that, Adda might be able to start getting royalties for writing the song. Would you be willing to sign a statement saying you knew she wrote it?"

"I sure would. Ernie can't hurt me anymore, and that son of his is worse than his father. If they think I'm too old to remember things, my Becky can vouch that I told her long ago."

~*~

Back in their hotel room, Trisha drafted two

documents reading and re-reading to make sure the statements were correct. She would surprise Rusty with them when he returned. Once drafted, Trisha telephoned Becky and told her about the visit with her mother.

"Would you consider signing the statement?"

"Sure. Mom told me they cheated Adaline out of her song. I'm not a primary source of information. I can only attest that she told me that years ago."

They would meet tomorrow morning at the nursing home.

29

Trisha slipped the signed statements into her briefcase. Her excitement mounted as she drove back to Asheville. Rusty would be taking depositions. Those documents along with the ones in her briefcase should provide significant evidence. They wouldn't go after the copyright and hold it up in court, but this added threat might be the tipping point that would convince Haven to settle.

The sun coasted toward the west, getting ready to set when they turned up the gravel driveway. Trisha almost slammed on the brakes when she saw Grant's car. What was he doing here? He had no key, so she found him waiting on the veranda.

Trisha parked and helped Adda up the steps, ignoring Grant.

Adda spoke through clenched lips. "Appears you have a visitor. I'll be getting on upstairs."

Trisha shot a look in Grant's direction.

He perched on his chair, ready to stand.

"You don't have go upstairs, Adda."

She drilled Trisha with her eyes. "I said I'll be going on up."

Trisha saw Adda to the staircase and watched as she managed each step. Then she turned around to face Grant, who stood in the front doorway.

"What are you doing here?"

"Can we talk, Trish?"

"There's nothing else to talk about."

He walked close to her. "There is. Please give me a few minutes."

Trisha glanced upstairs, remembering the scene Adda had overheard. She wouldn't let that happen again.

"Let's move to the summer room and keep your voice down."

Trisha sat in a chair, and Grant sat on the glider facing her.

"Trisha, I know we can work this out. Just give me a chance."

Trisha closed her eyes and sighed.

"Honey, I promise things will be better. We can live here. I'll commute. You've made this place beautiful. I'll talk with my mother. She'll treat you with respect, or she won't see us."

"Grant ..."

"You can have the singer at the wedding." His eyes moved toward the upstairs, indicating Adda.

"She has a name."

"Adaline. She can sing at the wedding."

Trisha walked to the glider and sat beside him.

She put her hand on his arm. "There's not going to be a wedding at which to sing, Grant. I'm sorry. Really sorry. I wanted it to work, but it didn't."

He pulled her close. "I'll make it work. Anything you want."

His eyes pooled with tears. She had never seen him like that. She'd never seen her pap cry, even when her parents died. Nor did she remember ever seeing her dad cry.

Grant melted into her arms. "Don't leave me,

Trisha."

Overwhelmed with guilt, she put her hands around his head as it rested on her shoulder. He wrapped his arms around her. They sat that way for a few moments.

Trisha wriggled out of his arms. "I heard the door."

He held tight. "I didn't hear anything."

She broke out of his grip and walked through the kitchen. No one was there. Did she hear the sound of gravel? She looked out the front door. It must have been her imagination. That was just as well. She needed to end this.

Trisha returned to the summer room but remained standing. She had to get Grant to leave. This was only making things harder.

"You need to go. If this marriage is meant to be, we'll know in time. Right now, I can't make that decision."

Grant stood to join her, grasping her hands. "So can't we just postpone? We don't have to set a date. You can wear the ring, and we'll just wait until you're sure."

"You're making this hard."

"I'm trying to make it hard. I don't want to lose you. At least tell me we'll keep on seeing each other?"

She shook her head. "Not right away. I need time. You need to give me some space."

"How much time?"

"I can't answer that." Trisha wiggled her hands out of his grasp.

He rubbed his temples. "Then how will I know? How am I supposed to know when to call, when to come, if you won't tell me how much 'time you need'?" His fingers moved as quotation marks.

"Are you mocking me? You don't even try to understand me." Trisha stepped toward the door to the backyard and opened it.

Grant pushed the door closed. "Trisha, it's a logical question. You're not making sense." He stepped toward her, arms crossed. "You're telling me if it's meant to work, we'll know, but you need time, and I'm not allowed to know how much? You need space, so I can't come around. How am I supposed to know when? And what am I supposed to do now? Just wait?"

Trisha heard Rusty's voice from just a few short days ago. *Take all the time you need. I'll be waiting.* She moved away from the door toward the kitchen. "No, what you need to do now is let yourself out." She walked into the kitchen. Then she closed and locked the door.

~*~

The following morning, Trisha heard Adda's footsteps and moved from the kitchen. She still worried about Adda and those steep stairs.

Trisha waited as Adda took one step at a time, grumpy as a bear. "What that man wanting? You taking him back?"

They walked back toward the kitchen where Trisha had started breakfast. "That's what he wanted, but no. I'm not."

"Good. I don't like him."

Trisha smirked. "Somedays I don't like him either. How do you want your eggs?"

"You can scramble mine. Where's Rusty?"

Trisha broke eggs into a bowl. "Nashville. I told you that. The attorneys will get sworn statements from your old friends."

"I thought he done that already."

Trisha poured the eggs in a skillet and reached for a rubber spatula. "This is the legal paper. Both attorneys will be there. They record the statement and ask them questions. The last time was just so Rusty would know if they were good witnesses."

It was the longest she had gone without hearing from Rusty. She kept looking for a message or e-mail the last two days. Maybe he would text when he arrived in Nashville. He flew this time instead of driving. He might be able to relax a little more.

Trisha thought about him standing right here, moving her aside, and loading her dishwasher. She said she wasn't ready for a relationship, yet she ached for his nearness.

After flipping the eggs and sausage onto two plates, Trisha carried them into the dining room where Adda worked at the puzzle.

"Adda, have you ever seen *Gone with the Wind*?"

"Is it the picture show with that Scarlett lady and some scoundrel that leaves her alone in the war?"

"That's the one."

"Ain't seen it, but I heard about it."

"Get ready for a real treat. We'll pop some popcorn and watch it later today."

Trisha kept her phone beside her during the movie. No call. No message. She couldn't stand not knowing what was happening in Nashville.

Margaret Mitchell's war-torn story had Adda on the edge of her seat.

"Why that woman sure be shaming herself trying to get someone else's man?"

"I think Scarlett O'Hara was accustomed to getting whatever she wanted."

Trisha checked her phone again. When she could stand it no more, she picked up the phone and texted. "What's going on in Nashville? Hope all went well. Adda and I are watching Scarlett tear down her draperies to fashion them into a dress."

"That Rhett's a no-good scoundrel," Adda said early on in the film. Later on, she wept. "He sure did love that child. Loved her like I loved my Enam."

Thirty minutes after Trisha's text, her phone dinged.

Depositions done. Uneventful.

That was brief. Maybe he's with someone. Trisha ventured one more text.

"When will you be home?"

Don't know.

None of this sounded like Rusty. He must be out and unable to message. Perhaps he'd call later. It would be better to hear his voice.

But a call never came. No call or text or e-mail. Not that day or the next two days. Trisha refrained from contacting him. Five days passed—two at his work retreat and three in Nashville. Why wouldn't he call to update them, to check on her? Something was wrong.

"Where's Mr. Rusty?" Adda asked.

This was the same question on Trisha's mind, but she was getting tired of Adda asking.

"I don't know, Adda. You have a phone. You call him," Trisha snapped.

Adda pressed her lips together and turned away from Trisha.

As Trisha climbed the stairs to her bedroom that night, the sound of Adda's voice in her bedroom stopped her. She moved to the door and listened. Adda spoke loud enough that Trisha had no problem hearing one side of the conversation.

"Ain't seen you here and we's wondering when you be getting back...If you already back, why ain't you been here? We could make you a real fine dinner...All right...OK...Good night, Mr. Rusty." Adda laughed. "OK, just plain old Rusty. I keep forgetting 'cause my mama always taught me to say mister."

Rusty had the gift to make Adda laugh.

Trisha hung near her own door to see if Adda would come out into the hall. But soon the bedroom light went out.

The next morning Adda told Trisha she had hit the button for Rusty on her phone. "He come back to Asheville two days ago, but he said he's powerful busy. He's gonna call me tonight, so I brung this down with me." She lifted the phone from her pocket and showed Trisha.

Trisha swung her head away so Adda wouldn't see the tears.

Later that evening, after Adda closed the door to her bedroom, a cell phone ring sounded. Trisha lurched for her phone. But it was silent. The ring must have been on Adda's phone.

Moments later, Adda's voice echoed in the hall as she answered. Trisha walked to the veranda and curled her legs up on the chair. *So Rusty Bergstrom, all you wanted was the chase. You just needed to know you could win.*

30

Trisha woke to bright sunshine streaming through her bedroom window. A perfect day for a wedding. She would have been waking, excited to have her hair and makeup done, to slide the protective covering off of the satin dress and slip it over her shoulders.

What was Grant doing today? Was he thinking the same thing? It wouldn't be long before he moved on, if he hadn't already. It would help him to save face. Appearances were important to him.

Adda had been out of sorts. Rusty always knew how to diffuse the cantankerous side of her. Since he'd been gone, Trisha and Adda had been brusque with each other. She'd grown to love Adda, but she'd never expected to live with her indefinitely. What if the suit failed? Adda couldn't go back to singing, and Trisha would never put her out. She had no idea what the future held.

She must get a job. There was no one to take care of her if she failed, no safety net. She'd be sitting for the bar in another month. Today she would study. Responsibility had always defined her until she let it slip away, sidetracked by smooth, empty words. No more distractions. No more excuses. She'd take the test and pass it. She wouldn't fail at another thing.

Trisha studied all day. At three o'clock, she took a

break and went to the veranda. Three o'clock—the exact time when Mendelssohn's "Wedding March" would have started. All heads would have turned as she walked down the aisle—alone. Most of them would have gotten their first glimpse of Grant Ramsey's bride. His guests. His family. His friends.

Outside, the gravel crunched. She'd pave that once she got a job. If Grant's car turned that bend, she'd walk inside and lock the door. She was in no mood for drama today. As the car came into view, her heart leapt. *Rusty. Why now? Why on this day?*

He parked and stepped out of his car. Then he stood there and watched her. With slow measured steps, he reached the veranda. No easy, carefree gait. No bright eyes or laid-back grin. Neither spoke as he took his time with the three porch steps and stopped at the rocking chair. Before he sat, he turned the chair to face hers.

His somber expression remained. "I didn't think I'd see you here."

Trisha looked away. "Sorry to disappoint you. It is my home."

He leaned forward, his arms propped on his knees. "I thought you'd be at the church."

She swung around to face him. "What?"

"Trish, you're not getting married?"

She turned away again, looking out at the grassy field.

Silence hung heavy between them before she faced him again. "Is this your idea of a joke? I cried in your arms in case you've forgotten."

"I didn't forget. I thought you two had reconciled."

As she looked at his face she arched an eyebrow.

"What in the world made you think that?"

Rusty sat back and ran his hands over his face, up through his hair, blowing out a rush of air. "Oh...I've messed this up." He turned back to face her. "Trish, I saw you with him, here in the summer room. I came before I left for Nashville. You were holding him like you never wanted to let go. It crushed me. I turned and left."

She crossed her arms. "And you didn't think to ask me about it? Didn't think I'd have the courtesy to tell you if that happened?"

"Sweetheart, I..."

"I'm not your sweetheart. It's obvious you aren't here to see me, since you expected I'd be gone. Adda's upstairs." Her arm swept to the door.

Rusty leaned forward. "Trish, it hurt so bad, just seeing you, imagining you in love with him. I fell apart. I'm so sorry."

Trisha glared at him. "You know what hurt so bad, Rusty? I lost everything—everyone I cared about. My parents, Grandma, Pap, Grant, and then you. For three weeks I had no idea why. I searched my mind trying to figure out what I said or did."

Rusty left his chair and hunched in front of her. "Trish, I'm so sorry."

Her mouth formed a tight line. "He begged me. Would you expect me to be so cold-hearted that I wouldn't hug him, give some comfort after three years together? He cried, Rusty. I couldn't ignore that."

"Oh, Trish, I was wrong. I made a terrible mistake. I should have had the courage to ask you. All I knew at that moment was the pain."

Trisha softened as she turned her gaze to his. She looked into stormy oceans of blue filled with turmoil.

"I needed you, Rusty. You disappeared, and I didn't know why."

"Would it matter if I told you he wasn't the only one who cried that night?"

Trisha turned pleading eyes toward him. "Rusty, I can't handle anymore guilt."

He nodded. "You're not responsible for that. I am. I jumped to conclusions and hurt us both. Will you ever be able to forgive me?"

Would she ever be able to forgive him? The betrayal was so fresh, she couldn't see past it. Yet his expression held its own pain.

She pursed her lips. "Probably. Someday. Just not this day."

"Would it help if I told you I got a ticket that night for doing eighty-five on fifty-five mile per hour road?"

Her eyes widened. "Rusty Bergstrom? Mr. Perfect broke the law?"

Rusty stood and leaned down, resting his cheek on the top of her hair. "Far from perfect. Oh Trish, I've missed you."

She stood to meet him but stepped back, creating space between them. "When I told you I needed time, I didn't mean without you in my life. I meant before we let this go deeper."

"I know that. I'm such an idiot." He reached for her hands.

"Well it's about time you be coming back to see us." Adda stood behind them, hands on her hips, scowling at the scene.

Rusty released Trisha, walked over, and embraced Adda. "How's my girl?"

"This girl's been wondering why you ain't been here."

Rusty held his arm out to Trish and motioned for them to step inside.

Adda's presence changed the intimacy of the scene. The old Rusty emerged. "I'm here now. Let's sit down and talk about having a trial."

"Now you know I ain't having no trial."

"Let's just talk."

They all sat at the dining room table. Rusty took the seat closest to Trisha.

"We're at a standstill. Robert Pitney's a bulldog. He won't budge to discuss anything except a trial. Adda, we can win this in court. Will you consider taking it to trial?"

"Rusty!" Trisha shouted as she leapt to her feet. "I forgot. Wait here."

She ran to get her briefcase and pulled out the signed statements, handing them to Rusty. He looked them over. "These are dated three weeks ago. Why didn't you tell me?"

She opened her mouth to speak, but he stopped her. "Never mind. How'd you get these? How'd you find Wanda Jean when my staff couldn't?"

"A little inside help." She reached for Adda's hand. "So can we refile in federal court?"

"We threaten to. If we need to, we'll file. This means I have some work to do. There was an amendment to the copyright act sometime in the 70s allowing songwriters who were work-for-hire to reclaim their rights. Some pretty prominent cases came out of that amendment. If we can prove she wrote it, we don't have to sue for the money. We just reclaim it. He turned to Adda. "Any chance you have a will?"

"Don't need one. I ain't got nothing to be leaving anyone."

"You need one now. We need to show a beneficiary so they don't think they can tie this up until it disappears. Do you want to leave your niece, Edith, any money that might be left?"

"If'n I get money, I want to pay you your fair wage first. Ain't right to do all this work for nothing."

Rusty grinned. "Well, Adda, you can't do that. We signed a contract."

"Well, I'll just give you some anyways, like a present."

He shook his head. "I can't take it. Here's how my firm works. All of the attorneys do some pro bono work, just to help someone out. It's a good thing to do. We aren't allowed to accept payment or gifts. It's in my contract at the firm, so if you offer me a gift, you could get me in a lot of trouble."

"Well, I ain't wanting to get you in trouble. I'll be needing to give some to Trisha for my living here all these weeks."

Trisha reached for her hand. "Adda, I have all I need. You take care of yourself and your niece."

"Well, I guess you can make up that paper, but I ain't got nothing if Frank won't agree."

"OK, ladies. Let me go get busy, and we'll give Haven a punch in the gut."

Rusty stood to leave.

Hands on hips, Adda asked the question they both wanted to know.

"When you coming back?"

Rusty rushed over and kissed her cheek. "Soon, Adda. Very soon."

He turned toward Trisha and hesitated before placing a kiss on her cheek. "I promise I'll be back." He leaned in close, squeezed her hand, and whispered, "I promise."

~*~

That evening, a text came through.

Saturday night and I'm still at the office. I miss you.

Lawyer to client—paying my fee will also help as evidence for our insanity defense.

Have you forgiven me yet?

Trisha grinned. *That might take a while. I rather like you being indebted to me.*

Please try. I'm not me without you.

~*~

Adda went up to her bedroom and listened for Trisha to go back downstairs, then she hit the button on her phone for Rusty.

"You get that paper ready for me to sign yet?"

"Not yet, Adda, but I'm working on it tonight. I'll bring it over tomorrow."

"I'm wanting to change it."

Rusty laughed. "Change it? It's not even written yet. What would you like it to say?"

"You thinking I'm getting me some money?"

"I'm hopeful, Adda."

"Then I want Edith to have enough to let her stay where she is, and I want Trisha to have what's left."

Rusty was silent.

"You still on this phone?"

"Yes, Adda. I'm here. Are you certain that's what you want? Does Trisha know?

"No, and I ain't wanting you to tell her."

"Adda, I can't write that will. Someone else will have to do it."

"Why can't you be doing it?"

"Let's just say, conflict of interest. Can we do it this way? I'll write what we talked about. You sign it so we'll have something on file. Wills can be changed. Once the lawsuit is done, I'll send someone from my firm to see you. Then you can write it anyway you want. It's best for me not to know."

"And you're sure I can change it?"

"Yes, I'm sure."

Adda pushed the button to end the call. "Conflict of interest? Just more legal mumbo jumbo."

~*~

When Trisha and Adda came from church, they saw Rusty sitting on the veranda reading over his documents.

"Working on the Lord's day?"

"I'm sure He'll forgive me quicker than you will. We've got to get this done. I need to file the will in the morning before I send the letter to Haven." He turned toward Trisha. "And we need to talk."

They moved to the dining room table. Rusty pulled out the will, placed a copy in front of Trisha, and motioned for her to read it to Adda. Trisha read it and explained that it left all assets, including future royalties, into a trust fund for Edith's care, stating that she would remain at her current facility or one of equal or greater quality in the event that her current facility no longer offered services to meet her medical, emotional, and social needs. It would be under the administration of a guardian ad litem.

"Where's it saying I can change this if I want?"

Rusty interjected. "It doesn't say it on this document, but the law allows you to change your will, as long as you're of sound mind."

"Ain't nothing wrong with my mind."

Trisha patted her shoulder. "You thinking of getting yourself married, Adda?"

Adda brushed her hand down. "Ain't nobody gonna be marrying this old lady."

Adda picked up the pen and signed on the line Rusty had marked. He slid the paper into his folder and returned it to the briefcase.

"Adda, that's all I need from you right now, but I need to talk some things through with Trisha."

"You asking me to leave?"

"Not at all. I just didn't know if you'd want to sit and listen to all of the lawyer talk. We can move to the summer room if you want to work on your puzzle."

Trisha stood. "Why don't we do that, and then I'll fix us all some lunch when we're done."

Rusty and Trisha moved to the summer room. Rusty sat on the glider, leaving room for her beside him. His three-week absence still stung. She moved a chair perpendicular to his seat.

Pulling his papers out, he placed them on the glass top table in front of him.

"As I said, the Copyright Act had been amended in the mid-70s allowing songwriters who were work-for-hire to reclaim the song rights after thirty-five years. Heirs can reclaim those rights as well. Once Adda's identified as the songwriter, they can't dispute her entitlement to the royalties. There are notable cases on file where song rights had been reclaimed. Billy Joel, Michael Jackson, Bruce Springsteen. We need the court to recognize Adda as the songwriter. Thanks to you, that's a slam dunk. Wanda Jean's a credible witness. She was an integral part of Haven, part of the inner circle. This document," he pointed to Trisha's signed statement, "is huge. She even helped Adda correct the original draft. At minimum, we'll get those royalties. And of course Ernie Gillen didn't enact the controlled composition clause limiting royalties since they were going to him. Problem still is the timing. They can tie this up for a long time if they choose to."

Trisha glanced at the notes, but he had summarized them for her. "So what's different now, except we have more assurance for some obscure future date?"

"After talking with one of the partners, I think I made a tactical rookie error. I deflated our request thinking that would bring a quicker settlement. The advice I received is the opposite. It's a poker game. My low bid told them I didn't have a good hand. The bigger the scare, the quicker they'll be to settle. Bid big, and they have to decide if you're bluffing. If they settle early, they'll get away with less than if they wait until you show your hand."

"So what happens now?"

"I send a letter to Haven letting them know I have new evidences and plan to refile in federal court seeking a transfer of copyright to Adda Mae Marsh, or her stated heir, retroactive to the inception of the song. I mention possession of two signed statements of verification that Adda wrote the song. I'm not identifying their names but will note that they are highly credible sources. If we file and it goes to discovery, they'll get that information. I'll reference the copyright act and some significant cases. Obviously, they'll already be aware of those cases, but I want them to know that I know."

Trisha rubbed her temples. "But can't they just wait until discovery to see if you're bluffing?"

"They can, but by then the press will have it. If it's filed in federal court with this sizable request, it'll be noticed. Every newspaper and entertainment magazine will sensationalize it." He gave her a sly grin. "I'm telling them Monday morning that I plan to file the following day if we don't have it settled. And I may just mention an AP reporter who's anxious to see what I file first thing Tuesday morning."

"What will you ask for?"

"Seventy-five million."

Trisha laughed. "Not funny. What will you ask for?"

He grinned. "Not kidding, Trish. Seventy-five million."

"Rusty! That's crazy."

"I know. Crazy enough that they'll want to end it. My courtesy letter will let them know I plan to file immediately unless they're prepared to settle right now."

31

Monday afternoon, Trisha's phone rang. A familiar warmth filled her when she saw Rusty's name.

"I sent my e-mail at nine this morning. They replied ten minutes ago. They're ready to settle."

Trisha let out a cry. "That didn't take long. That's wonderful."

"Robert Pitney called to see what we have. I told him he'd have to wait until discovery but assured him we have a slam dunk. He must have believed me. I have a conference call in my office tomorrow morning at nine o'clock to discuss settlement."

"I hope this ends it. I don't want to move forward. This is getting bigger than I ever imagined it would be."

"So, do you want to join me?"

There was a note of excitement in his voice. "I can't get involved in those kinds of negotiations."

"So be a fly on the wall. You don't have to say a word."

Trisha paced while she talked. "Will anyone else be in your office?"

"Nope."

Her stomach tensed. "Who will be in on their end?"

"I suspect it will be both Robert Pitney and Frank Gillen."

"Maybe." She bit her lower lip. "I haven't left Adda alone here with all of these stairs."

"We'll take her to my place. It's close to my office and all one level. You'll be back with her in less than an hour."

"And I can be a silent observer?"

"It's audio, not video. No one will know but me."

She sat in front of her tea cup and let out a whoosh of air. "OK. I'll do it."

~*~

Trisha met Rusty outside of his condo, right in the heart of Asheville, a few blocks from his office. She had never given much thought to where he lived. The interior might have been described as minimalist. Simple furniture, few embellishments, many books, the polar opposite from her grandparents' home where she grew up.

Trisha could see his drums set up in the next room, a guitar propped next to them. *What else don't I know about this man?*

Rusty turned the television on for Adda and showed her how to change the station.

"We'll be back in a little over an hour. Help yourself to anything you'd like."

They made the short walk to Rusty's office. Trisha had only been there once before. That was the day she started the ball rolling, and she hoped this would be the day it ended. Never had she imagined the journey ahead of her. Trisha felt as tight as the drums in Rusty's home. She didn't want to react when she heard the dollar amounts. She would have to work hard to remain quiet. Rusty stood behind her and massaged her shoulders.

"Stop worrying. It's in God's hands. Let's take a minute to pray."

They joined hands and Rusty prayed.

"OK, sweetheart, let's get this done."

He stood and went to his phone, hit speaker, and placed it on his desk.

A male voice answered, identifying himself. "Robert Pitney."

Rusty sounded like he had called an old friend. "Robert, how are you today?" He winked at Trisha.

"How am I? I'm sick of this frivolity. We're talking settlement just to end the foolishness."

"Is Frank with you?" Trisha's hands clenched together, her knuckles white from squeezing them.

"I'm here, Bergstrom."

"Hello, Frank. Glad you could make it. My client isn't present but she's authorized me to speak on her behalf."

Robert spoke next. "We'd like to know what you have before we talk settlement. It'll be available as part of discovery. Why not just tell us now?"

"We can certainly do that, gentlemen. It was my understanding that you wanted to avoid the press." He shot Trisha another wink.

"Let's leave the press out of this, Bergstrom."

"Easier said than done, Frank. You know how vigorous they can be when they smell a story. You may be aware that my client had an unfortunate intruder. That police report brought the press nosing around. They're just waiting to see what I'm up to."

Muted voices sounded from the other end of the call.

Robert Pitney spoke for them. "We're prepared to offer a settlement before this goes federal."

"I'm listening." He looked up at Trisha with a grin.

"You asked for 1.5 million. We know that's always a starting point for negotiations. We're prepared to give you 50% of your original request. That would be 750 thou."

"I can do the math, gentlemen. But you're overlooking new evidence and a new suit sitting here waiting delivery to federal court. If you recall, the amount is 75 million, not thousand." Trisha's hand flew up to cover her mouth. Rusty placed a finger over his own, reminding her not to make a noise.

"That's absurd," Frank Gillen bellowed.

Rusty stayed cool and composed. "I'm sorry. Did you receive my e-mail? I delineated the breakdown supporting our request."

"She's seventy-five years old. Why would she need that kind of money?"

"Well, we both know that's not how the legal system works. What we're looking at is what Adda Marsh rightfully earned had she been treated fairly by Haven Records. How she uses that money is her discretion."

Robert took over. "Nobody's going to give that woman a settlement like that."

Rusty bristled. "By 'that woman,' you mean Adaline—the one who put your record label on the map? I think we'll have the support of the courts, not to mention favor in the press. By the way, did you notice the comps I listed? Isn't Mikisha Rose one of your artists? She's pulling in eighteen mil annually and is nowhere near Adaline's sales. It's all public record. I don't believe Mikisha was ever nominated for a Grammy."

Muted conversation could be heard from the other end of the line. Robert returned. "We'll agree to the full amount of the first suit—1.5 million."

Rusty winked at Trisha. "Wonderful. That will be good to satisfy the civil suit. We'll still plan to file for the copyright in federal court."

"Don't play games, Bergstrom. What do you want?"

"We want what we asked for. I believe you're really asking what we'll settle for."

"Just give me a number." Trisha kept her hands over her mouth, eyes wide with anticipation.

"My client would rather have this finished without involving the Associated Press. They tend to sensationalize lawsuits of this magnitude. We're willing to sacrifice to avoid being tomorrow's front page news. One third of our request. Can you do the math?"

"Don't be offensive, Bergstrom. So you're asking for twenty-five mil?"

"That's my calculation."

Frank Gillen piped in. "Five million. No more."

"Sounds like a starting point. Let's make it seven point five, one tenth of our request. Providing we have a transfer of funds within seven days, and one hundred percent of song rights returned to Adda Mae Marsh effective from the date of the settlement."

Whispers sounded from the other end of the call.

"We'll do the 7.5 if that includes the civil suit. Dispersed in installments. Four mil now and the balance in equal portions over seven years." Trisha gasped, drawing in air and holding it until Rusty winked at her again.

"A little cash flow issue? I think we can work with you on that. I'll finalize this and draft the agreement. Gentlemen, it's been a delight doing business with you."

He hung up the phone, and Trisha jumped as if spring loaded. She threw her arms around him. "I can't believe it. Rusty, you were so calm. And they were so mad! I can't believe this is happening."

"Calm down, my dear. It's not our money."

"I don't care. Look what you did for Adda."

"No, look what you did. I was dead in the water until you got those statements. You, Counselor, nailed it down." He smiled ear to ear. "Let's not tell Adda she's a rich lady until we have the signatures."

Trisha stilled and swallowed the lump forming in her throat. Her head shook in disbelief. "You're amazing."

He reached for the lock of hair falling onto her forehead and tucked it back. "Does that mean I'm forgiven?"

"Let's just say you're a step closer."

They walked back to Rusty's. Adda was engrossed in a game show on TV. She turned when the door opened.

"So did Frank give you any of my money?"

Rusty chuckled. "Not quite yet, Adda. But he agreed to send some later this week. Let's wait to see if he signs the papers."

Adda never asked how much.

~*~

Two days after the conference call, Trisha watched the driveway, waiting for Rusty's car to crunch the gravel. He had called late in the afternoon to tell her he received the signatures. The wire transfer would be made tomorrow. Tonight, Adda would know she was a wealthy lady.

Adda sat working another jigsaw puzzle. Trisha glanced at her cold coffee, forgotten as she matched the colors and shapes.

Trisha saw Rusty's car and went to the door to meet him. He juggled a box and a briefcase. Lowering the box to a dining room chair, he set the briefcase on the floor beside it.

"Adda, where's your memory box?"

"Upstairs in my room. Why you wanting that?"

"If I remember, it was pretty beat up after they tossed your room."

"It got smashed some, but I smoothed it out. Is that an extra box you brung?"

Rusty didn't answer but started toward the stairs. "OK if I bring it down?"

Adda eyed him and then nodded. "You be careful with it."

Rusty sprinted up the stairs and back down again, carrying the mangled cardboard box.

"Adda, memories of a lifetime need to be stored with dignity." He opened the new box he had carried in and lifted out a silver-plated treasure chest. It had a handle on the top and was engraved with "Adda Mae Marsh" on the front.

Adda stood and walked to stand in front of it. "That's a mighty fine-looking place to keep my treasures." She ran her hands over the smooth silver, touching the engraved name. "That says my name, scratched in right there. Mr. Rusty, this is mighty fine."

Trisha stood beside her. "How about if we move all of your things into here and throw this old box away? And, we have a couple of things to add to your box if you'd like them there. You said you wanted something from each of us."

Adda had already lifted the lid off of the old box and opened the chest. "Well, I kept me a remembering for Mr. Rusty."

His brows lifted. "What did you find?"

"Remember I told you how all them braids wasn't my own? When we took them out and brushed my hair back, I slipped one of those swatches of pretend hair in this box. It'll remind me of our surprise day when I got them braids." She lifted the extension out, holding it up to show.

Trisha touched the lock of the hair extension. "What a great idea, Adda. It surprised me when I opened the door and saw you. Now I have something for you if you'd like it for your memory box." She went to a drawer in the hutch and pulled out a picture. "Do you remember me taking this picture with my phone?" Trisha held it before her.

"That's me and Wanda Jean."

"Would you like this to remember our trip to Greenville?"

She lifted the lid and placed it inside the silver chest. "Yes, ma'am. I wanna be remembering that."

Rusty put his hand on her back and guided her to her chair. "Well, I have something else for your box. Sit down and I'll get it." He went to his brief case, extracted a paper, and sat in the chair beside her. Trisha stood behind, her hand resting on Adda's shoulder.

"I received this today. It's signed by Frank Gillen. He's agreed to a settlement. This top part is a little mumbo jumbo," he grinned at Trisha, "but here's the important part right here. Trisha, do you want to read it through for her?"

Trisha stood beside her and finger traced while reading aloud. "Copyright for 'Just Call Me Baby' is hereby transferred from Ernie Gillen to Adda Mae Marsh. All royalties from the date of this statement will be dispersed to Marsh and her heirs. A settlement of 7.5 million U.S. dollars is payment to satisfy any and all past songwriter, recording artist, and performance royalties. Said settlement will be disseminated as follows: 4 million U.S. dollars immediately, 3.5 million in equal payments over seven years, payable on the last calendar day of each year."

Adda's mouth opened. She looked from Trisha to Rusty and back again. "You saying million? Like in a millionaire?"

"Yes m'lady." Rusty smiled. "You're a wealthy millionaire." He gave a mock bow.

There were tears in Adda's eyes for the first time ever. She had shared plenty of painful stories. She wailed when they trashed her room, but there'd been no tears until now.

She reached her left hand for Trisha's and her right hand for Rusty's and spoke through her tears. "And you done this for me for no reason? Ain't never had no one 'cept Minny that didn't want nothing outta me. 'Til Miss Trisha Mills comed to hear me sing. The good Lord sent me an angel that day."

Trisha sat and faced her. "You sing like an angel, Adda. So many years when I was sad, you sang like you understood—like you were singing right to a broken-hearted little girl. We shared our sorrow. Now God gave us joy together."

Rusty squeezed Adda's hand, his eyes locked with Trisha's. "God doesn't waste our scars."

32

The following Sunday, Rusty, Trisha, and Adda went to Pap's old church. Jimmy's eyes raised in question when he saw Rusty with Trisha. They worshipped together in the very traditional church, sharing an old hymnal while the pipe organ sounded. Older adults in black choir robes led them as they sang ancient hymns that had become so familiar. Trisha could count the people in attendance if she were so inclined. But regardless of the numbers, the worship style, or the music, the heart of this congregation reflected the love of Christ.

When they walked back to the car, Rusty turned to Adda. "We have a little surprise for you. First, I'm going to take my two best girls to lunch. Then we're going to visit Edith. Would you like that?"

"Oh, I been wanting to see her. She won't know me, but when I see her, it helps me remember Minny. Lordy, I miss Minny."

"When you're done visiting with Edith, we can talk to someone about getting you a room in the senior community center. Is that still what you want?"

"I'd like that a lot. I guess being a millionaire means I got enough money to go there?"

"Oh, you have enough money. You have enough to build your own senior community center."

Adda tilted her head. "Why would I be wanting to

do that when they got a good building already built?"

Rusty draped his arm around her shoulders. "Just teasing you, my dear. We'll get you the best room they have available."

Trisha touched her arm. "Adda, if you're not sure, you can stay with me until you make up your mind."

She lowered her chin. "And keep walking up and down all them steps? I'm mighty grateful, but a little room will be nice."

The facility was expansive. Green space provided a fresh look, the look of new life. Beautiful flowers and shrubs greeted visitors at the door. Edith's building offered the highest level of nursing care. Another building offered mid-level assisted living.

The section with the most independent living had two options. Adda could choose from a small cottage home in a quad of four or a spacious two-room suite inside the larger community living center. A guide gave them a tour of both.

Trisha stood back and watched the tenderness Rusty showed to Adda. "What would you prefer, Adda? You can pick whatever you want."

She stood outside of the larger building and looked back and forth between the cottage homes and the community living center. "I'm fixing to be near other folks. I like doing them puzzles, and sometimes they might be wanting me to sing."

"So you want in the building?"

"Iff'n it ain't too much money."

Rusty turned toward the guide. "We'll get her set up in one of the suites. Can we see which ones are available?"

There were three to look at. While they walked the hallways, Trisha stopped to look in the great room. A kaleidoscope of colors scattered across the table while two ladies attempted to interlock the puzzle pieces. Two others played a game of Scrabble while another was knitting.

Further down the hall they passed a chapel with a beautiful stained-glass window and chairs crowded together. Outside the chapel, an easel held a poster displaying a picture of a large thermometer measuring the success of their fundraising efforts. It obviously caught Adda's eye. Trisha stopped with her to look, while Rusty and the guide lagged behind talking about her admission.

"What's that meaning? That red ain't too high."

"I think they want to build a new chapel. This one looks pretty small. They're raising money for it. As they get more money, the red will go higher."

"Do I got enough money to give them some?"

Trisha smiled. "Adda, you have enough money to build the chapel."

"Well then, tell Rusty to give it to them. Can't have people sitting all over each other when they're worshipping. That ain't fittin'."

"Adda, you have enough, but I didn't mean you should do it all. They need $58,000."

"Would that be leaving me enough to stay here?"

Rusty and the guide had joined them. "Would what be leaving you enough?"

Trisha motioned to the poster. "She wants to pay for the new chapel."

He flashed her a wide grin. "Splendid idea. What better way to use some of your money."

The guide looked from one face to the next. "Are you serious? All of it?"

"Yes ma'am. Rusty, will you get her some of my

money?"

He nodded. "They might give you naming rights."

The guide jumped into the conversation. "Yes, that's a possibility, with board approval."

"You mean like I get to call it what I want?"

"Like I said, the board would have to approve, but if it carried a name in memorial, I imagine that would be accepted."

Adda looked from Rusty to Trisha. "Kinda like my remembering box?"

"Exactly."

"So I could call it after my Enam Job?"

Trisha swung her head toward her. "Oh Adda. That would be so beautiful. The Enam Job Marsh Memorial Chapel."

Trisha looked toward the guide who gave her a slight nod. "Adda, we could have a beautiful plaque made with his name, an imprint of a baby, and a few words."

Rusty jumped into the conversation. "The world was blessed with Enam for three short days before he went to the arms of the Savior."

"I like that. You go getting that plaque made and get them some money to be building that new chapel."

"Yes ma'am. I'm on it."

Trisha and Rusty exchanged looks. She dished out orders like a rich lady.

One week later, as Adda moved into her new room, Trisha hugged her, holding on for the longest time. "I love you, Adda. I'll come to visit you often."

"Thank you, Miss Trisha Mills, for stopping to hear me sing."

Rusty stepped in and hugged her. "Can I visit, too?"

"You better be coming with Trisha. She got rid of her man 'cause of you. And get that fella from your work to come see me like you promised."

"Yes ma'am." She stood in her doorway and watched them walk out. Trisha slid her arm through Rusty's.

"What was that about someone from your work?

Rusty shook his head with what appeared to be mock annoyance. "Attorney client confidentiality."

~*~

Autumn had made its entrance with a blast of color. Trisha pulled a throw blanket over her to stop the chill that came with October. They sat on the mountain-view side of the veranda sipping chai tea while Chester breathed a contented purr from his cat seat by the window ledge, his tiger-stripes curled into a spiral. Wind chimes whistled a song from the cool breeze.

"Well, sweetheart, that's three times you've bested me. First you find Wanda Jean when I couldn't, you passed the bar the first time you took it, and now you land a job less than two months later. What's next? Do you plan to make partner before me?"

"Ha, I've been at my job one week. I don't think we're ready to talk partner."

He reached for her hand, folding her florescent pink nails inside his grasp. "Have I told you I'm proud of you?"

"I think I heard you say that once or twice."

They sat for a few minutes, their hands still holding to connect the space between their Adirondack rockers. It was all Rusty had asked of her—that and a peck on the cheek when he said good night. True to his word, he gave her time.

Trisha couldn't change her life story any more than Adda could erase her suffering. She had no family. Her youth was spent with two older adults engrained in an aging church. Grief had prevented her from seeking more. Until Grant came along. She had clung to him like a lifesaver without knowing what real love looked like. Now she knew. Love looked like Rusty Bergstrom. Rusty embraced her history, her limited heritage. Grant had tried to expunge it.

Rusty had awakened in her what Grant never could. A wellspring of life bubbling up and flowing over. Trisha broke the connection of their joined hands and stood to walk inside.

"I'll be right back."

Within minutes, she opened the French doors from the dining room and called out.

"Hey." When Rusty turned, she crooked her finger and moved it back and forth, bidding him to follow. He stood and shadowed Trisha into the living room. She walked to the shelf and hit play on her MP3 player. Adaline began the soft notes of her signature song, "Just Call Me Baby".

Moving to the center of the floor, she held her hand out to Rusty, the start of a smile forming. He met her in the center of the living room and secured her hand. His eyes never left hers until he lifted their hands to twirl her under them. Then she drew close, her arm circling his neck. She laced her hand through the fluttering of hair that still curled near his shirt collar while staring up at sky-blue eyes. Heavenly eyes. Always lit with merriment. He stepped with fluidity to the rhythm of the music.

"So, where did you learn to dance so smoothly?"

The side of his mouth raised in a smirk. "Cotillion. Thirteen years old. Tammy Wiseman stood a head taller than me with glasses and braces. She corrected every step I took." There was amusement in his blue eyes.

"Sounds painful, but it worked. You dance like Fred Astaire."

"By eleventh grade I grew taller than Tammy. She shed the braces and turned the glasses in for contacts. She's quite a beauty today, and not so bossy. You'll like her."

Trisha leaned back, a question burning in her mind. "And why would I be meeting her?"

"She married my brother. Those are her children's pictures you saw on my desk."

"Ahh. Did she break your heart when she married your brother?"

Rusty pulled her a little closer. "No, it was never like that. God was saving my heart for someone special."

Trisha broke from his gaze to rest her head on his shoulder. She began to sing along with Adda, her whisper-soft voice close to his ear.

I just want to walk hand in hand, Let everybody see that you're my man. And everyone will know that I'm your lady. Her lips found the tender spot below his ear, traveling to kiss the pulse beating on the side of his neck. *But I just want to hear you call me baby.*

Rusty pulled back. She looked up at him and met his gaze again. His eyes were sapphires filled with longing, his voice rich with emotion. "So would you say we're having a meeting of the minds here?"

"I think you could make that argument." She touched her lips to his. "Unless you think this is undue influence."

"Oh, it's definitely undue influence. I might make an argument for duress."

Her head tilted. "How so, Counselor?"

Their lips brushed together. "One party holding undue mental power over the other, who, at the moment, is quite helpless."

"Really? Would that argument hold up if both parties were quite helpless?"

Rusty leaned in to caress her cheek with his lips. "Do you think that's the case?"

Trisha freed her right hand and looped it around his neck. "Without question."

"Then meeting of the minds it is. Shall I draw up a contract?"

"Oh, I don't know. Why don't we just seal it with a kiss?"

"I think that will work just fine. Baby."

Acknowledgments

Although writing may be a solitary activity, the road to publication is not. Many hands have contributed to this work of fiction. I would like to give my heartfelt thanks to my family for their continuous encouragement and support.

Thank you, Kristen Heitzmann for your critique and helpful suggestions. Your books are an inspiration to many aspiring novelists.

My knowledge of the legal process is limited to its portrayal on TV dramas and books. Thank you to attorneys Bernie and Susan Ellis for correcting my misconceptions and for providing accurate legal verbiage.

I'd like to express my gratitude to my writing group, Cross N Pens. It's a joy to partner with you. Thank you, Cynthia Owens and Tim Suddeth for your careful editing and helpful suggestions.

Early readers are an important part of the process. They're the first to read a manuscript fluently and provide valued feedback. Thank you Lesa Fischer and Larri Manos for filling that roll.

I am grateful to Pelican Book Group and am delighted to be part of their network of authors. A very special thanks goes to Megan Lee for her skillful editing. I'm so grateful for your expert help.

Above all, I thank God for the privilege of writing. May He be forever praised.

Prologue

*Then the righteous will answer him, 'Lord, when did we see
you hungry and feed you, or thirsty and give you something
to drink? When did we see you a stranger and invite you in,
or needing clothes and clothe you? When did we see you sick
or in prison and go to visit you?'*

*The King will reply, 'Truly I tell you, whatever you did
for one of the least of these brothers and sisters of mine, you
did for me. ~Matthew 25:37-40 NIV*

I sat bolt upright, not quite sure what had roused
me. Did I hear voices and a slamming door downstairs
or just imagine them?

The sirens screaming in the distance were real. The
alarm clock glowed 4:15 AM. in neon red. I lay wide
awake with no sleep left in me.

Climbing out of my bed, the November chill sent
shivers down my arms. I inched the bedroom door
open. Night sconces cast shadows in the darkened
hallway, fingers of light reaching down the wall. Thick
carpeting absorbed the noise of my steps. The sirens
still shrieked their warning call somewhere far off. My
stomach churned. I held my hand over it to ward off
that sick feeling.

Lights on the first floor sent a softer glow up the
stairway. Reaching Edwin's door, I rotated the knob.
Light didn't penetrate into the dark room, but small

fissures from the gap in the door confirmed an unused bed, still made from yesterday, neat and smooth, pillows plumped like Leticia always left them. How could he be out at 4:15 in the morning? My heart raced, my mind grabbing at any possible explanation. A choked sob arrived from below. I hurried toward the stairs. As I stepped down the wide, curved staircase, my hand gliding on the smooth, polished surface of a massive wood railing, Leticia appeared at the bottom.

"Go back to bed, Scott." Red eyes and a husky voice betrayed her as she climbed toward me.

"Where're my mom and dad?" Where was Edwin? Leticia touched my shoulders to turn me around and motion me back upstairs. I lay awake until daylight, my pulse racing, unable to still my trembling hands.

****

I didn't see my parents in the morning. They made poor Leticia break the news to me. How typical. The second person to tell me was the morning news anchor. After a cheerful "good morning" and a wide-angle shot of a brilliant fire-orange sunrise, he affixed a somber expression for the next segment on his scripted card.

"Edwin Harrington, sixteen-year-old son of the prominent defense attorney Charles Harrington, was found dead last night from an apparent overdose. A man from the night cleaning company discovered Harrington's body under the bleachers of the Ravenwood High School's football field."

I waited to hear my name. But he didn't know. He couldn't, because no one did. I took my secret and hid it deep inside my guilt.

1

Scott Harrington

The Tenth Street Bridge spanned overhead with a thousand metallic arms reaching skyward in the eerie darkness. It crossed the Monongahela River, connecting Pittsburgh to the South Side. The insufficient cardboard wouldn't hold my 6'2" frame, so I curled my knees close to my body to keep out the chill of touching cold concrete. Every joint throbbed. The acrid scent of puddled asphalt burned my nostrils.

I sat up and readjusted my backpack against the concrete pylon. Raindrops sparkled like diamonds in the glow of streetlamps, which also illuminated the other men. Three slept well, as evidenced by the heavy snoring. A drunken slumber, if the discarded bottles were any indication. About ten feet from where I sat, another man stretched flat on the icy cement, wide-eyed yet oblivious to anything around him. The dark of night swallowed the blackness of his face, but his large white eyes held a wild and unrelenting stare at the grating of the bridge above. Where had his trip taken him?

The fifth man appeared no older than a teenager. Wide awake, his gaze darted from side to side, nervousness cloaking him like a well-worn jacket.

Sandy-colored hair, shaggy and unkempt, escaped his steel-gray hoodie. No cardboard insulated him from the bite of the cold surface. A crumpled up sweatshirt served as his pillow. If it weren't three in the morning, I might have attempted a conversation. But voices at this hour would be an intrusion.

Tight fingers gripped a backpack bulging beyond the capacity of the zipper. Was he concerned that someone would take his belongings if he succumbed to sleep? Perhaps I was the naïve one. Maybe he watched to see when everyone else slept and pilfered what he could. Was that why his bag was overstuffed? I pulled my backpack closer and readjusted my head to protect it. It wasn't much, but it was mine.

Glancing in his direction, I took care to avoid eye contact. He looked like Richie Cunningham from *Happy Days*, a touch of red in the sandy-colored hair and a pale complexion. But he wasn't a clean-cut suburbanite kid with his own bedroom and a doting mother. Where were his parents? Wasn't there anyone he could turn to?

An occasional car infringed upon the night sounds as it rattled the trestle above. I closed my eyes, imagining I was somewhere else, someplace sleep would come. My childhood home, the pretentious estate with all the grandeur of old money. What would my father think if he could see me now? Those were memories I didn't care to visit. Much better to focus on my own little home, the comfortable living room, the smell of wood burning in the fireplace. A place where my mind could escape. Cozy and simple, the feet of my recliner raised as I sank into the soft brown leather, swallowing me with comfort. The TV hummed with a sportscaster's dialogue while I drifted into the shadows of my mind, almost forgetting I was lying on a thin piece of cardboard under a cold bridge.

The inclination to compare myself to others was a part of my nature I couldn't seem to overcome, and it could be exhausting. Charles Harrington made certain that I never forgot that I didn't measure up to Edwin. There was one brief moment when a flash of insight helped me understand. My father wielded it as a motivator. Nothing would have been enough, because then I might have stopped striving. It's hard to overcome a lifetime of indoctrination, so over time, that insight faded.

There were times when I thought I'd mastered the tendency to compare myself, when I was satisfied with who I'd become, but then I'd find myself in the company of someone whose accomplishments diminished mine or left me standing in the shadow of my father's censure.

The opposite was true on this night as I slept under a bridge for the first time. I fought the tendency to feel somewhat superior to the five men who shared this underpass. I came here to blend in, to assimilate into this culture, yet the egocentric part of me wanted to make sure everyone knew I didn't belong here. But that attitude would be a detriment. I needed to guard against it to accomplish anything.

Sometime before morning light, I slept. I woke to discover two of the snoring men still fast asleep, while the third relieved himself on the other side of the pylon. He paid no notice of me, finished his task, and disappeared into the hazy fog. The man with the wild eyes closed them in sleep. A bare stretch of concrete remained where Richie Cunningham with the hoodie had been. I checked to ensure that my backpack and blanket remained intact and found both secure.

Judging from the predawn light, it was around six o'clock so I'd gotten only two or three hours of sleep. Rising, my body was unbendable until I began to stretch the stiffness away and then blood flowed to my limbs again. Desperate for a bathroom and a hot cup of coffee, I began walking.

****

The yellow brick of St. John's Episcopal Church still held its original charm. It had graced this corner for over a hundred years, with beauty and architecture unparalleled by the new wave of nondescript churches. A white cross peeked down from the cupola, bidding all to come. Walking past the grand oaken doors, I tried to envisage what stood behind them, imagining rich maroon carpeting cushioning dark pews, all illuminated by the rainbow prisms from a thousand pieces of stained glass fashioned to depict the garden of Gethsemane and Jesus with the children.

Then it hit me. I envisioned the interior of my childhood church which, as teenagers, Edwin and I coined Fellowship of the Elite. Worshippers showing off their designer fashions and glittering jewels. How discordant would it be to visit a Sunday service dressed in these frayed jeans and in obvious need of a shower?

The doors to St. John's remained locked throughout the week. I walked the manicured path to the side of the church, breathing in the fragrance of fresh grass and withering flowers, a contrast to the stagnant scent of auto exhaust and concrete. A simple sign posted on the gray, metal door noted the hours for breakfast. They began serving at six. I prayed the door would open when I turned the knob, and it cooperated, the heavy metal scraping the surface of a frayed welcome mat. I entered the oversized room with its large industrial kitchen and the welcoming aroma of coffee.

A small portion of the space in the vast room had been set up with tables where pancakes were being served. People already occupied some seats, even at this early hour. Most of them scattered throughout the area with their coffee and pancakes, spaced for solitude. I needed human interaction. Scanning the tables, I chose one with two men and carried my cup and plate over to join them.

"Good morning." I sat down without asking permission. A grunt and a nod came from my left.

The man seated across the table rewarded me with a hearty welcome. "Howdie do." He flashed a grin as wide as his voice was loud. I glanced around as a few heads turned our way. "Always a good mornin' here. We get the best coffee and hotcakes in town. Name's Pete. This here's D.J." His attempted introduction brought another grunt.

Pete's grin revealed sparse and decaying teeth. Age spots peppered his arms, and red cheeks bookended a bulky, bulbous nose. His booming tones continued to reverberate throughout the room, oblivious to the fact that he displaced the quiet.

"Good to meet you, Pete. I'm Scott." I muffled my words hoping he'd get the message. "So Pete, anywhere else someone like me can get a meal around here? This ain't gonna last me 'til supper."

"No sir-ee, Scotty. That it ain't." His voice still

thundered. "Couple'a places you can try. If'n I were you, I'd head on down to Stanwix and try the shelter there. Or you can try Hope House. It's a place that lets a feller stay and tries to get him turned around, like learnin' new job stuff."

I knew about Hope House, but it wasn't what I needed. "So how does the Stanwix Street one work? I'm kinda new at this. A little down on my luck right now."

"Well, ain't we all." His eyes sparkled despite the bloodshot streaks. "Ain't we all. First time you go, you gotta tell 'em some stuff about you and sign a paper agreein' to their rules. After that, you just sign in when you go. You can get a good, hot meal and a bed for the night."

Right about now, a bed sounded like heaven. I'd have traded my pancakes for sleep, but Pete's response squashed that dream. Besides, I didn't come here for sleep, I came for information.

"Doors open at five o'clock, first come, first serve. Can't be late 'cause them doors get locked when they have enough people to fill the beds."

Could I make it until five?

"Listen here, Scotty boy. You come along and stick with me, and I'll show you the ropes. But get eatin', boy. We gotta hurry," Pete bellowed again.

No one had called me Scotty since I was nine, but I didn't correct him. I'd walked into an opportunity, someone loose-lipped, willing to show me the ropes and let me stick with him. But why the hurry? It felt like hours of daylight stretched before us with nowhere to go.

I didn't rush my pancakes, but instead watched a few people come and go through the metal door. When the clock on the wall showed seven o'clock approaching, Pete's agitated hand formed little circles in front of my face, a motion saying, "Hurry." Determined to take a cup of coffee with me, I picked up our Styrofoam cups and asked, "Black or cream?"

Pete flashed his easy grin. "Black and sweet. I take mine black and sweet."

His chuckle led to a fit of coughing. I hesitated for a moment, not sure if I should do something, but he motioned me away with his hand. I turned in the direction of the man he called D.J., but he flipped his empty cup upside down on the table without glancing up.

After we exited the church's side door, Pete stopped to light up a cigarette from the pack tucked in his shirt pocket. We walked through the midst of the morning rush hour with cars at a stand-still, drivers waiting to get past the red light. Dense pedestrian traffic hurried in all directions. Pete could move for an old man, but I kept up, intrigued to see our destination. He darted to a city bench near a busy intersection. Plopping on the bench, Pete reached his weathered hand into a plastic grocery bag he toted around with him. He produced a large and rugged piece of cardboard with "Homeless and Hungry" scribbled on it in black marker. He stationed the sign in front of him and reached in to retrieve a large plastic cup, the kind you might get with a convenience store soft drink. It had "God Bless You" written in marker across the front.

I stood there for a moment, my jaw slack. Hungry? We had just finished devouring a huge plate of pancakes. And panhandling? I'd never imagined myself begging on a street corner. I'd always taken some pretentious pleasure in being a giver, not a taker. But today, this is what I needed to do.

I took the final gulp of my coffee, shook out the residual liquid, and moved toward the bench, only to meet Pete, extending his hand and blocking my movement.

"No siree, Scotty boy. One to a corner. Nobody'll be feedin' the cup for two of us." He reached into his plastic bag and retrieved another smaller piece of cardboard with "Homeless and Disabled" printed on it in amateur block letters. Pete held it out in my direction. "Now limp a little and get on outta here. Find a corner a block or two away with some different traffic. I'll see you in a couple'a hours. We ought'a have enough to get us a burger and some refreshment for tonight, iff'n you know what I mean." With a gleam in his eye and a suppressed grin, he turned his face away, looking pitiful for the crowd.

My cheeks flushed red, I rotated the sign toward myself and walked to the next block. I didn't have to panhandle. I could eat at the shelter and didn't care about Pete's idea of evening refreshment. But Pete was crucial to my plan. He knew the streets. He'd be a big help to me. I couldn't go back empty-handed in two hours. So I located a busy spot near a crowded corner, void of a bench. I sat on my backpack on the ground and propped up my sign, holding the foam cup upright to receive my beggar alms. I tugged the visor on my cap and kept my eyes lowered in case someone recognized me. People stared at me pitifully, some swung closer to the building to avoid me, and a few pulled out coins or a one-dollar bill. Unsure of the protocol of panhandling, when the first person dropped some coins in my cup, I glanced up and said,

"Thank you kindly." That became my mantra of the morning. Two hours and $27.50 later, Pete sauntered up the sidewalk with a large grin. He reached for his cardboard sign as I stood to join him.

As I followed Pete into the diner, the word *retro* might have described the décor. But I'd been a preppy teen. Retro for me was far from this shadowy diner. Dark-green speckled plastic, patched with tape in numerous spots, cushioned the chrome base counter stools. I followed Pete's lead to a counter seat, but when it wobbled with each movement I made, I convinced him to slide into a booth. Stale cigarette smoke clung to the curtains and mingled with the heavy odor of grease drifting from behind the counter.

A waitress in jeans and a black polo with *Larry's Diner* embroidered on the pocket, spread two paper placemats in front of us and topped them with silverware wrapped in a napkin. Her nametag said *Kimberly*. "What'll you have?"

Pete's booming voice echoed through the diner. "I'd be right grateful for some of that there coffee." He pointed toward the coffeepot behind the counter. "Then a big old burger and fries."

The pancakes still sat heavily in my stomach, but I ordered a grilled cheese sandwich.

Pete and I sat over a $3.80 lunch for almost two hours. Each time she went past our table, Kimberly refilled our coffee cups and wiped up the coffee spill and stray cigarette ashes from the shaking of Pete's rheumatic hands.

"So Pete, are all of those people who were in St. John's homeless? Or do some just come for the breakfast?"

Pete took a drink from his coffee mug, his hand

shaking as he lifted it to his mouth. "People got all kinda different places they call home, Scotty. Some might have a place of their own but need help gettin' food now and then."

"How about you? You live on these streets or do you have a place somewhere?"

"Me and D.J. mostly stick together."

That didn't answer my question, but Pete followed that with a coughing spell. When he recovered, he lit another cigarette and started in on a story about the old steel mill where he once worked.

When the lunchtime foot traffic began to pick up, Larry's Diner filled to its meager capacity. Pete got up to leave, magnanimously slipping thirty-five cents on the table for the waitress. The haphazard cluster of bills in his hand indicated that his take from panhandling far exceeded mine. An old man must elicit more sympathy than a young man, even with a proclaimed disability.

"I'll catch up with you later, Scotty."

"Hey, Pete. Hold on a minute. Where will you be eating and sleeping later? Do you go to the place on Stanwix?" I couldn't afford to lose this connection. When and where might I hook up with old Pete again?

"Naw. Ain't fer me. Me and D.J. got us a vacant building over on Liberty. A storage shed in a parking lot. Don't think nobody checked that ol' lock out in a year. You come on over if you can't get you a bed at the shelter. Beats being under the bridge." He slipped out the door and disappeared into the pedestrian traffic on the city sidewalk.

Settling back in the booth, I accepted Kimberly's offer of a coffee refill despite the fact that I was already over-caffeinated. With seven hours until the shelter opened its doors, I finished my coffee and set out to find Pete's vacant building. Perhaps I could sneak a few hours of shut-eye. None of my plans for the day would happen without some sleep. Why in the world did I decide to do this?

We hope you enjoyed this preview of Kathleen Neely's The Least of These. Look for it where books are sold.

A Devotional Moment

The Lord your God is in your midst, a
warrior who gives victory;
he will rejoice over you with gladness, he
will renew you in his love; he will exult over
you with loud singing ~ Zephaniah 3:17

Sometimes, the decisions of our past create circumstances that threaten the well-being of our future. When those decisions are our knowledgeable, free-will choice, we must accept the consequences of those decisions even as we strive to right ourselves. But what do we do when our present hardship is because of the choices others have made? Perhaps we were taken advantage of. Perhaps we were at the wrong place at the wrong time—or associated with the wrong people. We must remember that God is always present, always waiting for us to lean on Him, no matter what the circumstance.

In **The Street Singer**, the protagonist collides with a woman who once held fame and favour, but now lives in misfortune and poverty. She finds solace in the memories of a better time, when her place in life was secure. But her present circumstances demand a humility that can inspire others to greatness.

Have you ever found yourself in a situation where you gave all, but got hardship in return? If you answered yes, and are harbouring bitterness, anger or heartbreak; let it go. God is standing in your midst waiting to be your champion. No matter the situation, if we are truly striving to be good, if we live honest, upright lives, He will fight our battles for us, obtain justice and victory where it seems none exists.

LORD, HELP ME TO CHOOSE WISELY IN MY LIFE DECISIONS. SHOW ME THE BELIEVERS, HELP ME TO SEEK AND DISCOVER THEIR TRUTHS, SO THAT WE MAY HAVE A GODLY RELATIONSHIP. TEACH ME TO SEE YOU IN ALL ASPECTS OF MY LIFE. IN JESUS' NAME I PRAY, AMEN

Thank you…

for purchasing this Harbourlight title. For other inspirational stories, please visit our on-line bookstore at www.pelicanbookgroup.com.

For questions or more information, contact us at customer@pelicanbookgroup.com.

Harbourlight Books
The Beacon in Christian Fiction™
an imprint of Pelican Book Group
www.pelicanbookgroup.com

Connect with Us
www.facebook.com/Pelicanbookgroup
www.twitter.com/pelicanbookgrp

To receive news and specials, subscribe to our bulletin
http://pelink.us/bulletin

May God's glory shine through
this inspirational work of fiction.

AMDG

You Can Help!

At Pelican Book Group it is our mission to entertain readers with fiction that uplifts the Gospel. It is our privilege to spend time with you awhile as you read our stories.

We believe you can help us to bring Christ into the lives of people across the globe. And you don't have to open your wallet or even leave your house!

Here are 3 simple things you can do to help us bring illuminating fiction™ to people everywhere.

1) If you enjoyed this book, write a positive review. Post it at online retailers and websites where readers gather. And share your review with us at reviews@pelicanbookgroup.com (this does give us permission to reprint your review in whole or in part.)

2) If you enjoyed this book, recommend it to a friend in person, at a book club or on social media.

3) If you have suggestions on how we can improve or expand our selection, let us know. We value your opinion. Use the contact form on our web site or e-mail us at customer@pelicanbookgroup.com

God Can Help!

Are you in need? The Almighty can do great things for you. Holy is His Name! He has mercy in every generation. He can lift up the lowly and accomplish all things. Reach out today.

Do not fear: I am with you; do not be anxious: I am your God. I will strengthen you, I will help you, I will uphold you with my victorious right hand.
~Isaiah 41:10 (NAB)

We pray daily, and we especially pray for everyone connected to Pelican Book Group—that includes you! If you have a specific need, we welcome the opportunity to pray for you. Share your needs or praise reports at http://pelink.us/pray4us

Free Book Offer

We're looking for booklovers like you to partner with us! Join our team of influencers today and periodically receive free eBooks and exclusive offers.

For more information
Visit http://pelicanbookgroup.com/booklovers

CPSIA information can be obtained
at www.ICGtesting.com
Printed in the USA
LVHW091555200319
611280LV00003B/576/P